Sean Patrick
O'Mordha

For All Time and Eternity:
waters from the deep

For All Time and Eternity:
Waters From the Deep

ISBN-978-0-9829842-6-0

Cover Design by B. H. Moore

Produced in the United States of America

Celtic Publications
Sparks, Nevada:

Dedicated to:

Ashton Michael Moore

Always in our thoughts and prayers.
May you continue to enjoy reading
throughout your life.

Other Publications
by

Sean O'Mordha

A Pirate's Legacy:
(series)
For Glory, Truth and Treasure
The Urchin Pirate
CIC (The Canary Island Commandos)

Death by TOP Secret

Incident at Beaver Creek

Print and eBooks available from:

**oldguey.webs.com
celticpublications.xipherzero.net
smashwords.com
Amazon.com**

Author's Note:

    <u>For All Time and Eternity</u> draws heavily on ancient writings, Hebrew and modern scripture, and Biblical commentary from the past 1000 years. In the Book of Deuteronomy (12:3–4) a person is exhorted to destroy idolatry. It adds, "You shall not do such to the LORD your God." The understanding of this verse is that a person should not erase the name of G-d. As a result, scriptural students see the words "God" and "Lord" often written as "G-d" and "L-rd". This is so that individuals will avoid the risk of sinning by erasing or defacing His name. Within Judaism, the general rabbinic opinion is that this admonition only applies to the sacred Hebrew names of G-d, not to the word "God" or "Lord". Out of respect, and to avoid erasing G-d's name, even in a non-forbidden way, many religious commentators continue to write the name "G-d" or "L-rd" in this manner. As a product of their teaching, so does the author.

SPO

For All Time and Eternity:
waters from the deep

Chapter 1

The wet pillow barely muffled the boy's sobs as the throb in his head only intensified the searing pain in his heart. Gradually anger replaced tears as he began viciously beating the pillow. Overcome by remorse for harboring such hatred, the tears returned. So the pendulum swung, until exhaustion yielded to the empty, numbing feeling of hopeless despair.

Sitting up on the edge of the bed, he swung bare feet to the cold, wood floor, and then stiffly walked to the large window to stare through the rain-splattered pane at the glistening asphalt street four stories below. As he slowly opened the window a blast of cold, wet air sprayed his face and chest exposed by a ripped T-shirt. Staring down at the street, his usually active mind was like a radio tuned between stations—nothing but dull static. He lift his left leg over the sill and out into the chilled night air.

Δ   Δ   Δ

The greatest lesson Dr. Roger Elam learned in youth was community service as reflected in an Eagle Scout project followed by a two year, church mission. Community service was as much a part of life as family, church, and work. That's why every Tuesday and Thursday he boarded the psychedel-ically-painted CitiTrans bus headed for the inner city. Twice a week for eight years he rode that par-ticular bus, but hadn't really looked at the world beyond the badly scratched, Plexiglas window. Instead, he engrossed himself in catching up on professional journals, reviewing reports, or making notes about the direction to guide the martial arts class at the YMCA. Today he looked because of a comment his partner made that afternoon.

Roger and Solomon Friedman began a close friendship in middle school. After high school, Solomon left for Israel while Roger went on a church mission to Chicago before beginning college. The first day of graduate studies nine years later, Roger sat at a long, scratched, and well-worn, wood table across from a heavily bearded student, the *payos,* side locks of hair, hanging past his shoulders in a tight curl. The *yarmulke* on the crown of his thick, curly hair was the brilliant blue of the Jewish flag. Other than a white shirt closed at the collar but sans tie, the rest of him was clothed in black. As their eyes met, recognition was instantaneous. The professor was less than elated as the two hugged and practically danced around the room, having to clear his throat several times—loudly—to get class started.

Despite forming a partnership upon completing doctoral studies, the two saw little of one another during hectic, daily schedules. To compensate, they popped into each other's office at least once a day to share a provoking thought.

Today, Solomon's message delivered at he stuck a bearded head into the open door was, "Man is G-d's only creation that can appreciate what has been made for him—if he takes the time to look."

Standing at the bus stop a block from their office situated on a hill overlooking the city, Roger looked—really looked—at the neighborhood beneath a canopy of sycamore and black walnut. Nestled side by side, the well maintained, turn-of-the-century homes had been converted into offices like his, or upscale condos with small landscaped and manicured yards. The curbs were packed with shiny, new cars, mostly Bimmer, Lexie, and Jag types. A pimple on the end of this prosperous nose was a battered Jeep Ranger that hadn't seen the business end of a car wash since tumbling off a Toledo transport. Unlike the suit and tie profess-sional types dominating the street, its owner was a cut-offs and sandaled photojournalist with as much character as his off-road transportation.

From this hillside advantage, he could see over the thousands of trees and checkerboard rooftops to the harbor and a line of grayish-black clouds rolling in from the sea. It made for a beautiful painting, but as the bus traveled into the city, the beauty rapidly faded. Trees thinned until becoming almost non-existent. The rooftops became houses and buildings not so well cared for. Each stop portrayed an incrementally depressing picture of careless deterioration. More "FOR SALE" or "FOR RENT" signs appeared. Single dwellings changed to dilapidated tenements interspersed with grungy storefronts, warehouses, burned out buildings, or weedy lots. A light rain began to splatter the bus' huge, scratched window as the thick, gray clouds darkened the demoralizing picture.

As the bus approached his stop, Roger pulled the frayed chord and moved to the back door, gripping the overhead handrail to prevent an unceremonious toss into someone's lap. A teeth-grating screech of brakes brought the vehicle to a stop. When the back door opened with a hiss Roger grabbed the vertical, chrome bar and swung down to the sidewalk to the greetings of some boys clad in judo uniforms entering the double, front doors of the Y. That they were unafraid to wear the martial arts garb in public was a testament of how far the program had come. Detractors were few and enviously silent.

In the basement, locker room a high-spirited din ebbed and flowed as other boys quickly exchanged street clothes for the heavy, cotton uniform called a *gi.* Predictably came the unmistakable crack of a towel, followed by the inevitable yelp, thud of bare feet across the thin carpet, and laughter. When a clip of profanity sliced through the air, Roger coughed loudly.

"Oh, geez! Sorry, Sensei," an embarrassed, falsetto voice squeaked from somewhere amid the locker jungle.

Profanity was all too inherent in the language of the ghetto streets. It was a way to shed childhood and appear manly before the onset of leg hair and deepening voices. At least when Roger was present the boys refrained from using such language.

Suddenly he caught the glint of a platinum-blond head flash through the door followed by the slam of a metal locker door. An eerie silence cast its shadow over the room as boys scurried to leave. Roger peeked around the edge of his row of lockers. It didn't look good.

"Hi, Manny."

A sullen grunt returned Roger's greeting as the new arrival peeled off his T-shirt and slammed it into the tall, narrow cubicle. Roger watched silently as the boy continued to disrobe revealing more bruises—back, upper arms, thighs. They hadn't come from his program.

"Trouble again?" Roger asked, sitting on the end of the dressing bench near the young man.

"Yeah," the boy snapped curtly.

"Are you going to be okay?" Roger's tone was gentle.

Manny spun around and glared at his teacher. The fire in those penetrating, sky-blue eyes was unsettling, but it had been there before, lately, too often. Over the years, the two had painfully worked on anger control with some success, but over the past few weeks, things had seriously digressed.

"No," he growled, slamming the door with a loud bang, rushing past his mentor while pulling on his uniform jacket. "We're going to be late."

Δ   Δ   Δ

Perched on the windowsill, Manny idly bumped his heels against the brick wall while looking down at the occasional car or truck gliding passed his apartment building that faced the main street to his left. A voice penetrated the static in his mind—the radio station had become tuned in and the announcer's message was clear.

"What's the use, kid? This whole life thing has been one, big, meaningless joke . . . on you," the announcer said. "Things are never going to change. What you did has bound you to a life of pain and torment. You committed a major crime. Yeah, the laws of man exonerated you, but the laws of G-d will not. No, you didn't kill anyone, but you might as well have. Those guys will never be the same again. How many times have you dreamed of seeing them lying on the ground, crying, bleeding? You will never forget that. G-d makes people remember their sins so they feel the need to beg His forgiveness. Look at all those times you did something and asked forgiveness. You continued to remember and feel bad. What's the use of forgiveness if you are going to continue remembering, so why prolong the misery?"

"Go to Hell?" Manny shot back in protest.

The voice remained calm and condescending. "Hell? There is no such place. All that fire and brimstone, and screaming souls stuff was invented thousands of years ago by pathetic Greeks trying to explain things they didn't have the mental capacity to understand. Ever since, frightened, niggling men trying to cope with things beyond their grasp have held onto that lie and even embellished upon it as a way to control people. The teachers in your school are right. Man is nothing more than a complicated mass of atoms that came together over millions of years. G-d said it himself. Dust Thou are and unto dust Thou will return. That's it. You are just so much dirt. Look at the life you exist in right now. That's hell. Why prolong this agony? Since you are nothing but a pitiful conglomeration of atoms, why not disband them and let the process start over so the next person they form can have a shot at happiness."

Manny felt the windowsill slide beneath him as his legs inched further out.

Δ Δ Δ

Manny and Roger's friendship began when the nine-year-old first slipped into the Y's gym looking for something to do. An impish wisp of a kid with fine, long, silver-white hair accentuated by a dark mahogany tan, his bright eyes twinkled with curiosity. It was Roger's first day to teach martial arts and eleven boys eight to fourteen had just started warm-up exercises. Manny leaned against the wall close to the door.

"Ready for a quick exit if necessary," Roger guessed.

While issuing warm-up instructions and counting cadence, he backed to where the boy stood.

"Want to join us?" Roger asked, keeping his back to the wary youngster.

"What is it?"

"Judo mostly. A kind of fighting."

"Why you wearin' PJ's?"

"We work pretty hard. Saves time if we get tired and want to take a nap," Roger quipped, flashing a quick, over-the-shoulder smile.

The kid looked up at Roger and broke into the wide, toothy grin that would be his trademark on better days

Walking back toward the class Roger issued a casual challenge. "Give it a try."

"I gotta wear PJ's?"

"Makes it easier to play."

"Ain't got none."

"Got 'em at the front desk for borrowing. No charge."

The kid bolted through the twin doors soon reappearing with a white bundle tucked under his arm. Unabashedly tossing off street clothes while standing next to the wall, the boy didn't know how to fasten the extra-long, white belt. Still counting calisthenics Roger trotted over, knelt in front of him, wrapped, and tied it. A fiercely independent ghetto kid, he would normally rebel at such treatment. Roger's casual manner didn't trouble him at all. It was in, tie, and back to the group, nothing special.

Manny joined the line. Two hours later a sweaty urchin with an infectious grin showered. That was the first time Roger saw the bruises. He'd heard all the excuses before so said nothing. Not then.

Two nights a week, two hours a lesson was a lot of work, and Manny was one of the few who showed up consistently and worked, worked, worked. He borrowed one of the Y's uniforms until Roger quietly arranged for the bony kid to be an

"Assistant Sensei" and earn one to keep by conducting warm-up exercises. Afterwards they'd go for a soda or ice cream. They became friends. The bruises came and went sporadically and so did the anger. The two grew close. Only then could Roger safely broach the abuse issue. Still it wasn't easy. The fierce denial and a score of excuses muddied the discussion, but eventually, through trust, the truth came forth.

After his mother's death, the boy's father began hitting the bottle and Manny. In the guts of the city that was too common, and Social Services wasn't interested because it meant taking yet another kid into custody. Then what? There was no place to put them.

Walking the three flights of stairs from the basement to the second floor gym seemed harder than usual this night for Roger. He was disheartened. Every time there was trouble and a new set of bruises appeared, it provoked a setback in Manny's disposition. Before, his cheerfulness returned in a day or so, but since that unfortunate incident last year Manny's depression lingered just below the surface despite repeated counseling. His primal demeanor remained morbid, dark, and ominous.

Roger quietly slipped through the double doors into the characteristic bloom of joyful bedlam. Manny stood alone in one corner. Everyone sensed his anger. Most of the kids understood too well. They had their angers, too.

While impossible to give him space, they had nothing to fear. Manny never vented on other kids.

"Hey, it's not their fault. They take enough stuff as it is. They don't need more junk on their load," he once explained, not exactly in those words, but that's the way Roger preferred to remember.

On spotting Roger, the order to line up rang out followed by the mad rush of twenty-three kids scurrying to take their place in one of three horizontal ranks. Roger stepped onto the mat, bowed, and assumed his position in front as chaos evaporated into a respectful, but anxious silence.

Josh Redding, a college social works major, who joined his team last year, took the kneeling position on Roger's left. Manny sat on Roger's right. Both Brown belt rank, each was ready for promotion to Black belt. Manny was better, but had grown distant and unmotivated over the last couple of months. The anger grew as well. Tonight it seemed stronger than before and especially worrisome.

That first day in Roger's class, Manny was a runt next to other boys his age. Height came grudgingly slow. Then one day Manny showed up at Roger's house. He had visited before, for a couple hours, but this time he stayed. The bruises gradually faded.

Roger's wife had always been appalled at the boy's condition. Sure, his muscle tone was excellent from all the workouts, but, as she said, "He's too thin. He needs some meat to go with the muscle." One month made a difference. By the end of nine, he'd not only filled out, but also gained a couple inches vertically. He also started acting like a normal teenager. That in alone could be disconcerting except for this kid it was such a positive move.

Unfortunately, with the sweet came the bitter. Living with the Meir's family, he had become another son and an older brother to Roger's children. Wherever they went or whatever family activity they undertook, Manny was included. Continuing to attend his inner-city school Manny's grades blossomed as well. He was happier than he'd ever been until trouble unexpectedly reared its head.

As Roger swung the family van into the drive following a Sunday morning at church all the kids rubbernecked out the windows. A police car and Welfare Services van waited at the curb in front of the house. During Manny's protracted stay with Roger and Elsa, his father had granted permission for them to seek foster home placement for the boy. That meant one less mouth to worry about feeding and more money for booze. The caseworker had been belligerent from the first, her antagonism toward their religious beliefs poorly masked. Roger persevered until she brazenly brought up the polygamy issue and all but accused him of harboring more wives.

Roger was Mormon. The polygamy issue died over 100 years before, but ignorance and bigotry hadn't. With his face the color of the red stripes on the American flag displayed on the woman's desk, he pushed his chair back, stood up, and left the room, going straight into the Director's office without knocking.

The director reprimanded and quietly removed the woman from the case, but relations with Social Services spiraled downhill from there. There were other problems and irregularities, which could not go unchallenged culminating in a formal investigation of the division. That's when they came to take Manny back. Not that his father cared. Roger had talked to him and received written permission for the boy to live with them. Social Services put pressure on him to "demand" the return of his son to avoid criminal abuse charges.

Tears flowed freely that morning. Roger's children adored their older brother. Elsa disappeared behind their bedroom door, her sobs barely muted. Seated alone on the patio, Roger's heart ached as he recalled Manny's face peering out the van window as it pulled away. It was the first time he'd ever seen the boy cry, too.

That following Tuesday evening, as the regular Judo class began, Manny walked in and silently took his spot next to Roger. Later, after showering, Manny told Roger to drop the foster care plan.

"Maybe they'll just go away and forget all about me, again. I'll just stop by . . . to visit . . . if that's okay?"

Roger stopped, pulled the boy close, and hugged him tightly. He could hide his tears, but not the crack in his voice as he said, "Of course."

Δ   Δ   Δ

Manny slipped closer to the front edge of the windowsill. Misted rain splashed over his body. It was cool, but couldn't quench the fire deep within, searing his heart. Bare feet dangling in space, he idly alternated bumping each heel against the rough, brick facade while peering down at the shiny, black street. Would he create a crater or crack the pavement when he hit, like in the cartoons? Probably not. Just a big mess, yet, four stories was a ways up.

"My luck I'd hit feet first and end up a cripple, easy prey for the ol' man and those guys over on Van Allen Street bent on revenge," he moaned to himself.

Gazing down at his T-shirt, anger welled up again. The picture of a little boy with the words "I'm somebody, 'cause G-d don't make junk," was ripped. It had been a gift from the Elam children. He loved it as he loved them. Peeling if off, he angrily hurled the balled remnants into the air, watching it arch out and down to splatter on the pavement. The movement caused him to slip a bit further.

Grabbing the sill, he rooted himself.

"Oh, what the . . ." he stifled the curse word and chuckled. "Well, Mr. Kreutzer and Roger, you two did a good job. I can't even spit out a good cuss word anymore."

With a sigh, he pushed off the window ledge, dropping to the iron fire escape platform several feet below, the cold ridges digging into the bottom of his bare feet. As they were sufficiently calloused, there was nothing more than a minor discomfort.

Slowly walking down the serpentine steps so as not to create undo noise, he reached the bottom platform. Swinging out onto the vertical ladder his weight would force it to the sidewalk, but the screech of the rusty pulleys would also wake the entire neighborhood, so he leaned over, grabbed a smooth, round bar along the bottom edge and let himself down. Swinging back and forth, he dangled momentarily before dropping the last few feet into a puddle of water that splashed up. It felt cold as it curled around his calves, but good.

Looking toward the alley behind his building, he hoped to see Cherry standing beneath the street light, but she wasn't there. She hadn't been there for several months now. Some said she'd quit and gone home. Others said she'd been arrested. One rumored she'd been killed by a trick and dump somewhere. Manny wished he knew. She had been a friend, too. A good friend.

Chapter 2

Cherry's spot was beneath the street lamp, mid-block by the alley running behind the apartment building. Manny's dad had a fourth floor front while the girl had a second rear. That was convenient to her work. If a trick didn't have a place to go, they went up the back stairs.

A runaway at fourteen, she looked closer to thirty than twenty, and talked using slow, simple sentences with a limited vocabulary. Drugs, booze, and men had taken their toll, but the prostitute was someone with whom Manny could confide inward feelings he felt uncomfortable sharing with anyone else.

Having an abusive background in common, whenever Manny had trouble sleeping—which lately was often as teenage hormones played their games—he'd slip down the fire escape and the two would talk. If a customer showed up, Manny walked away so they could contract business in private. If the trade was slow, they talked uninterrupted until morning light. Sometimes, local boys came around with a ten spot for a trip up the alley. Something being better than nothing, she accommodated by leading them into the dark, cave-like tunnel splitting the block. There, across from a dingy, bare light on a recessed, concrete receiving dock she'd mollify their lusting itch. Ten bucks, ten minutes, no frills.

One evening Manny tossed and turned repeatedly, his whole body tingling as if charged with electricity. Eventually he slipped quietly down the fire escape almost zombie-like and headed for Cherry's spot. It was vacant and his heart sank until hearing muffled voices in the alley. A few minutes later, a couple guys emerged. One gave the thumbs up sign and grinned. Both giggled as they hustled away. Cherry appeared, stuffing some bills into her tiny, shoulder purse.

"Hello, Manny," she greeted in her high, nasal pitch.

"Hi, Cherry," he replied in a hoarse whisper as beads of sweat formed on his brow.

Manny was a mess. He was sweating, yet shivering. It felt as if something was scratching him deep within the gut while every muscle in his body drew up like a bowstring ready to snap. His mouth was dry and tongue felt swollen. His breath was shallow and rapid to match a heartbeat. Taking a deep breath, he summoned up all the courage possible.

"I got ten dollars," he sputtered.

Cherry's smile was so slightly to be nearly invisible. "No."

"No?" he squeaked in protest, "I'm as old as those guys."

"Manny, you're like a brother," she replied tenderly, stroking his cheek lightly with her fingers. "I could never do that to my brother."

Within that tender moment an old Chevy rounded the corner. She kissed the boy on the forehead and stepped to the curb as the rusted sedan pulled up. Leaning into the opened passenger window, she began transacting a business deal as Manny turned away and disappeared into the shadowed alley. Sliding into the car she turned, smiled, and waived. He never saw her again. Sometime later, a kid with a new slingshot put the street light out.

Δ   Δ   Δ

Standing beneath the fire escape as a steady mist continued, Manny looked and hoped with all his heart to see the girl, but she wasn't there. The street was as dark as his soul. The City didn't make repairs around here often. "A waste of time," they postulated sarcastically. And who could possibly make repairs to his broken heart?

Turning to the corner, the young man looked diagonally across the street where a dim light shown above the Corner Deli. At this time of night, Mr. Kreutzer would be hunched over his desk, studying Torah. Over the years, Manny often sat beside him at a wooden table learning more than just to read and speak a new language. There was a room there, too, where he often stayed until his old man sobered up and asked him to come home. It had been a safe haven, until tonight.

"And don't get any ideas of running off to that old fool across the street or I'll put him out of business—permanently." The last words his father spewed out before throwing him into the bedroom earlier that evening were not a hollow threat. Sober, Manny's dad was a gentle giant, but in a drunken stupor he'd hurt that beloved, old man.

Drawing up a quick breath to stifle a sob, the boy turned the corner and passed the entrance to his apartment building. As a cold gust of wind sprayed more mist in his face, he burrowed hands deeper into tight, cutoff jean pockets, hunched bare shoulders, and headed north until coming to the end of the long, block directly across from the YMCA. He stopped. The Y was one of only three places which had provided shelter and comfort, and now he was forbidden to go there as well.

As a tear trickled down his cheek he stepped from the curb splashing more water up the legs, crossing against a red light. Traffic was almost non-existent this late.

"Too, bad," he thought, continuing a slow tour of the neighborhood. Run down by a speeding car would be an easy out, drawing out an amused vision of himself flying through the air to land unceremoniously on the hard pavement.

Δ   Δ   Δ

Roger was truly grateful to have Josh Redding working with him in the Judo class. That allowed him time to give individual attention to students. Tonight he paid special attention to Manny, but the young man's despondency wasn't readily apparent as he worked with the younger kids. Finally, with the first hour and a half instruction and practice finished, the time arrived everyone looked forward to most, the traditional one-one-one matches.

As the students knelt around the edge of the mat, Roger shifted his attention between the matches and Manny sitting on the opposite side of the large rice mat. He was looking for some sign of encouragement, but Manny's eyes remained riveted to the floor at his knees. If anything, his countenance seemed to darken. It had been a while since the boy's father beat him. Obviously, it happened again, but this time something seemed to trouble him worse than usual. Roger was beside himself. The authorities were disinterested and impotent. He could see the boy seemed on the edge of breaking. Despite never taking frustrations and anger out of any of the other Judo kids, what would happen when Manny went over the edge? Roger watched and fretted until it came time for his star pupil to compete. Normally a boy selected an opponent of equal or greater ability. Roger chose instead.

Josh Redding placed second in recent regional competitions against a national contender. Manny could score high points when he maintained concentration and focus, but when that didn't happen he was as vulnerable as a lone sheep on open range. Roger sensed tonight was not going to be good. The boy might as well have shouted out his intentions before attempting execution. For that reason, Josh continually bested Manny, and out of frustrated desperation, Manny badly telegraphed a roundhouse foot sweep. For an instant, Roger thought Josh hadn't picked up on it until inches from what would have been a terrible blow to his ankle. The college Junior hopped lightly over it while simultaneously shooting a left fist into the boy's shoulder. This caused Manny to lean backward severely. Josh followed up with a snap of the right foot. Manny had left himself wide-open, left foot high in the air, precariously balanced on the right. Josh's foot swept away that lone contact with earth. Manny landed on the mat with a devastating impact everyone around the mat felt as well as heard.

The expression of surprise on his face reflected the fight for air. Arching his back several times, Manny gasped before rolling onto his knees. Roger was on the verge of jumping to his side, but fought down the urge. He had a proclivity to "mother" these kids, too much. Besides, in Manny's state of mind he would spiral completely out of control.

Within a minute Manny began breathing more normally, staggered to his feet, shook off the effects, and went right at Josh again. Roger was always amazed at his resiliency. Now Manny attacked, blindly charging as Josh retreated backward. Reaching out as if to stop the charge by pushing against his opponent's chest Josh suddenly rolled onto his back pulling Manny down with him. Planting a foot on the hip, Manny was hurdled up and over to crash almost spread eagle on his back above Josh's head—*Tomonagi*—the "cowboy throw," but Josh didn't follow through. He should have continued rolling backward which would have placed him in a sitting position on Manny's chest to apply a double chokehold. Instead, Josh hopped up and readied for another stupid mistake while casting a furtive look toward Roger. What to do? Let Manny win? Just defend or beat the pulp out of him? Josh didn't know. Neither did Roger. This was one of those no win situations he really hated. He halted the match.

"What are you doing?" Manny screamed hysterically. "I can take him."

"I want some time to play, too, Manny." Roger replied with tender calmness.

The boy just stood rigid, staring at Roger. Chest convulsing violently, he began to hyperventilate, and then tears welled up, spilling down his cheeks. The anger vaporized as a drop of water in a hot pan as the boy buried his face on Roger's chest. Clutching the long, tangled, white mop of hair Roger held him close. Every kid in the room watched in silence as Roger escorted the sobbing boy from the mat to a quiet corner as Josh took over and proceeded through the closing ceremony.

Each participant cast a quick, unobtrusive glance toward the pair seated in a remote corner as they left the gym, respecting their space. At one time or another most had been there, too.

Δ   Δ   Δ

The Y really had been a salvation, giving him alternatives to a dead-end, ghetto existence. With head bowed, long, straight strands of hair plastered over his face, Manny continued walking north. The next couple blocks were nothing but a series of stores where weary people attempted to eke out an existence, locking their precious goods behind a folding, iron gate each night to go to what they called home, a more or less dingy apartment not unlike his own. Occasionally the shop windows were permanently boarded up—a sign of futility's victory.

Suddenly the ramshackle facades gave way to a rusty, badly bent, chain linked fence encircling a vacant, corner lot. It had been a car dealership, or so the old people said, "Burnt up one night. A real sight. Flames as high as the old hotel. All kinds of explosions inside."

The owners had the debris hauled away and the ground leveled off. That was in the days property was worth something, but no one bought it until lost to back taxes. No one knew who owned it now. No one cared. The kids used its gravely surface as a playground, mostly baseball using a Whiffle Ball because the real thing flew too far and hit things it shouldn't. Somehow, there was always a ball available. In his early years, Manny spent lots of time watching other kids play. Always too small, they didn't let him participate much. That was the impetus to become more active in Judo. Size didn't matter.

Coming to the corner, he stopped short and stared at the building across the street. Behind a new, reinforced, chain linked fence with a razor wire top, the abandoned Excelsior Hotel loomed six stories into the black night. It had almost gotten him. Others weren't so fortunate. Older residents called it Hell's Castle. Straining to see the penthouse on top Manny wondered if Benny's ghost was up there, as some swore. Using a secret entrance, gangs still used it as part of their initiation, and there were those stupid enough to go inside that harbinger of death on their own.

Closed, abandoned, vandalized, and gutted by scavengers it was still dangerous, but Benny had made it home. The penthouse was actually much as it was in the old days, except dingy from age. That's where he lived, worked, and entertained. Then something evil moved in. Manny was there when it happened. He felt an icy sensation as the malevolent thing passed his hiding place.

Suddenly the hairs on the back of his neck bristled a warning. Shoulder brushing the fence in a futile attempt to keep away from the castle, he turned the corner and walked head bent down along the vacant lot. He moved faster toward the next corner, but invisible, icy tentacles stretched out to encircle his soul, trying to ensnare him again. Manny began to run. Despite the cool drizzle, sweat peppered his brow. His legs felt weak and rubbery. Breathing became laborious. Despite being in perfect condition, he could barely move. Rounding the corner, he fought desperately against the invisible force trying to drag him back toward the edifice. It had captured him once, but he escaped. It still wanted him. Suddenly something splattered on the pavement at the foot of the hotel—a brick? He bolted into the shadow of the first building next to the vacant lot and broke free.

Leaning against the metal gate protecting the business, Manny doubled over fighting to regain his breath, as the bump on his temple pound painfully. That's when he detected the sound. There was something in the alley next to where he stood, something approaching,—a thin, sporadic shuffle—something incorporeal coming toward him. Manny lurched to the center of the wide sidewalk and took a defensive stance just as he had done before. Just as before!

That dreadful memory pounced upon him from deep within where he so painstakingly buried it. He didn't want trouble. He was minding his own business, returning from an errand for Mr. Kreutzer.

"Not again!" he groaned to himself.

A puff a wind whipped a ball of brown wrapping paper out of the alley. Manny watch it blow into the street, listening to its raspy shuffle, wondering why it wasn't wet. He chuckled, first to himself, then audibly. Again, he bent over gripping his knees for support, slowly shaking his head in relief. Gradually his heartbeat returned to near normal as did his breathing. Gathering himself together, he headed back toward his dad's apartment, trying to push the nightmare back where it belonged, wishing the headache would join it.

Rounding the last corner, he came to the alley behind his apartment building. He glanced toward Mr. Kreutzer's second story window. The lights were off. It would be after 11:30. Torah study finished, the old gentleman retired until five, ready to greet the first customer at seven with a cheery smile, a hot cup of coffee, and a bagel fresh from the oven. Manny wanted to say goodbye to him, too, but the old man could see into the boy's heart and stop him. He was very persuasive.

Manny's eyes slowly ascended the fire escape to his own window, debating whether to return there or go to his room down the hall from Mr. Kreutzer as he had so many times before.

"No, that would resolve nothing," he thought as another wave of depression passed over him. "Besides, I can't let any harm to come to Mr. Kreutzer."

His eyes continued upward until gazing at the black hole that had once been a street light. He wondered about Cherry. He really wanted to talk to her. She was a good listener, and just talking out loud afforded Manny the opportunity to hear himself and work out the problem.

Chapter 3

The practice room became strangely silent after Josh hustled the last student out. Seated in a far corner, Roger was startled and concerned at how violently Manny's whole body quaked as deep-rooted bitterness retched itself to the surface. Once seemingly freed, a silence enveloped and bore down like a heavy weight so that the two made their way down to the dressing room in silence. At the second level, they stopped briefly to peer through the round, glass window in the gym door. Beyond, a dozen kids were engaged in a half court, pickup game of round ball. When a couple of incoming participants acknowledged Manny, there was a delayed response. The anger was gone, but he seemed preoccupied and distant. Roger worried. Once, years earlier Manny began retreating into a make-believe world as an escape. That might be expected in a troubled pre-adolescent, but become real problematic with a sixteen-year-old.

"Wanna shoot some hoops?" one of the boys asked.

"Huh? Oh, no thanks. I need to pump some iron."

Keeping turned so they could not see the red, swollen eyes, Manny continued down the stairwell with Roger in pursuit to the empty, basement, weight room; empty except for the smell of stale sweat permeating the air. It rankled Roger's nose. The janitors kept the building clean, but not even a new air vent seemed able to handle the pervasive smell.

"Man, these things hold a lot of water," Manny said, dropping his heavy, cotton jacket on the floor.

"That will add to the problem," Roger joked to himself.

As a counselor, Roger instinctively knew when to listen so sat on the end of a weight bench and waited. Manny silently cinched up the heavy leather, lifter's belt, and lay on one of the narrow benches at the Universal. Reaching over his head, he set the weight pin at 200 pounds. With exaggerated huffs and puffs he began the first set of ten lifts, each press executed effortlessly. Before starting a second set of ten lifts Manny remained sprawled on the bench, allowing appropriate time for his muscles to recuperate and work on breath control.

"How much do you weigh now?"

"One-eighty-seven."

"Not bad. You're pressing over your weight."

"That's nothing." Reaching over his head, he pulled the adjustment pin out, reinserting it in the 250-pound hole. Adjusting himself under the bars, he took several deep breaths and began pushing upward. Steadily the weights moved to their apex then down, back up and down, stopping after completing a eighth lift and then using measured breathing to replenish the cells.

"You've been spending a lot of time around here."

"I guess. There's a lot of stuff a guy can do on the streets. Most aren't exactly uplifting. Beats walking around or wasting time just hangin' out."

After completing two more sets of ten at the original two-hundred pounds, he sat up, wiped the sweat from the bench with a small towel, and moved to the incline. Setting it at the steepest angle, he locked toes under the stirrup pads with his head on the bottom end, and began sit-ups.

"How many of these do you usually do?'

"I do fifty at this angle, but tonight's a twenty-five count." He did three sets, again resting between each.

Returning to the Universal he toned legs and arms, working different muscle groups, religiously following a routine set up with the Y's weight trainer. From there Manny moved to the showers to rinse off the sweat prior to 20 laps in the pool, which was more to Roger's liking. His own modified weight lifting program was boring and ill followed. Afterwards they slipped into the Jacuzzi.

"You've come a long, long ways since that skinny, little street kid walked into my class and thought he'd be runt of the century forever."

"Yeah. Didn't seem like anything would happen," he replied before slowly submerging for a long minute.

So, how tall are you now, six foot?"

"Nah. Not quite five-eleven, but like Elsa says, give a plant nourishment and love and it'll grow." Manny's mood suddenly darkened. "It's getting time to close this place. We better shower."

"Oh, bother!" Roger chided himself. "You blew that. I've got to get him to open up."

They showered in silence, but that troubled silence was broken while toweling off when Manny said, "I don't get it. A guy turns sixteen and he can quite school, but he can't be on his own."

Roger's heart jumped into panic mode. He'd worked so hard to keep the boy in school.

"You thinking of quitting school?" he asked, trying to stay calm.

"I thought about it a couple times. Those jerks in the legislature must be on crack. I can quite school, get a job, and have babies, otherwise I'm forced to live at home until eighteen."

Roger went around to his locker. By raising his voice a little he continued the conversation. "Yeah. It's crazy, but that's pretty much the way the law reads."

"They won't let me move to a foster home, not permanently. Not for more than a few weeks at a time."

"The idea is to keep families together at all costs."

"Not very insightful is it?"

"In some cases, no."

"Any chance Social Services' will change their minds about you guys?"

Roger grated. "Not much. You want to come home with me tonight—for the weekend?"

A long silence settled over the room. Roger thought he heard a muffled sob.

"It's late. He'll be passed out 'til noon. It'll be okay."

"I wish you'd come visit us again. The guys at Church have been asking about you. They're planning a campout end of the month. Elsa's concerned you aren't eating right."

There was an uncomfortably long silence then he came around to Roger's side.

"You know," Manny said softly, his voice cracking under the strain of suppressing a release of his emotions again. "I've never once said thank you. I've been thinking about that. You and Elsa have been really great, more than a guy could ever hope for. I love you both." Squeezing Roger in an enveloping hug, Manny turned and was gone.

Roger stood motionless—dumbfounded— as a single tear welled in the corner of his right eye, dispelled when some of the basketball kids filed into the locker room. It had been such a touching moment that Roger tried clinging to it as long as possible, but it troubled him, too. It had seemed so . . . final.

Throwing his wet uniform into the locker, he slammed the metal door shut with a loud bang, bolted up the steep, concrete steps to the main level, and burst onto the street. Manny was nowhere in sight. He looked again in both directions. Nothing. The deli where he usually hung out was dark except for a dim light in a second story window. He looked across toward the apartment building. There was a light on in the fourth floor, front. Roger worried, but Manny was probably right, his dad would be passed out by now. It'll be alright by morning. He'd stop on the way to work so they could have a bagel together at Mr. Kreutzer's deli.

Re-entering the Y, Roger retrieved his sweaty clothes and stuffed them into a duffle bag. In a way, he felt silly. He had panicked. Over what? A boy showing gratitude? Yet, a feeling of foreboding gnawed his stomach. Everything seemed okay, for now, he reasoned, besides, he barely had ten minutes before the bus came that would take him back across town and home.

Δ   Δ   Δ

The walk about the neighborhood had resolved nothing. If anything, it strengthened the decision. Wet and cold, Manny really wished Cherry was around to talk with. But then, he'd already made up his mind. Roger and Mr. Kreutzer were like an uncle and grandfather. He often confided in them and trusted their opinions, but Cherry had a way of letting him discover his own answers.

In his "runt years," when he used the fire escape to leave by what he referred to as the midnight door, Manny had to climb up the back stairwell to the roof and then down the fire escape on the side of the building to get back into his room. He continued to use that route even for the last year when becoming tall enough to reach the bottom rung because of the horribly loud, screeching noise the ladder made whenever lowered. Looking toward the blackened alley he suddenly didn't care how much noise he made.

With an almost effortless spring, he leaped up and wrapping fingers on the bottom rung of the ladder hugging the brick wall, and pulled it down. There was no shriek as expected. It lowered smoothly and silently. Climbing up, he paused briefly on the platform and touched the cable. Rubbing thumb and forefinger together, he was remotely surprised. Oil! Now why would someone have oiled the ladder? Nothing else in the building was cared for.

Chapter 4

Still heavy with sweat, Manny religiously folded the wet Judo uniform into a neat bundle, bound it with the brown belt, tucked it under his left arm, and gently closed the locker door. He couldn't linger, but neither could he leave without expressing gratitude to someone he loved and respected so much.

After giving Roger a hug, he bolted up the carpeted cement stairs and out into a light rain. Tucking the bundle under the left arm, he jammed hands into jeans pockets, and hunched his shoulders against the cool drizzle before leaving the shelter of the Y's front canopy.

Forging quickly along the rain-soaked street from each island of light cast by the street lamps to the next, his only company was a drunk staggering from a tavern, and a small cluster of street kids huddled in a doorway looking for something to do on yet another pointless night. Recognizing Manny, one of the kids flashed a friendly street sign. He returned it with a nod. He wasn't into that sort of thing even if it was a way to walk these streets and avoid trouble. Kids knew to leave him alone and keep clear, even the punks trying to gain access to some gang, or just out to make a reputation, especially after a year ago when some toughs made that mistake.

"What happened is unfortunate," Roger said, "but you have every right to protect yourself."

Still, Manny silently cursed himself before crying to sleep that night and awaking many nights afterward as nightmare flashes of the incident haunted his sleep. Nothing anyone said, no amount of prayer removed the weight of guilt from his shoulders. Entering the apartment foyer, he climbed the creaking, wood stairs with its wobbly banister, quietly entering his apartment. Manny saw the top of his dad's head sticking above the sofa back. The TV was on. He wasn't asleep.

"Where you been, punk?' the middle-aged man grunted, staggering to his feet, a can of beer in hand.

"Why did his father have to drink? Why was he always so angry at Manny? What had he done?" Manny asked himself those questions almost every night.

"Down at the Y."

"Down at the Y. Down at the Y," his dad sneered, crumpling the can, and giving it a toss at the overflowing wastebasket. He missed. "You're always at the Y. You can't stay home and clean up this filthy place like I told you."

"I'll do it now."

"Yeah, you will after I beat some respect into you."

This time when his father's fist launched toward his face Manny didn't even think. The punching bag at the gym had been his father. It always had been, but after the last beating he vowed there would be no more. His hand intercepted the fist stopping it with amazing abruptness. For a moment, both stood silent. His father was surprised by the move. Manny was surprised at how easy it had been. Slowly he lowered the man's arm.

"No more," Manny said softly.

His father was no featherweight. The times he did work, it was moving furniture. He was big, he was strong, and once more out of control. It would be so easy, so very easy. Manny wanted to strike back, but he couldn't. Blocking the blows was easy, but that only inflamed his dad's rage. Unexpectedly the man hurled something. The move was sudden, catching the boy off guard. The blow to the side of his head sent him down. The ensuing fists and kicks bruised him as he once more curled into a ball until the fury was spent.

Δ   Δ   Δ

Slipping back into his room through the window following the walk, Manny felt fatigued. Like all the times before, he quietly peeked out the door. His ol' man was passed out now. He closed it deliberately, threw off his damp clothes, and lay on the bed. The pillow was still damp from his tears following the beating. There he dozed an hour or so before rising again. He'd finally resolved on the decision to leave. It meant leaving everyone he loved, but there was no other way. He had to escape to a place from where no one could force him back. The voice in his head was partially right, "start over."

Stripping off his boxers, Manny carelessly tossed them into the open closet. Pulling on a clean pair from the dresser, he then pulled a bundle from the top shelf of the closet, another Judo gi that he began putting on almost religiously. Then why not? This was going to be a special morning. He thought about Roger's offer. Staying there had always been wonderful, but his ol' man would just use the cops to force him back. He couldn't retreat to Mr. Kreutzer's deli either, not after the threat to harm the old man. He couldn't endanger either of them, yet he had to be free. Two more years of this was impossible. When the sun rose in an hour he'd be far from the grasp of this hell.

Sliding legs into the baggy trousers, he pulled the drawstring tight, tied a bow, and tucked the loose ends inside before slipping into the heavy, cotton, canvas jacket. Closing the front and wrapping the new, brown belt around his waist, he tied it off in the prescribed square knot. Next, he swept his long, damp hair back, fastening it into a ponytail that lifted high off the crown of his head to cascade down to the base of his neck. Finally, he secured the white headband with its gold emblem of a flying crane, an unusual gift Mr. Kreutzer brought back from one of his frequent trips to Israel.

Reaching once again onto the closet shelf, he pulled down another bundle. This was the Samurai sword he'd found at a pawnshop months earlier. Measuring two feet long it was badly tarnished, but after an application of silverware cleaner the slightly curved blade shown brilliantly, reflecting light better than a mirror. However, it was the surprise discovered while cleaning the cracked leather wound around the long handle.

Carefully pulling the hardened material free he exposed the true grip. It was the most exquisite thing he had ever seen, an inlay of different woods depicting a crane in flight and wrapped with tiny cords of blue and gold. It was breath taking. That the emblem matched his headband was intriguing. Some wino had traded it for a bottle of booze claiming it to be a WW-II souvenir. The pawnbroker paid ten bucks for it and charge Manny nearly fifty. It was worth hundreds.

Sliding his left hand across the hilt, a short dagger effortlessly appeared from a hidden compartment into his hand. It, too, shown with gleaming brilliance even in the dim streetlight outside the window. When a Samurai's long sword failed him, this short blade was there to rectify disgrace—the fallen warrior's friend. Manny stared at it for a long time before returning the blade to its secret home and sheathed the weapon in its plain, lacquered leather scabbard. Slipping the sheath strap over his shoulder, the weapon hung down his back, the sword's hilt close to his right ear. Exiting back through the window, Manny quietly descended the fire escape. Each step on the serrated metal rungs bit at his bare feet, but he ignored the discomfort. He seldom wore shoes in the summer; walking the hard, hot pavement toughened them for competition.

The streets remained fairly deserted at this time of morning except for delivery and garbage trucks scurrying back and forth trying to complete their rounds before the melee of cars, buses, and humanity jammed the traffic system into locked submission. It was noisy. It would get worse, swelling into a cacophony of chaotic pandemonium. Through this overture Manny headed for the one place he knew would be a quiet haven—the city park nearly a mile away. In the southwest, lightning struck out from a grayish-black cloud moving in from the ocean. He was oblivious to it.

Leaving the rough, cement sidewalk wandering through the park, he strode on the soft, cushioning grass, feeling it reach up to curl around and caress his feet. The sensation radiated inward, momentarily soothing a soul immersed in a rolling boil. Eventually those feet brought him to the Japanese garden. Passing beneath the squared entrance of heavy timbers, he strolled slowly along one the winding paths, around the pond, and up a short incline to a bench located under a wood latticework covered with interwoven vines. This was his private place, so quiet, so restful, so away from reality. It was a place to think, a place to dream, a place he always had to pry away from. He didn't want to pry himself away this time. He just wanted to dream.

The lightning moved closer, the rolling thunder booming like a great, bass drum of an approaching parade band. Manny gazed into the pond. Three large Koi meandered neared the shore, ghostly shadows in the murky water illuminated by a stone lantern. Withdrawing the sword, Manny knelt on the wet grass and laid it in front of his knees marveling at the pallet of colors reflected with each ensuing flash of lightning. Lightly touching the blade with one finger, he absently tried to touch the tiny lights darting across the smooth, tempered surface, but like a little mouse he once tried to catch, they were too elusive.

Once again, his mind found rest and escape, until a sharp crack of thunder shook him from that world of dreamy solitude. Startled back to reality, Manny loosened his belt and pulled the flaps of his jacket apart. Reverently, he slid his right hand across the hilt feeling the dagger spring from its hidden scabbard into his palm. Slowly he raised the razor point to the hollow just below his breastbone.

His mind dwelt on how history was filled with companions. Anthony had his Cleopatra. Romeo had his Juliet. Manny? Manny had his despair.

"Well," he thought, "I may not have a woman to share my history, but I'll have their end. In a moment the hopeless misery and pain of this life will be done."

Then a strange thought entered into his mind. Something he'd heard somewhere, in church perhaps.

"Into Your hands I commend my soul." The words were loud and clear as if someone was whispering into his ear, unlike the radio voice he heard earlier in his mind. The words repeated more softly as if urging him to say them. "Into Your hands I commend my soul." It seemed appropriate.

Feeling the point touch his skin, he repeated the words, "Into Your hands I commend my soul," the words exiting his mouth more as a plea. Gathering in a deep breath, he steeled himself, and gazed toward three solitary boulders in the pond. Curiously, they began to glow oddly as the hairs on his neck prickled. His skin tingled. A bluish light reflected from the blade of the long sword. Leaning his head back, he looked upward. From the heavens, a shaft of brilliant, swirling, white, blue, and orange light sped down aimed directly toward him, its elliptical mouth gaping to devour.

Chapter 5

The spiraling shaft of light was a curiosity, a momentary distraction. Refocusing on the intended course, Manny glanced down at the knifepoint against his breast, drew in a deep breath, and squeezed his eyes shut. An immediate searing sensation pierced his breast, radiating throughout his body, enveloping him in a twisting, wrenching, burning torment. He hadn't counted on such pain. He wanted to take it back. Just as suddenly, there was nothing–no feeling, no thought—just a hollow, weightless emptiness. Opening his eyes, Manny found himself enveloped in a fog, or something like fog. Thick. At least it seemed thick. Depth had no meaning. Reaching out, he drew pieces aside like opening the multi-layered folds of a curtain to

45

reveal more of the same entwining, amorphous, grayish stuff. He moved his legs to step forward, but there was nothing to take hold of and propel him in any direction. It was like being on wet ice. He wanted to move. There was a compelling urgency to move, but how?

"Why is it so hard to concentrate?" he gasped.

Manny perceived snatches of random thoughts, but just as he was about to gather one in, it evaporated into the haze. Sweat began beading on his forehead. Fuzzy, indistinct images continued to materialize, shimmer, and fade away. Frustration and desperation peaked, but by drawing in a long breathe he fought those feelings down, forcing himself to relax as his old, marital arts masters taught. After a time the images came into better focus, remaining long enough to be recognizable. They were memories—his memories—passing as if on a merry-go-round in slowed motion, sweeping in, continuing out of sight.

A little boy playing in an abandoned building slips. A wall panel topples onto him. He can't move. The heavy weight pins him to the floor. He kicks. There's no one to see him. He screams. There's no one to hear him. "Don't play in that place," a woman's voice admonishes. He had sneaked in. No one knows he is in the building.

"Mommy, I can't move," the little boy cries out. "Help me mommy. I can't breathe!"

He fights desperately to move. Buried alive! The fog spilled over and swallowing the tiny body while flooding Manny's mind with oppressive tangles, lifting him upward, floating, twisting, forcing him into a spin. His stomach sickened.

"Please, G-d, help me!"

Light. A pinpoint appeared off in the nebulous distance. Manny's mind reached for it, choking down the urge to vomit. The sickness dissipated with the fog as the light gradually drew nearer, radiating outward, surrounding him with a hurtful brilliance. His mind asked, "Is this heaven?" He felt heat and groaned. "The other place? Probably. You don't do that kind of thing to yourself without some kind of punishment." He remembered Father Bradley's derisive sermon at the funeral of a young girl who found escape with a handful of pills. Funny what a bony, post-toddler remembers. He was with his mother then—when she was alive. "Why was the Priest so mean?" he asked.

His body contacted something solid. He's was no longer floating but lying on his back, a light overhead so hurtfully bright he dared not open his eyes. Rolling onto one side the light dimmed, becoming more bearable. Cautiously opening one eye, he blinked repeatedly until the vision cleared revealing a black speckled pink and tan-colored wall. Carefully turning his head that one, opened eye followed the wall upward. It was a huge boulder. Rolling onto his back, the light again became overwhelming. Squeezing eyes closed tight, Manny continued onto his other side where the light became more bearable again. Slowly opening first one eye then the other, he blinked repeatedly until the vision cleared. He was gazing at a black speckled pink and tan-colored wall.

"Either I made a wrong turn or I'm stuck between two boulders with a horribly, bright light straight overhead," he reasoned.

Desperately trying to understand what was happening, that old nemesis, panic, began to creep in and sweep over him. Ever since trapped in the abandoned Excelsior Hotel, confinement terrified him. Oprah Winfrey called it Claustrophobia! Turning onto his stomach, he slowly pushed himself up on hands and knees, fighting off another surging wave of hysteria. An infernal buzzing sound like a radio between stations echoed in his ears. He waited a moment for the announcer's voice to return. When it didn't, he gently shook his head trying to make it go away. It did, replaced by the faint throbbing that plagued him since the fight with his old man.

Rising to a kneeling position, Manny slowly looked around, and determined he was in a narrow gap between several huge boulders. The light, still causing his eyes to hurt from its brilliance was the sun directly overhead. There was a way out. The panic evaporated, but not far. It was never far, ever ready to leap from its perch and seize him in its tentacles. Sitting back on ankles, Manny looked down. Pulling the gi's lapels apart, he ran two fingers over his chest—smooth, brown skin, unblemished.

"Well, maybe that speaker in Roger's church was right. When a person dies the body returns to its normal, whole self," Manny thought.

Reaching out, he placed a hand on each flanking boulder and cautiously stood. They weren't nearly as large as appearing from ground level. That's when he heard the commotion. Leaning to peer over the rounded rock on his left revealed five men yelling and throwing rocks at an old man they pursued up the broad, rock-strewn incline toward Manny's position. One of the men was huge— absolutely huge—but his awkward, lumbering gait easily tread the terrain forcing the others to keep up.

Gaining the rock directly below Manny, the old man was trapped as the five closed in, continuing the pummeling of stones and epithets, until the big one raised a spear and hurled it. Reaching over his shoulder, Manny withdrew the sword while springing over the rock. A sharp crack of thunder split the clear sky.

Dropping in front of the old man, Manny swung the blade to intercept the projectile, neatly severing the massive, iron point from its shaft. The attackers froze, mouths agape at the sudden appearance of the white robed figure until the giant roared something at his accomplices who charged in mass.

It was déjà vu as Manny flashed back to a year ago. He hadn't meant to hurt them.

Δ   Δ   Δ

Manny glanced out the window. The inside of the glass was clean. Nearly a century of accumulated dirt, smoke, and exhaust on the outside smudged the streetlights, and that was impossible to reach. The final pot clinked against another as he put it in the little cupboard. It was later than usual, but he didn't care.

"There. All done, Mr. Hauptmann."

"You're gonna' ta make someone a fine wife, Manny," the old man jested in his splintered American-Yiddish accent, pushing his battered chair from the table with a nerve-grating screech.

"It's getting pretty late. I better head back to the deli. Is there anything else I can do?"

"What else? You've cleaned up, fixed a meal, changed the bedding, and now you go home to wash my dirty laundry. In this tiny place what's left to do? I have no money, you know."

"*Mitzvah*," Manny replied with a twinkle in his bright, blue eyes, referring to the Jewish concept of doing good to others.

Three times a week for the past year and a half Manny visited the elderly man. Mr. Kreutzer used to do it when his friend could no longer walk the five blocks to the deli for a cup of coffee, bagel, and social interaction, but Manny became increasingly concerned. It just wasn't safe. There was a time old people could go about unharmed. They didn't have anything of value, but that all changed. Gangs roamed the streets in search of devilment, which now included hurting people just for fun. At first Manny accompanied Mr. Kreutzer once a week, but the elderly man made other trips alone, for a while. Actually, the visits were fun and made Manny feel good.

"In the service of man you are in the service of G-d," they each declared in Hebrew and laughed.

Manny liked Mr. Hauptmann. He was funny, and more enlightened than his wisecracks portrayed. No one told him to make these visits or do the chores. They just seemed to come naturally, but the longer he stayed the more jokes and stories the old man remembered, and the more Manny laughed, something both needed in their lives.

Placing gnarled hands on the table, the ancient figure pushed himself upright and tottered over to the boy as Manny gathered up the small bag of laundry. He was short, quite short, and towering over him was a bit embarrassing for Manny, but that only encouraged the old, vaudevillian stage manager to launch a barrage of jokes.

Reaching up, he placed a rough, open hand on each of the boy's cheeks, pulled his head down, and kissed his forehead. "You're an angel my young friend. One of His very special ones."

An unsettling feeling buzzed through Manny with that declaration. He struggled with the thought.

"The G-d of Abraham protect and bless you, Manny Guzman. Shalom."

"Shalom," Manny replied equally soft.

Mr. Hauptmann had been in good form this night as Manny puttered around the tiny, efficiency apartment working extra slowly as the old man reminisced about his life backstage, conjured jokes, and relived stories to captivate the young visitor, not once repeating himself.

"John and Helga are sitting on the porch when Helga says, "John, when I die, will you re-marry?"

"That's a terrible thing to think about," John says, and wouldn't talk about it, but Helga keeps asking the question for several days. "John, when I die, will you remarry?"

Finally, he gives in and says, "Yes. I guess I would."

"Would you sell the house?"

"No. I wouldn't do that."

"Would you sell our bed?"

"No."

"Would you let your new wife use my golf clubs?"

"No, that's not a problem. She's left handed."

Manny laughed so hard he had to grab the miniature kitchen counter to keep from falling down. That's why it was later than usual when he stepped into the cool night and begin the walk home—the safe one above Mr. Kreutzer's deli.

Usually he scurried pass the backside of the block square Excelsior Hotel, but for some reason it didn't frighten him this night. It was as if he were surrounded by a virtual army of friends as he remembered a couple of particularly funny jokes Mr. Hauptmann shared, muttering them aloud to re-enjoy their hilarity, and share them with whom-ever was on his shoulder—maybe that guardian angel both elderly friends, Mr. Hauptmann and Mr. Kreutzer, talked about so often. Maybe, he thought, Benny's ghost was close by. He liked a good joke, too, so Manny made a point to speak up.

"Hey, Benny. There were these two old guys . . .. Ah, Benny what happened? How'd you really die?"

He owed his hermit friend in the hotel more than anyone knew. He never told anyone, not Roger, not Mr. Kreutzer. It was a debt that would go unpaid. It had been nearly five years since his friend died there. Chased by an angry mob, Benny fell down an open elevator shaft. At least that's what they said. Manny was suspicious. There was another person in the hotel that day. He had been seen going in, but not coming out. Manny saw him and felt the evil.

Crossing the street, he passed the vacant lot used as a playground with its dark, shadowy places. That's when he heard it—a soft scraping noise behind him as four gang bangers moved from the shadows.

There was no doubt they meant trouble. Spreading across the broad sidewalk Manny could see the chain, ball bat, and pipe dangling at their sides. The leader tossed the first insult about Manny's love of Jews. Another brought up his drunken ol' man before starting in on Judo. Manny backed away. They advanced, trying to encircle him. That's when the leader flashed a knife.

Manny hadn't wanted to hurt anyone. Not ever. When a Judo opponent once fell wrong and dislocated a shoulder Manny became visibly upset. He didn't want to hurt these guys, but knew a couple of other kids they sodomized. That was the first time Manny had ever used his training outside the dojo–the training hall at the Y. He'd hurt them—badly. He hadn't meant to. As the ambulance carted the last away, the fifteen- year-old slipped into a dark corner to throw up.

"You are allowed to protect your life and that of anyone else who's threatened," Roger counseled.

Mr. Kreutzer echoed similar sentiments from the Torah. "The law of *rodef* stems from the Book of Leviticus, Chapter 19, verse 16. G-d does not say that you are allowed to defend someone who is threatened with great bodily harm, it *requires* such defense be made, either by those standing nearby, or by the person being threatened, using the least force necessary to stop the offender."

"High sounding excuses!" Manny snorted to himself. Within seconds, he had crippled one boy for life. The other three were more fortunate. Their bones would mend in time. The police said he was justified. They had weapons. They were looking for trouble. They reaped their reward.

"Yeah! Manny, the reaper!" his mind screamed itself to sleep that and many ensuing nights.

Δ   Δ   Δ

The night of that incident, Manny secretly vowed never to use martial arts against another human being except in competition. That covenant seemed hastily made as the four men ahead of their giant friend closed rapidly, blood-chilling screams on their lips, weapons waving over their heads intent on serious mayhem, thirty yards away and closing rapidly.

Roger was well versed in Jujitsu, but limited instruction to its more salient forms of Judo and Karate. However, he saw to it that his favorite pupil received special, supplemental instruction from other martial arts masters. Manny became well versed in the art of the Japanese sword, but preferred the staff. It was less lethal.

Absentmindedly returning the sword to its scabbard slung down his back, he looked at the spear's decapitated shaft lying on the ground. A terrifying, maniacal scream shook him to the present. The first attacker wielding a club was barely fifteen feet away. Oddly, the boy with the ball bat had attacked first. Instinct took over. In one, smooth motion Manny squat, gathered up the shaft, and turned it on end. The man's belly ran into the blunt end doubling him over with a loud grunt. Manny spun the other end around and slammed it down into his shoulder. There was a muted crack as the attacker careened sideways into the rocks, the blood-curdling scream of attack turned into a cry of pain, exactly like the boy with the bat.

Taking one-step forward, he met the next two attackers. With blurring movements, the first rouge fell heavily backward as the staff swept his feet away; the second became airborne as he catapulted across the dirt and loose rocks. The last one, carrying a short sword, hung back, but upon charging, found himself flipped up landing so hard on his back the air exploded from his lungs. A neat series of pirouettes allowed Manny to land blows across the shoulders of the second followed by a cross check with his bare foot along the third man's head. By this time, the sword carrier began breathing again while crawling on all fours only to be leveled by a strike to his ribs, which audibly gave way.

During the brief seconds his companions were overpowered, the leader, the size of a one-story building, stood silently fascinated by their blistering fast demise. Regaining composure, he launched a charge amidst a frightening bellow.

Standing his ground, Manny poised for action, focusing on the attacker's deep-set, black eyes. They were just like the boy with the knife on the street—the one he paralyzed. A great sword hung from the giant's enormous hand. Momentarily frozen by the memory of what he had done to the teenage attackers, Manny ducked just in time as the air split overhead and rumbled like the flight of a hundred bats. It was a moment's curiosity before he shot the end of his stick between the giant's legs and with a great heave, lifted the man's right leg into the air. His momentum was already flowing in that direction and Manny just aided it some more, throwing the giant head first into a boulder. Even with a thick, leather helmet to protect his skull, the collision sounded like the watermelon Mrs. Henderson dropped on the sidewalk in front of the deli.

The giant staggered upright, promptly careening backwards drunken-like. In almost burlesqued, slow motion the black eyes rolled upward as he crumpled in spiral fashion to the ground. The battle was over. Five bodies lay scattered on the ground, writhing, moaning, or motionless as a sudden rush of nausea swept over the victor. Wobbling back to the boulder from which he had leapt, Manny ducked around the edge and threw up. His actions to protect the old man had been instinctive, but what he'd done made him physically ill just as before. It was only then, as the nausea abated, he had time to reflect on the strangeness of the whole affair. These guys certainly weren't from the streets he knew.

Except for the big one, the attackers were dressed in short skirts of animal skins, a couple had coarse-woven shirts, three wore thin, leather soled sandals laced up the calf, one was barefoot. The colossus was covered by thick layers of dusty, dark, sweat-stained leather—helmet, jacket, and pleated skirt. The middle parts of his hairy legs around the knee were all that lay exposed. Something resembling a calf-high boot protected his feet. Turning around, the fellow he'd just saved looked like a slightly taller Mr. Hauptmann the day Manny found the old man eternally asleep in bed clothed in a long, grayish nightshirt with black and red stripes, and old fashioned, leather slippers on his feet. Blood trickled from a cut just above the outer edge of the man's right eye and from temple in front of the thick hairline.

"Are you okay?" Manny asked.

"Yes, praise the father of Adam. Thank you."

"What's their problem?"

"Servants of the evil one. My work is nearly finished and their day of judgment is fast approaching. Perhaps, they feel the only way to stop what is to come is to kill me, but that cannot happen. The Holy One said he would send a protecting angel to set a staff in defense of His servant. However, let us not press our luck."

Looking down at Manny's bare feet he cast a glance at one of the prone attackers. "I live some distance up the mountain. The rocks can be difficult to traverse without foot protection. Perhaps we should purchase some from one of these men."

Manny looked at the nearest man. His flimsy sandals laced well up the calf look as disgusting as the feet they sort of covered.

"No. I'll pass, thank you."

"As you wish. Come, then. There may be others."

"Why don't you let me dress those wounds . . .," Manny began, but was left to fall in behind as the elderly gentleman shuffled off around the jumbled pile of boulders and up a steep incline. Frankly, Manny was surprised how well a person of such obviously advanced years could move over the steep, rocky terrain as little clouds of dust billowed up from beneath the swirling hem of the long nightgown.

Δ   Δ   Δ

Mr. Kreutzer was pretty spry for seventy something. He lived frugally, but was generous to a fault; candy or an occasional ice cream cone to the kids, a cup of coffee or sandwich to some down and outer, interest-free loans or credit until the next paycheck, expecting no interest and certainly never demanding repayment.

At least twice every day he swept the sidewalk on both sides of his corner business, often a neighbor's space, too. That's how he came to see the scrawny kid from the apartment across the street begging a quarter for a hot dog. Leaning the threadbare broom against the brick wall of his store, Mr. Kreutzer marched up to the barefoot urchin and grabbed him by the collar.

Manny remembered squirming, but felt like a dangling, limp, cloth doll. The old guy was surprisingly strong. Without a word, he literally dragged the boy into his deli and plunked him down at the counter.

"You don't move from there," his deep voice rumbled.

Manny watched through big eyes, too petrified to move, as the deli owner prepared a hot pastrami sandwich and a large glass of milk, and then slid it in front of him.

"If you ever get hungry, you sweep this floor. Don't ever beg for money. That's not right."

No one ever took offense at Mr. Kreutzer's stern admonishments. Perhaps it was the way his words came out. One knew he meant business in a very loving way.

Manny wasn't the only kid who swept floors or did any of a hundred different jobs around the place for something to eat, other than sweets. And it wasn't too hard to sit cross-legged in a semicircle on the floor around one of the metal wire chairs Mr. Kreutzer occupied in the middle of the store on a slow afternoon. This was when the bearded, old man donned a little cap on the back of his head, and read stories from the Torah—his Jewish Bible. He was a marvelous storyteller. After reading a few passages, he would retell the story with such captivating detail every boy sat motionless, hanging on each word. However, Manny and the old man quickly developed a special relationship as the boy spent increasingly more time at the deli, even accepting a room upstairs when things got too bad at home. Within a year, Manny was reading Hebrew.

The parish priest and neighborhood evangelical minister didn't like Mr. Kreutzer's impromptu religion classes. Where they bullied and dictated what to believe, the old man's stories guided young minds to internalize an understanding of what was morally right.

One day a man tried to rob the deli owner, striking him in the face with a fist. The people who saw it didn't vocalize their outrage. When the police arrived, they had to grab the would-be robber and hurry him away in a police car to save his life. People loved and respected Mr. Kreutzer and stood ready to protect him.

Δ   Δ   Δ

As the old man in a nightshirt traveled along a wisp of a trail through a barren wasteland of rock and grass, Manny often stopped to scan behind them. "There may be others" was worrisome, but after several miles and an hour and a half, he was confident no one followed. The young man was also grateful that the trail proper was devoid of the broken rocks strewn between tall blades of grass beyond its edge.

For a time he had grave misgivings about turning down the acquisition of footwear, however the trail itself was composed of fine dirt and actually comfortable to travel. The old man maintained a steady pace often forcing him to keep up. Although the trail traversed rolling terrain, the trend was mostly up. Despite being in good, physical condition, Manny's body was beginning to complain. That was disconcerting as his traveling companion showed no signs of tiring. Just when he felt a real need to ask for a short break they exited the forest and approached a cluster of tents nestled in a shady clearing, sheltered from the blistering sun. A dog barked and lumbered toward them.

The Mastiff-sized creature circled the pair, sniffing the air warily before stepping next to the old man for a welcomed scratch behind the ears. Manny was well aware how the dog placed himself between his master and the stranger. Despite basking in the affectionate attention, it kept a cautious eye on the new arrival.

"This is Calēb. He is very protective, and very spoiled," the old man said.

As the dog checked out the new arrival, a man chopping firewood nearby began to walk toward them. Drawing near he spotted the dried blood on the old man's face and garments and cried out, "Father! What happened? Are you alright?"

"Yes. Yes. I am fine. Just some followers of the evil one tried to harm me, but I told you Elohim, blessed be His Holy name, would send an angle to protect me," he replied casually, as if this were nothing out of the ordinary.

"Thank you, My Lord," the man responded, bowing especially low. Manny squirmed uncomfortably. This was the first time anyone ever bowed or addressed him so formally.

"This is my third son, Yafes, the beautiful one," the old man introduced.

Manny stretched forth his hand and was not disappointed when the young man's grip nearly popped the fingernails off his hand.

Yafes was tall, somewhat more than Manny, with the lean, hard look of an athlete. His shoulders were broad, chest deep, narrowing to a well-sculptured, six-pack, and hips that flared into long, powerful legs. The way he strode toward them imbued grace and confidence with a touch of cockiness.

"A diaper," Manny quipped to himself. "Out here in the sticks and with all these people around clothed from head to foot, even if in nightshirts, he runs around in a diaper."

Sure, during the hot day of summer Manny kicked around in cutoffs and felt a bit silly when the reflection in the weight room mirror shown a deeply tanned body accentuated by a milky-white tush and thighs. This Adonis was the color of burnt, gold amber, and bore neither tan lines nor hair except the thick, curled mop on his noble-looking head. A beardless face was finely chiseled and youthfully handsome.

"And this is my first born, Shem," the old man continued as a second joined them.

He might have been shorter than Manny, but his barrel chest and biceps stretched the gold, black, and red striped fabric of the full-length nightshirt. Manny prepared for another finger-crunching grip, but was surprised at how gently the man's hand engulfed his. With eye contact, he instantly knew this was someone in complete control, possessing a confidence needing no out-ward manifestation. Shem's glistening, mahogany-colored eyes seemed to have the ability to pene-trate the soul, while exuding genuine kindness.

"The one over there by the dark woman is my second son, Cham," the proud father pointed to another who had not bothered to bestir himself from where he lounged under the shade of a tent flap.

"I pray you will stay and receive our thanks and hospitality," Shem invited.

"Uh, yeah. That'd be okay, I guess," Manny replied.

Manny was feeling tired following the struggle through the veil of fog and encounter with the bandits, followed by the long, uphill climb under a sweltering sun. Besides, where else would he go?

"Come, then. Cool and refresh yourself in the shade, then we shall eat," the one called Yafes replied, adding, "You do eat food?"

"Whenever I can," Manny responded a bit perplexed by the question. He hadn't eaten since . . . well he had nibbled a cold hot dog yesterday noon, or at least what he thought was yesterday. At the reminder, his stomach knotted with hunger and grumbled noisily. It was embarrassing. That may be why they quickly offered a small, wooden tripod seat with a sheepskin cover to sit upon.

The old man sat on another stool as an equally old woman hustled out of the tent carrying a wooden bowl and cloth to clean his wounds. The ever-attentive Calēb lie between them, keeping one eye on the newcomer. Manny stretched forth his hand to make friends with the animal, but it would have none of that, growling softly while rippling his lips.

"This is my wife, Naahmah. She fusses over me too much," the old man said.

"Once again you are fortunate to escape," the wrinkled woman muttered affectionately, casting a pleasant smile of greeting toward Manny.

"Hello, My Lord. My name is Miriam, wife of Shem," a strikingly beautiful, young woman introduced herself, having appeared suddenly from the same tent the old man's wife had come. Knelling his, feet Miriam grabbed his right foot, pushed up the pant leg, set it into a large bowl, and poured in cool water. Manny was so startled and petrified he didn't know what to do or say as she began washing his foot. No one, especially a woman, had ever washed his feet, except his mother before she died, when he was a toddler. Patting the moisture dry, another girl, a bit older, came forward to apply something from a small, earthen jar and rub in on. It felt slightly oily and tingled. Its perfumed aroma wafted up and swirled about his nostrils.

"My name is Naashon, wife of Yafes," she introduced herself.

"In all the excitement I have been rude. Please, I beg your forgiveness, My Lord, but I have never inquired of your name," the old gentleman apologized as they were skillfully administered to.

"Manny. Well, actually Peter Guzman, sir. My middle name is Emanuel, that's why they call me Manny." He caught himself practically babbling, an irksome, nervous habit, and quickly silenced his flapping tongue.

"Your appearance certainly was a surprise. Oh, I knew you would come, but dropping out of the sky like that. You should have been there, my children," the old man detailed excitedly, waving his arms as if drawing a picture. "When those rogues set upon me I was guided to a particular rock. With no escape, I waited for the Holy One, praise be His name, to fulfill His promise. As I began to pray there came a great crash of thunder and my guardian angel drops from the sky directly before me, and with one swing of his mighty sword strikes down a giant's spear intended to end this mortal life. My heart very nearly jumped from its breast with surprise and thanksgiving."

"I'm sorry. I didn't mean to scare you. I was behind the boulder and that was the quickest way to intercept the spear."

"You caught a spear," Cham asked, a sarcastic note of skepticism in his voice, obviously having not listened.

"Oh, he did not catch it," the old man replied boastfully. "He used his sword to cut off the point in mid-air, and then used the shaft as a staff to dispatch the attackers."

"And just how many attackers were there?" Cham asked, a vague sneer curling one side of his lips.

"Four sons of men and one giant," their father continued, not allowing Manny any opportunity to speak.

"You defeated a giant? With only a staff?"

"Oh, yes, and very handily, too," the old man continued boasting of Manny's deeds as the boy felt the heat of blush fry his cheeks.

Without an opportunity to respond, Manny grew increasingly uncomfortable.

"If you would excuse my curiosity, My Lord," Yafes interjected as they finish tending their father, "but you seem a little young for an angel of the L-rd."

"A what?"

"Please, Yafes. My jubilation is obviously making of gurest uncomfortable. Please accept my sincerest apologies, My Lord."

"Please, sir, just call me Manny."

"By all means, My ... I mean Manny. Now, let us wash our hands and partake of a fine meal. My wife and daughters are very good cooks," the old man said, wiggling his bushy eyebrows several times and smiling broadly from beneath a thick, chest-length beard.

Manny always felt nervous around strangers. Coupled with the strangeness of the surroundings and lack of food his stomach had constricted into a knot. The tantalizing aromas issuing from the fire pit amplified the hunger pangs and tied off the knot into fist-sized lump. Famine overcame nervous-ness as he struggled to keep from ravishing the generous portions laid out, richly seasoned meat, vegetables, and bread in wooden bowls.

"This is very good," he managed to say between mouthfuls.

"Would My Lord like more drink," the dark-skinned wife of Cham asked.

Turning to lift his wooden bowl to the pitcher she bore, Manny was confronted by voluptuous breasts straining the fibers of her dress. His eyes lifted upward. A slight smile slithered across her full, red lips.

"Ah-h, thank you," he stuttered.

She reminded him of a black Cherry. She had large breasts, too. That's why she was so popular. Even during their innocent talk Manny found himself staring at them, wondering, fantasizing, catching himself, and feeling ashamed, yet finding his eyes and mind wandering back.

"This is a pretty good drink. Tastes like grape juice," he said trying to divert his thoughts.

"Our father makes it himself," the Olympian Yafes, replied, puffing out his chest with pride. He'd thrown a tunic over his body before sitting, but it did little to hide the physique. "No one has the knowledge of acquiring the juice of grapes as does our father."

The old man cast a fleeting scowl toward the boastful son. The message was clear and sharp, and Yafes responded by busying the food in his bowl.

"A son proud of his father's accomplishments is a blessing," Manny replied, remembering something Mr. Kreutzer had said, wishing he could possess a modicum of such pride.

The old man stared at Manny a moment, smiled faintly, and nodded agreement before ripping off a bit from a chunk of meat in his hands, and poking it through the beard into an open mouth, using the end of a finger.

Parched from the heat and exertion, Manny continued to quench his thirst from a never-empty bowl of grape juice until a light-headed and fuzzy sensation slipped up from behind and slapped him on the back of head. It hadn't dawned on him that the drink might not be plain grape juice.

"Excuse me," he slurred, "is there a bathroom around here?"

"Bathroom?" Shem asked.

"A place to relieve one's, ah . . .?"

"Of course! How thoughtless of me. Here we have held you almost captive with our talk not considering your bladder," the old man responded merrily, his cheeks displaying a dusting of a red blush.

If that drink was truly what Manny now suspected, then the old man had to be as inebriated as he, more so since he consumed nearly twice as much.

"I need to make such a journey as well," Shem replied standing up. "Come."

Seated, Manny felt fine other than being a little light-headed, but upon standing, he staggered. Stepping off the soft ground cover, the warmth of the soil penetrated the soles of his feet, radiating upward to stimulate his woozy head, and kindle the overfull feeling of his bladder.

"We are very grateful to you for saving our father today. Although we have said that, it cannot be said enough," Shem said softly as they walked away from the tents.

"I'm just glad I happened to be there. He's nice. I like him."

"So do we."

"He reminds me a lot of Mr. Hauptmann."

"Who?"

"A really nice, old man I once knew."

"We worry about him, but our lives are in the hands of Adon Olam, praise be His name. Are you really an angel?"

"No. At least I don't think so," Manny replied hesitantly, not sure what his status was just now.

"You look and dress somewhat like an angle, and in some ways act like one."

"I wouldn't know any of that."

"When G-d speaks with me, He is often attended by several angelic beings. They, too, have long, white hair like yours, and wear white robes something like you do, although fashioned differently and of much finer material," he continued, lightly stroking the fabric of Manny's gi with his fingers.

"I think it is just a coincidence . . . Wait. You said you speak WITH G-d!"

"Yes."

"Face to face?"

"In a way."

Shem's reply was so matter-of-fact and straight forward as to disarm Manny completely. He'd heard Father Bradley repeatedly say that G-d didn't speak to people any more. Mr. Kreutzer said He only spoke to *tzaddiks*—enlightened, holy ones.

Roger said G-d spoke to His children all the time, but they didn't listen very well. Manny tended to believe Roger, or maybe he wanted to believe that G-d was still alive and concerned about His children, concerned enough to still speak with them at least once in a while, except He didn't visit the ghetto.

After walking some distance from camp where they could privately relieve themselves, Shem motioned Manny to follow and slowly headed around the foot of a hill out of curiosity, and not particularly wanting to be alone.

"I like to take a walk after a meal such as we are having," Shem said.

Manny followed, but his temple started pounding incessantly from the exertion, and his head felt as if filled with helium. Mostly he wished the circular gyrations would just go away.

"My father was ordained to the Holy Priesthood of Yahweh, blessed be His holy name, and commissioned to bring forth the word of warning unto the people. No more will our Father, He who created all that can be seen, touched, and smelled tolerate their sinful ways. Man has grown too wicked. I know they will not repent. So does father, but still he goes forth trying to persuade them to return to the right ways."

"How long has he been preaching?"

"This is the 120th year now."

"120 years! How old is your father?"

"Six hundred years this next moon."

"Okay. Okay. I knew it. This is one whopper of a dream or one very cute joke . . ."

"I'm sorry. I do not understand," Shem replied, honestly bewildered.

"Hey, look. Last night, this morning, I don't know . . . whatever," Manny retorted, feeling very confused and flustered, "I was trapped. I couldn't take any more beatings from my ol' man. The law forced me to stay. There was no way out. The last thing I remember, before seeing your father, I was on my knees ready to rip my guts out and this light coming at me . . . I don't know where I am. You're all really swell people, but nobody dresses like that in public," he babbled, pointing at Shem's gown.

"The Holy One, praise be His name, obviously brought you here to save my father."

"I'm glad about that. Is this a really weird dream or am I dead, or what?"

Shem stroked his thick, black beard in thought a moment before answering, "I would say you are not dead, but perhaps for a purpose known only unto G-d, His chariot of light was sent to snatch you from the gates of death and to bring you here."

"To save your father?"

"Yes, and perhaps to save you, too, I think"

"I'm sorry but this is getting beyond me. I wish G-d would explain all this."

"Ask Him."

"Yeah. Right. Like He walks around here all the time to talk to."

"He does quite often."

"You mean He could be somewhere around here now?"

"Yes."

Again, Shem's genuine, straightforward answer struck Manny like a blow to the midsection. He had to change the subject.

"Okay, okay. By-the-way, how come you all say 'praise His Holy name,' and stuff whenever you say G-d's name?"

"It is a reminder not to use His sacred names too liberally and always with reverence."

Exiting the thick grove of trees they had been walking through, Manny stopped short and lost the ability to breathe. Here, high up in the mountains with only a stream of water nearby, sat a passenger-sized, wooden ship.

"Shem? I didn't get your father's name," Manny ventured hesitantly as a really strange feeling began to swell up like a huge wave and a warm gust of wind swirled over him.

"It's Noah."

Chapter 6

Manny knew he was alive, but if not for the barest hints of shapes, the thought that he was lying in a coffin entered his mind, and that was enough to feel claustrophobia coiling to leap from its perch. He blinked repeatedly. No change. He rubbed his eyes. Still no change. Panic seeped in. He remembered the fight with his dad, the blow to the head. Had he have been blinded? Depression began replacing panic. What would life be like blind? One more reason to die, but he'd have to do a better job pulling it off.

There was a blanket covering him, course woven, but soft. Was he in bed, his bed . . . in his dad's apartment? No, too firm. The cover didn't smell right, either. In his room at Roger's or Mr.

Kreutzer's, the sheets and blankets always had a fresh scent and a crisp feel. Mrs. Elam and Mr. Kreutzer were alike in that—ironed sheets. Well, Mr. Kreutzer "let" Manny iron the sheets, part of his "payment" for staying in the apartment over the deli. Actually, this cover felt . . . fuzzy? Revisiting the smell, it was different. Really different. Another pervasive odor invaded his nose, which was not immediately identifiable. It was rankling.

Fingers exploring further, he determined this could not be any bed slept on before. This was decidedly firmer. He continued trying to fight through confusion. When his father threw him into the bedroom, he landed on the floor and lie there for a time. However, this was not right, either. There was a shag rug beneath his back. More confusion. The floor in his bedroom in the apartment was bare wood. At Roger's, the bedroom had carpet, but not shag. Mr. Kreutzer's place had wood floors with area rugs. One of those was made of sheepskin brought back from one of his many trips to Israel.

"I must be at the deli," he thought, "But how did I get here? I couldn't make it across the street blind unless someone helped me." Another shot of the pervasive odor attacked his nose reminding him of the San Diego Zoo. "I must be in the apartment," he groaned, silently resolving to dung out the dirty clothes from the closet.

Gingerly touching his temple, Manny

remembered the fight. When his old man swung a fist—the first time—Manny stopped it. The man went ballistic. Reflexes took over as he blocked blow after blow. Frustrated, his old man went berserk. Then what? Oh, yeah. Something in the air. It glanced off his forearm and everything went crazy. He was on the floor, unable to move as his old man leaped in for the kill. Manny curled into a ball as so many times in the past. Fists. Kicks. The anger spent, Manny vaguely remembered being hurled onto his bedroom floor.

He must have passed out. Everything after that seemed so real, but it could only have been a very strange hallucination. In reality, he was back in his ghetto room to continue a life of more of the same, now blind, although he still couldn't place how Mr. Kreutzer's sheepskin rug got into his room.

His mind shifted to that night's events. The walk through the neighborhood. A farewell? No, not at first. "Be honest, yes it was," he said to himself. "You've contemplated suicide for nearly a year. This beating terminated constant waffling and set your resolve to escape the only possible way."

His mind continued to dwell on the walk. What happened at the hotel? Something tried to get him. That wasn't the first time, it was something real, not in the sense a person could touch it, but whatever it was, it seriously wanted him, whether dead, or alive, or in some way changed was immaterial. During the escape, Manny felt something akin to icy talons rooting about in his breast. He had experienced that sensation during special lessons from an old, martial arts master, but instead of using the defense, he forced rubbery legs to move until breaking free of the invisible grasp at the very place where he encountered the gang last year.

Yes, the fight. The thought of suicide began creeping into his mind after that event, becoming stronger with each of his old man's beatings. Their cries of agony, the sight of blood made him physically sick. The memory still wrenched his stomach, but permanently ending the nightmare dominating his thoughts wasn't right. At least that's what everyone important in his life said about suicide. "Life is sacred." They didn't have to endure the loneliness, the pain, the futility everyday of their life.

Was the park a dream? The misting rain, the thunder, the lightning added to the dispiriting feeling. The lightning. What was that coming out of the sky? That vision replayed with incredible clarity. Like some giant, writhing snake with an open mouth of orange, yellow, and red fire, it spiraled toward him. There was a burst of engulfing brilliance followed by a crackling sound, incredible pain, and the sensation of hurling through the air. Then there was the silence as he had never experienced, abruptly finding himself surrounded, no, more like embedded in a dense fog. The strike must have been close or he would have been toast because of what came after. Overwhelmed, his mind sought refuge and concocted a dream about Noah and the Ark, his very most favorite Bible story.

There were still unanswered questions, as how did Mr. Kreutzer's rug come to be on his apartment floor and under him? The sounds outside weren't anything he'd ever heard in the ghetto, and nothing smelled right. Things weren't quite right.

"What's going on? Where the heck am I?" he mumbled aloud as a twinge of panic crept back inside his mind and claustrophobia ruffled its wings.

Reality and delusion continued to swirl about in his mind. Confusion reigned. He tried to move, but his body felt horribly stiff and sluggishness as if lead filled every limb. With serious concentration, he willed his right hand under the blanket, running fingers over his chest. He breathed a sigh of relief. No holes. No bandages. Just smooth skin. Apparently he had botched the attempt ending up in a bed, but where? A hospital? His old man's place? Mr. Kreutzer's? Was it possible he found a way to Roger's house? Still, it didn't smell right, except perhaps for his dad's place.

Moving more of his body, the leaded sensetion slowly dissipated, but the whole seemed stiff and sore. Gradually legs and arms moved with lessening discomfort so he tried sitting up. That was a big mistake as a voracious throbbing slammed his head accompanied by violent spinning forcing him to fall back to fight off a tidal wave of nausea. Suddenly, a searing shaft of light shot through the room. His vision hadn't been lost, but now he was light blind as someone entered the room.

"Who's there?" he called out, fearful that if his old man he was absolutely defenseless.

"Good morning," a woman's voice replied with a sweet softness. "Feeling better this day?"

"Who are you?" he said, squinting to identify the visitor, silhouetted against an intense back light.

"I have been appointed to watch over you while you recuperate."

"That makes sense. Of course. I must be in a hospital after whatever happened," he thought, and then asked, "How long have I been out?"

"You have slept the night and most of this day. It is almost time for the evening meal," the melodious voice replied with a usual accent.

"What's your name?" he asked, becoming very interested in seeing the body that accompanied such a tantalizing voice.

"Does the young lord not remember? I am called Egypt, wife of Cham, youngest son of the Lord Noah."

"O-o-oh, this just isn't going to quit is it?" he

moaned, rubbing his throbbing temples with more earnest.

"The others work on that ridiculous boat. Thanks to you, it is my good fortune to stay behind," she continued, stepping to his side, and kneeling to apply a cool, wet cloth to his brow. It soothed the aggravating headache, giving immense relief.

"It's not a dream, is it?"

"A dream? We have only the nightmares caused by my husband's father. We are held captive by his demented ravings."

Manny tried sitting again. The throbbing lessened and the dizziness slackened, but only if he moved very slowly, although the suggestion of nausea hung about the fringes, eager to pounce like an expectant vulture.

He remembered the woman with raven-black hair, a bluish tint highlighting strands flowing around a finely sculpted face. He remembered the full, red lips and sumptuous body ill hidden by a tan sack of a dress. He remembered her well. All during the meal, he felt her eyes surreptitiously explore every inch of his body. Whenever he glanced up and their eyes met she didn't retreat, but let the corners of her mouth curl ever so slightly into a tiny, imperceptible smile. Manny felt the heat of a blush upon his cheeks. When her husband caught the exchange, he mimicked her smile and resumed stuffing his bearded face with food.

Egyptus must have had a basin of water because he heard the tinkle of liquid just before reapplying the cool, wet clothe against his neck and wipe it across his shoulders. There was a light fragrance. Then there was a tickle as a tiny droplet trailed down his spine. She slid the cloth down to catch it.

His relaxing muscles suddenly tensed as the wet cloth slid to the base of his spine, lingered, making little circles before slowly slipping back up to his shoulders, gliding onto his chest to massage his breasts. For a moment, he thought she was going to give him a sponge bath as the cloth continued onto his belly while her hot breathe tickled his right ear. His stomach turned into a knotted fist.

"Does the young lord wish to rise or perhaps linger longer upon his bed?" she whispered tantalizingly.

"I think the young lord wishes to throw up," he barely managed to sputter as he began to gag, the first time in his life grateful beforehand to upchuck.

Truly blinded by the searing light from outside, he reeled away from the woman and staggered outside. By squinting through one eye, he could just make out a group of trees not far away and bolted into them, losing whatever remained in his stomach upon reaching them. Although the gut now felt better, the rest of his body swam in a sea of trembling weakness.

Leaning against one of the trees for a while, he took slow, deep breaths until gradually subduing a spinning head and regaining some strength. The cooling shade also afforded Manny time to adjust to the light and think.

Nothing made sense. What he had rationalized as a delusion was happening. It then occurred that he must have suffered a concussion, and became stuck in a weird dream. Adding to the confusion, he hadn't picked up on these people's names because even Mr. Kreutzer used the Anglicized forms, and actually meeting these people was an impossibility. Upon seeing the Ark and discovering that he was in the presence of the great prophet Noah, the dream abruptly stopped to resume when he awoke in the tent.

No, that wasn't the reason it stopped. There was something else. A wind, comfortably warm, blew off the mountain and over him, and then it entered into him. There was a voice. Not Shem's. He had heard that voice before and felt peace and an ineffable joy, but as hard as he tried, Manny couldn't remember what the voice said. He shook his head . . . slowly . . . wishing the spinning and pounding would go away, and the world return to normal, so he could remember. And then the underlying problem dawn on him. He wasn't suffering the effects of any beating or concussion. He had a hangover. Glancing up, he saw Egyptus standing by a corner support of the large tent's awning, watching.

After a while he straightened and looked back at the cluster of black tents. The woman had busied herself about the main campfire. It was then Manny realized he was clad only in boxers as a flourish of embarrassment swept over him. Running around in underwear hadn't bothered him as a kid, but with puberty came self-consciousness, sometimes painfully so. Unfortunately, there wasn't much he could do about this situation. Gathering up as much courage and dignity as possible, hey strode past the woman and into the tent.

Again engulfed in blackness and blind again, his foot became ensnared in something to be unceremoniously dumped to sprawl face down on a pile of ultra-soft bedding. This was obviously a bad day and the best solution was to remain where he lay until light suddenly poured in as someone lifted and secured one whole section of wall.

Momentarily frozen by the sudden flood of brilliant light, he watched as the woman fastened the wall in place. As she moved quickly toward him, Manny barely managed to grab a blanket to cover himself.

"Ah-h-h, excuse me. Where are my clothes?" he sputtered.

"Right here, next to your bed. Let me help you put them on."

"Yeah, right. No thanks. That may be extending hospitality a little beyond what I can handle. If you don't mind, you know, stepping outside, I'll get dressed myself."

"Whatever you wish. My Lord has a beautiful body," she replied, sliding her hand up the length of his arm and down his chest until her long fingers reach his naval.

Manny nearly jumped out of his skin, twisting away in an awkward scramble for his clothes. Rising, Egyptus walked slowly toward the opened wall, casting a long glance over her shoulder. There was a hint of craftiness in that smile as she emitted a soft sound something between a snort and a sigh.

"There is food outside. The others will be back soon," she said, tossing the remark over her shoulder before disappearing.

For the first time Manny could see sheep-skins spread out over the ground to make beds on some sort of woven carpet. Quickly scanning the interior, he spotted his clothes neatly folded near where he had laid and put them on in a fumbling frenzy. He missed the sword entirely until stepping on it with a bare foot, all the while wondering how he had gotten into bed and more pressing, how he had gotten undressed. The parting remark about his body left him disquieted, especially considering the woman's not so subtle advances.

Outside, Egyptus tended to clay pots by the fire, but turning her head, cast a longing stare as the boy emerged from the tent. His head began throbbing again, not quite so hard, with a return of the dizziness. Finding a seat under the canopy, he sat down, and buried his head in his hands.

"Try some of this," she said, handing him a steaming bowl of what appeared to resemble thick oatmeal. He hated oatmeal. At that moment, his stomach wasn't too sure if it was upset because he recently threw up or was just plain hungry. He decided giving it something to ruminate over rather than its lining. Unfortunately, this pasty-looking stuff was the only thing available.

"Thanks," he replied. "Gotta spoon or something?"

"We use our hands," she replied, demonstrating with two fingers in scooping fashion.

"Well, then I better wash up," he announced removing himself to the cleaning area.

Returning to his seat, he peered into the bowl of mush, wrinkled up his nose, dipped two fingers in, and stuck them into his mouth.

"Hey, not bad," he said. "Tastes a lot better than it looks."

Egyptus flashed another wily smile punctuated by an enticing wink.

A lot of hookers plied his neighborhood, but this woman put them to shame. The sack dress of a coarse, light brown cloth barely touching her ankles was tight enough to suggest wide, curving hips, and long, graceful legs. The rest of her filled out the dress leaving little doubt the temptress was well put together. Smooth, dark skin and a melodious voice only emphasized a sensuous beauty.

"Cham's one lucky dude," Manny thought.

How many times in recent years had he lay in bed unable to sleep, fantasizing what it would be like to take a trip up the alley like other boys his age, to be uncovered in the presence of a woman.

"But not this woman. She's married. You better watch out Guzman 'cause she's obviously putting moves on you," he whispered to himself and shaking off the temptation.

Realizing he was staring, Manny quickly paid unusual attention to his food until Calēb trotted to the edge of the canopy area, sat down a few feet away, and stared at him, a sloppy, wet tongue dangling out one side of his panting mouth. He seemed a bit friendlier, but remained standoffish.

"Good day, my young friend. I am glad to see you have returned to the living." Manny recognized the merry, baritone voice of Yafes, or as Manny had learned of him through Mr. Kreutzer's stories—Japheth.

"Yeah, thanks."

"Father said you probably needed rest after the rigors of your journey."

"Right. And a little less grape juice. What was in that stuff?"

Japheth's laughter lightened Manny's depression. "It is from father's own vines. He is a master wine maker," Japheth replied proudly.

"Think I'll stick with water from here out."

Japheth leaned back and loosed a robust, baritone laugh that brought a smile to Manny's lips. "It must be difficult to travel such a long way and to do battle as soon as your feet touched the earth."

"It could have been worse."

Japheth raised an eyebrow. "Defeating a giant so easily? Perhaps father is right."

"Hey. I'm not an angel, okay? See, no wings. I'm just a guy that somehow is stuck in a really screwy dream. Besides, that giant fellow was too cocky and put himself off balance. I couldn't exactly miss the chance to dump him. I just hope he'll be alright. He hit his head pretty hard on that rock."

"Does it matter?" Shem asked, joining the conversation.

"I don't like hurting people."

"You are a good person Manny Guzman," Japheth replied. "I respect you very much."

Just then Cham appeared, sullen as ever. "It is still difficult for me to believe anyone could defeat a giant so easily, especially by a mere boy. I've never heard of such a thing," he said, a challenge craftily intoned to provide a back door to avoid giving offense.

During the meal last night, Manny quickly decided that Cham's, or more Anglicized, Ham's style to be confrontational with an air of guileless innocence with an easy out if challenged.

"Perhaps you could give us a small demonstration," Ham said, a sly glint in his brown eyes. "If you are feeling . . . better."

"Yes. Please," Japheth jumped in excitedly. "I love to wrestle. Perhaps you would like to . . . ah-h . . .," he proposed, holding his hands out, palms up, and rocking his body sideways.

Apparently, the oatmeal stuff was the cure because the hangover and pounding in his head had gone. "Yeah. Okay," Manny replied, eying Ham as Japheth began removing his sandals. "But I'm not too sure about taking on another giant right away. It might be best to pace my recovery and wrestle someone more my size. How about it, Ham?" Manny said.

The younger brother startled and started to back out, but Japheth clapped his hands together excitedly, almost squealing with merriment. "Yes, of course. Ham is very good. I am big, and strong, and can be very overpowering. It would not be good to exert yourself too quickly after all that has happened, but I must warn you, Ham is quick and very sneaky."

"Oh, really? I wouldn't have guessed," Manny said, sarcasm lightly touching his comment.

Manny really had no remorse having formed a dislike for Ham's arrogance and bad manners. He deliberately trapped him into the match. Besides, he had a strong suspicion Egyptus' advances may not have been entirely her idea. No, he had no remorse for what was about to happen.

Walking to a sandy area shaded by some white-barked Aspens, Ham begrudgingly peeled off his robe, leaving on a knee-length kilt, and removing his sandals. This allowed Manny to assess his opponent's physical build and it surprised him. Japheth was obviously the bodybuilder of this age, and Shem appeared fit as well, but Ham, on the other hand, was slender with no real upper body muscle. His stomach was slightly rounded and smooth. Manny felt a decided advantage. Slipping the sword and scabbard over his shoulder, he handed them to Shem. Of the three sons, he felt to trust Shem and Japheth, but not Ham, and for that, he felt badly, a little. Leaving the gi on would give Ham something to grip and an advantage. Manny fought down a cocky feeling, but it was difficult. Ham was going to need all the help possible.

Giving the customary bow from the waist, the traditional Japanese form of showing respect towards one's opponent, and a way of saying thank you for the opportunity to improve one's self, Manny prepared for combat. Ham ignored the gesture and immediately began a slow circle, looking for an opportunity to attack. However, Noah's youngest should have simply trumpeted his intentions like a charging bull elephant. There was no surprise when and what he was about to try. Manny countered assault.

"Well, done!" Japheth crowed with astonishment, "Whatever happened. Come on Ham, get off your back, and have another try."

When Ham picked himself off the ground a third time he was visibly upset. "I can't even touch you. It's not fair," he whined.

"Okay, if you want to get down and dirty, that's alright by me," Manny responded tauntingly.

The fourth throw put Ham high into the air before landing on his back, once again, but this time Manny dropped into a Judo pin, wrapping his right arm behind the downed man's neck, and locking the fingers onto the right shoulder. Throwing the weight of his own shoulder onto his opponent's chest, he immobilized Ham's right arm. All Ham could do was flop from the waist down like a beached fish.

"When you want to quit," Manny whispered in his ear, "just tap my shoulder."

Ham responded immediately. He'd had more than enough.

"Do you feel well enough to try me?" Japheth said.

"Yeah. I'm okay."

"You will not find me quite so easy, my young friend," Japheth taunted lightly, as he pulled his garment overhead, tossing it aside.

Once again, Manny beheld Japheth's physique. It was daunting, every inch rippling with muscle from a bull-like neck to his toes. Unlike

Ham, there was no hint of paunch. He thought Japheth posed a striking resemblance to pictures in one of his history books of an ancient Greek athlete or warrior, sans beard. Even Japheth's face gave Manny the feeling of déjà vu of those pictures, but that feeling took flight as the man reached to his back, fiddled with something, and nonchalantly removed his leather kilt, flinging it aside as well. To Manny's horror the man was obviously about to remove the diaper, too.

"Ah-h-h, are you planning to ah-h-h wrestle me like, you know, nude?" Manny stuttered.

"G-d created man in His image, the image of greatest beauty."

"Yeah, but I don't recall ever seeing Him, ah-h-h, you know, showing everything," Manny squeaked with embarrassment.

"Our guest is right, my brother," Shem interjected with a slight chuckle. "Although His countenance is beautiful beyond words, I have never seen our Heavenly Father, praise be to His name, appear other than fully clothed. Nor have I seen His angels appear in such manner either, except, of course, this night past which was an unusual situation."

Manny shot a panicked glance at Shem. "What did he mean by "except last night?"

"But I have never wrestled except . . ."

"Perhaps, my son, our guest is suggesting

that your splendor might be so overwhelming as to distract his concentration," Noah said with a soft chuckle while taking a sip from a bowl of grape juice as he joined the group.

Manny felt mortified. Confusion had beset him during the transition from puberty through adolescence. There were times he questioned his sexuality, as when he'd catch himself staring at another boy and feeling excited. That's why, for a long time, he evaded those feelings by waiting until everyone else had showered and left. When that was not possible, he went to the furthest end of the communal shower for more privacy. At Roger's house, privacy was impossible with the Elam boys practically attached to each of their big brother's legs, hovering like bear cubs around a honey log. At least the doors had locks.

As a child, he generally ignored or considered girls a nuisance, until a couple years back his attitude became decidedly different. The night he asked Cherry to go up the alley Manny had awakened from a dream. He couldn't remember the details, but he was aroused and sweating, despite being a cool night. His whole body felt like a volcano ready to explode.

Now, here was Japheth squaring off across the stretch of sand, legs apart, fists on hips, no more than a diaper about his loins. Manny felt uneasy. Embarrassed? Aroused? Guilty? Ashamed? Angry? Enveloped in spiraling consternation,

Noah's teasing didn't help.

"Does the angel from Heaven plan to wrestle my brother fully clothed?" Ham taunted. "A pity to see such fine cloth become soiled."

"Mind your own damn business, loser," Manny hissed under his breath as blue eyes shot fire in the man's direction.

"Perhaps I could hold your coat so it will not become soiled or damaged," Ham continued undaunted.

Manny pulled the tail of the heavy, canvas jacket from beneath the brown belt, slid if off his shoulders, and handed it to Shem. "It won't tear," Manny responded curtly.

Japheth smiled. He wasn't the only one with muscles. Manny just felt self-conscious about exposing himself in public, but the nearly daily workouts had transformed his own youthful body into a powerful framework. Forcing feelings of discomfort aside, he focused on his opponent. Japheth was not only the epitome of the glory that would be Greece; he was also confident, agile, and smart. It was obvious the man was planning to wrestle in the traditional style on the ground, but he had no intention of cooperating. That would be suicide.

At first Manny evaded each lunging attack like a bullfighter, frustrating his adversary. That was his strategy in competition—size up the opponent, watch for repetitive moves, and wait patiently for them to make a mistake that would put them on the ground. It was a frustration to his opponents, who tried hurrying the game, but 'fighting' was like a fine meal, according to Roger. "Take your time and observe every nuance," he often said. Slowly Manny cleared the clutter from his mind and focused. Japheth landed with a dull, but solid thud in the deep sand.

Sitting up, the burly grappler slapped one knee and hooted loudly, "Well done, my friend. What happened brothers?" Everyone shrugged their shoulders in unison. It had happened too fast.

Manny felt better now, more confident than he had in months, more focused, more in tune with the environment. After the second throw, he was feeling a bit cocky. He wanted to try something he hadn't done for a long time.

Holding up his hand to delay Japheth's next lunge, Manny sawed his feet into the soft sand, slightly sideways to Japheth, and lowered the head-band over his eyes.

Casting a questioning look at one another, Ham said, "Surely you do not intend to . . .?"

Shoulders squared, Manny took in a deep breathe, and exhaled slowly. The first time another of his martial arts teachers introduced the technique, he instantly felt the mysterious power sweep over his body as every inch became sensitive to the surroundings, almost felt like entering into another realm. Raising his right hand, he curled each finger into the palm as a beckoning gesture. Japheth shrugged his shoulders toward the others and attacked, aiming straight for Manny's hip.

Manny's movements flowed with the charge and impending impact as his right foot slipped backwards. Squatting low, his shoulder caught Japheth's chest at the precise moment. The move had been so fast there had been no opportunity for the big man to react. Manny's butt caught him just below the hip, lifting, and catapulting him high into the air. Japheth landed hard on his back.

Deathly silence gripped the audience as Manny pushed the headband back to his forehead and adjusted to the light. Japheth lay flat on his back, eyes fixed heavenward. There was not so much as twitch.

"He is dead!" Ham shouted. "He has killed our brother!"

Japheth's outstretched hand waived weakly as he coughed to return air to his lungs.

"I am not dead," he croaked. "You will have to wait a bit longer to be rid of me anxious one."

The hulk gradually turned onto his stomach and pushing up to hands and knees, slowly shook his head so that the long mane of hair swept back and forth like a dangling dust mop. Eventually rising to a kneeling position, he coughed again, and stared at Manny, his dark eyes blurred, liquid pools.

"Are you okay?" Manny asked softly while kneeling next to the man's shoulder. "I didn't mean to . . ."

"I am alright," he coughed weakly. "Only my pride and maybe a few parts of my anatomy are bruised. You could see through that veil over your eyes, right?"

"No. I just knew how you would attack and felt it as you came."

As Manny stood, Japheth stretched out a hand for an assist up. Manny grabbed it, bracing his feet only to find himself suddenly wrapped in a bear hug against the man's sweat and sand covered chest. Lifted off the ground as Japheth stood, arms pinned, he could do little except squirm. He was almost defenseless. Japheth laughed, although weakly, as he hadn't regained all of the air in his lungs.

"You are a wonder, my good friend, but a bit naive, too." He set Manny gently on his feet. "Never trust an opponent until he is down to stay." And then wrapping an arm around the victor's shoulder, he gave another hug, equally firm, but affection-ately so.

Manny smiled feebly in agreement, until spotting some boards nearby. Silently walking over to the pile, he selected two, each nearly two inches thick, ten inches wide, and a couple of feet long.

"What kind of wood is this?"

"Gopher wood. We grow it to use on the Ark," Shem replied.

"Strong?"

"Very much so."

"Here, Japheth, hold this board," Manny said, handing it to him. "Put one hand on each end, and hold it vertically out in front of you. Lock your elbows and hold it tight."

"What are you going to do? Surely you don't plan to . . ." Japheth began, suddenly realizing Manny was indeed planning to break it with his bare hand. Seconds later, he stood looking at two pieces of wood.

"Now, hold this board the same way," Manny instructed. "Ham, you better stand behind Japheth and brace him."

Manny stepped back a few feet to focus his concentration before leaping into a flying front kick that shattered the board.

"Oy vey!" Japheth exclaimed. "Our enemies be spurned. Brother Ham, I think we are lucky to still be alive. Indeed, the giant and his friends had no chance at victory." Helping Ham onto his feet, he continued, "With an angel as this, there is no need for an army to protect our father."

Ham tried to appear unimpressed, but the awe was difficult to mask as he dusted sand from his burnoose. Ego bruised, he slunk into a sullen deportment testifying to being a poor loser. His behavior would have been worse had he known Manny placed him behind Japheth knowing full well he would be knocked down by the impact.

"That is very hot work," Bilnah remarked as she offered a container. "Would you care for a drink?"

"What is it?" Manny asked, quickly looking into the container.

"Some sweet water from Lord Noah's well."

"Thank you," Manny replied taking the bowl. After a test sip, he downed the contents. She was right. It did taste sweet. After a third bowl his tongue didn't feel three times its size with a coating of hangover paste.

"Thanks for taking care of me," he said, using his sleeve to wipe some remaining drops of water from the corner of his mouth. "Last night, I mean."

"It was the least we could do," Shem replied.

"Just out of curiosity, ah, who put me to bed?"

"We did, Shem and I," Japheth answered as they walked back to the tents.

Manny visibly sighed in relief.

"Angels have strange undergarments," Japheth continued, his robust voice returning and disconcertingly loud. That was not a subject Manny felt comfortable discussing publicly, especially with

Miriam following just behind them. "Those pictures, what animal are they?"

"Bugs Bunny." Manny replied curtly, feeling heat rise to his face, knowing he was blushing.

"Bugs Bunny? I have seen nothing arrive here like that."

"He's a cartoon character."

"A cartoon character? I do not understand." Japheth's interest was genuinely sincere and Manny realized embarrassment was causing him to be unintentionally short. "That meal sure smells good," he remarked, trying to change the subject.

Japheth sniffed the air while wrapping a burly arm around Manny's shoulders as they walked to the dining area and said, "Yes, and we have worked up a very good appetite," but like a dog with a chew-toy, he was not about to give it up. "The feel of the cloth is so very different. Our best weave is not nearly so smooth or thin. What is it made of?"

"You're really a curious fellow aren't you?"

"I love learning. I love nature and all the beauty it beholds because it has all been touched by the hand of G-d."

"My brother has a natural hunger for knowledge." Shem interjected.

"Wish I had a set of encyclopedias to give you." A few steps further Manny spit out, "Rayon," and exhaled a deep breath to ease his tension.

"What?"

"My underwear is made of rayon," Manny replied slightly exasperated. He had managed to change the subject then brought it right back.

Miriam bowed her head to hide a giggle behind a dainty hand. Realizing his folly, Manny shook his head and broke into a big smile. Japheth appeared confused for a moment before contributing one of his thunderous laughs.

Chapter 7

Approaching the cluster of tents, a pair of lions ambled out of the trees to their left as casually as if strolling over the African Belt. Manny jumped, but couldn't move to cover with Japheth still locking him in a side hug so he just froze in place.

"Hey, guys. Lions?"

"Well, there you are," Japheth replied with a matter-of-fact air while planting a fist on either hip. "Where have you two been these past several days? Have you been out hunting, my furry friends?"

The lioness turned her head to look at him while continuing across their path, with an almost, "What's it to you?" scowl. The male ignored the remark like a headstrong teenager coming in far past the appointed time.

Japheth's relaxed attitude and the way he talked, as if the lions were just a couple of oversized kittens, didn't do much to calm Manny's heart as it continued to pound a 20-K race. The sword was in reach, but he wished it was in his hands instead of Shem's.

"Seem rather docile. Pets?" Manny inquired.

"A special tranquility lies over the earth, at least about this place," Shem answered.

"A what?"

"Our L-rd has spread His hand over this part of the earth so there will be peace and cooperation among all his creatures chosen to be on the Ark. That is why the lamb can graze next to the lion and nothing will happen."

"But, don't they get hungry?"

"Yes," Japheth answered. "That is probably why these two have been gone, out searching for food not chosen to repopulate the earth after the great flood."

"And it is time for us to eat as well," Miriam announced as the big cats continued pass the tents, up, and over the rise, oblivious to the humans, finally disappearing in the direction of where the Ark rest.

Ham had already washed leaving the three men to eagerly clean the playtime dirt from their bodies, dry, and slip on clean shirts. Manny untied his belt, refitted the jacket, and retied it with the double wrap around his body and square knot. Gathering to eat each person knelt for prayer. Manny laid the sword on the ground parallel to his right leg silently surprised at how natural that action had been, as if he had done it all his life.

Side by side, husband and wife bent to their knees, forming a circle. Shem offered the prayer. "G-d of Adam, Master of the universe and of this earth, praise be your Holy name. Great is your glory and great is yhour power. May your love continue to abide with us, your children. Hear now the words of my heart.

"The Ark you commanded my father to build is nearing completion, the food stores have been gathered, and many animals have arrived. Our father continues to cry repentance unto an unfearing people as you have commanded. We await further instructions.

"We are grateful and humbled for the elohim you have sent in fulfillment of your promise to protect our father. He has shown us wondrous things and fulfilled his responsibilities with great measure. May your spirit continue to be with him and give him the strength and courage to face the difficult days that are to come.

"We are most grateful for your love and blessings as we continue to serve you. Blessed be your Holy name, now and forever and ever. Amen."

Each person's voice rose to echo "Amen." Manny was not accustomed to the expression, but as it came from his lips, it felt as natural as placing the sword at his side.

After a moment of silence, Japheth stretched out on his side by the meal spread out on the cloth before them, speared an apple, and bit off a big chuck that cracked like a bone being broken. Ham glared at Manny while stuffing something into his mouth as their guest reached for a glistening, brownish thing swimming in a light brown sauce and took a bite, a date, a fat, juicy date the size of a small kiwi, bursting with sweetness, some of the juice trickling down his chin. While the other men also stretched out on their sides to eat, Manny remained seated, legs crossed.

"I've never seen a sword quite like that," Ham remarked, using an elbow to point while shoving more food into his face.

His voice seemed uncharacteristically restricted and nasal, not a pleasant sound, and with his mouth filled to near capacity with food, not a pleasant sight, either. Manny wished he would at least close his lips while chewing to muffle the smacking sound.

"It was hand crafted by an artisan before . . ." Manny hesitated. To speak of world wars and such things of his time would be meaningless to these people and likely generate confusion. ". . . a long time before I was born."

"Angels are born?" Japheth jumped in.

"Born. Created. Whatever," Manny said, dodging the question. He was more interested in satisfying a more settled stomach than conversation.

"The metal appears very different," Ham continued.

"It's steel."

"Steel? What is . . . steel? I know only stone and bronze."

Manny chided himself for saying that, but a street kid had to be quick of mouth as well as feet to survive and answered, "Steel is a metal made on the forge of HaShem." Manny saw Shem shoot a concerned glance in his direction. He apparently used a term Shem took as one of G-d's names. "HaShem means, the Name," he quickly added, which seemed to satisfy the future Prophet who winked.

"Could I see it?" Ham pressed.

Manny guessed that was the direction of the conversation. "Sorry."

"Humph," Ham replied sullenly, and then seemed to perk up. "We are going to work more on the Ark tomorrow. Would you like to help?"

"Yeah, that might be fun."

"You could work with me. I really do need an extra set of hands on the upper deck."

Manny's street savvy peeked. Ham hadn't been particularly friendly, now all of a sudden he was acting like best buds.

"Good," Japheth interjected. "That would allow me to work on the third deck stalls near the back. Shem could help me while the women continue loading the food."

"If you're going to be working on the Ark you may want to wear something cooler. That garment is quite heavy and appears to be hot," Egyptus suggested as she brought more water.

Mumbling to himself Manny thought, "Sure, it'd be appropriate to wear something more practical, and I could just leave this sword here, too, for you to guard. Wrong."

"I am sure to have something for you to wear. We are about the same height," Japheth added.

"And much wider," Bilnah, said, referring to her husband's more mature size. "I shall find something tonight and change it to fit better so it will be ready when we leave in the morning."

"That's very kind of you," Manny said.

Throughout the meal Noah appeared unusually quiet, almost meditative. Judging by the redness of his cheeks Manny thought that he might be inebriated, but didn't move as if drunk. He had no problem directing a knife into the meat to slice off a piece for himself, and then silently offer another to Manny. He just seemed preoccupied.

Following the meal, Shem offered thanks to G-d for the fine meal after which the men lounged about a fire as the women cleaned up. When they finished Shem stood, briefly disappearing into a smaller tent set off from the others, returning with a large scroll. As he sat cross-legged, everyone gathered closer, or at least focused attention on him. Manny repositioned himself next to Japheth and Bilnah. Ham remained sprawled on his carpet as Egyptus slid in beside him.

"These are the words of our earthly father, Adam," Shem announced, reverently opening the scroll and slowly rolling the continuous length of thin sheepskin until coming to a particular place. Ever since Shem could read, he took on the responsibility to share the sacred writings with the family. After offering a prayer, he began to read.

"With the help of Eve, we built an altar two cubits high and four cubits wide. On each long side we placed a kneeling stone, one across from the other. I upon one and Eve upon the other we joined our left hands across this alter. Rising my right hand to heaven, I did supplicate the L-rd upon our behalf. Our hearts were heavy and tears stained our faces. This day our family was to give thanks for the blessings of the harvest. It should have been a day of great joy, but it was not. In the course of a moment, we lost two of our sons. Cain, in a fit of rage slew his brother Able whose blood soaked the earth, and Cain was banished forever from our presence by the command of He who created us."

Manny listened closely. He had heard the abbreviated story as retold to Moses, but these were the words of the man who actually exper-ienced that great loss. Manny had heard of this book lost long ago in time. Shem was reading from the Book of Adam.

Δ   Δ   Δ

Anyone looking upon the scene from a distance when Manny first saw the Ark would have seen him stand transfixed by the sight of the enormous boat, and then slowly turn to face the mountain towering over it. Canting his head slightly to the left it appeared as if he was listening to something before crumpling into Shem's arms to be laid gently upon the ground.

Coming as a warm breeze, a voice spoke to him, giving a complete understanding of who he was, where he was, and what he was doing in this place, the words sweeping over his mind like a great tidal wave. However, the young man's mind went into overload causing him to collapse into the future prophet's arms, but that was not the case.

Kneeling with Manny's head on his lap, Shem continued to gaze toward the mountain, listening to the voice. After a time Shem said, "Yes, L-rd, I understand. It shall be done as you say."

Scooping the young man up to cradled him in strong, brown arms to carry him back to camp. Noah was exiting the smaller prayer tent as he began descending the hill. By Caleb's alert, Japheth hurried to meet his brother and take the burden the rest of the way to camp.

"Ha, it would seem the L-rd's angel can't handle his wine," Ham crowed, not bothering to bestir himself from next to the fire.

"The L-rd spoke to him," Shem whispered to his father.

"Yes, I know. Your mother has prepared a bed for him in our tent," Noah said.

Setting Manny on a deep pile of sheepskins, the two men began to remove his clothes. As Shem untied the drawstring to his trousers, he paused.

"Does he wear an undergarment?" Japheth whispered.

Shem pulled the waistband down slightly. "He does."

Both were relieved, however, upon removing the pants they stared at one another and shrugged their shoulders. After covering their father's guardian with a blanket and placing the sword by his side, they left.

Δ   Δ   Δ

Shem was in many ways like Mr. Kreutzer with an unassuming attitude and a clear, firm voice. Black, penetrating eyes that saw more than just the surroundings seemed capable of burrowing to the very core of a man's soul. Shem knew who he was, what G-d expected of him, and possessed the dogged determination to carry on His work. The one difference was the beard. Like Mr. Kreutzer, Shem sported a full and very thick beard to the chest. While Mr. Kreutzer's was as white as Manny's hair, Shem's was black as coal, despite being ninety-eight years old, twenty years Mr. Kreutzer's senior.

After the scripture reading and prayer that second evening, Noah and Naahmah retired to their bed, as did Ham and Egyptus, while Bilnah and Miriam worked to resize the clothes for Manny. The three men continued talking into the evening. Manny had thousands of questions that could have kept them up for days, but most would have to wait as Shem and Japheth needed to rest for the next day's work.

A small oil lamp flickered near the rear of the tent providing the barest light as Manny quietly entered Noah's tent and disrobed next to his bed. Sliding beneath the cover, he snuggled in the soft warmth. He hadn't noticed the mountain cold as he sat by the fire and it chilled him while moving to the tent. Lying with hands clasped behind his head, he stared into the blackness above, continuing to reflect upon what Shem had read and taught from Father Adam's writings. On the other side of the large tent, behind a curtain, Noah's snores sounded very similar to Mr. Kreutzer—long, deep, and rumbling. Naahmah held her own with a slightly higher pitch that almost harmonized with her husband.

Suddenly, he remembered failed reciting his evening prayers. Noah led the family in prayer before retiring as Mr. Kreutzer and Roger did, but they also encouraged him to have personal prayer, so he arose, knelt, and quietly recited a prayer Mr. Kreutzer had taught. The rumbling snores faded into silence. Before the obligatory "Amen," he hesitated, and then continued less formally as Roger had taught.

"I'm really confused, G-d. Why am I here? Yeah, I'm supposed to protect Noah, but there's more. I think you told me, but I apologize for not remembering."

Manny stopped. The vision of the previous night on the mountain came to mind as clear as if he were there again. He sensed the cool, night breeze whispering among the trees, the pounding in his head from the walk—the effects of the grape juice—the sweet smell of pine, the distant lowing of creatures. He relived the shock of seeing the Ark and realizing he was in the presence of the great antediluvian prophet and his family. However, that wasn't the reason he passed out. He remembered the warm wind caressing his face and a gentle voice. Turning his head to one side to hear more clearly, all he remembered was, "Line upon line, precept upon precept my Cherub, blessed above all my children save one." As suddenly as it came, the voice was gone into the fluid mists surrounding him, replaced by the warmth of a penetrating love filling every cell of his body.

"Whose voice was that?" He desperately tried putting a face with it because there was the distinct impression of having heard it before. That was not a figment of any imagination. The voice had been real, as if the possessor stood next to him and spoke directly into his ear. And Cherub? What did that mean?'"

Almost immediately, the stereophonic, stentorian snores resumed. Slipping beneath the warm covers once again, Manny tried to reason all that had happened in the last couple days while the words of his unseen visitor echoed in the halls of his mind, but the sounds of his host became like the purr of a kitten lulling him into a deep, restful sleep.

The next morning Manny awoke to find one whole side of the tent rose again allowing a stream of early morning light in and Naahmah approaching.

"Good morning. Did My Lord rest well?"

"Yes. Very well, thank you," he responded taking a long, leisurely stretch.

"I was concerned. My husband breathes very loudly when he sleeps."

Manny strangled a giggle into a modest smile. "No more than Mr. Kreutzer back home," he replied cheerfully, thinking that she more than held her own in the duet.

"Here are the clothes my Japheth's Bilnah sewed"

"You are all very kind. Thank you," he replied, taking the large bundle and placing it next to his right leg.

Naahmah smiled warmly, turned, and left. As Manny watch the woman walk away, silhouetted by the incoming light, he noticed how gracefully she moved, the ends of her sack-like dress swaying in rhythm with each step.

Setting the bundle on the ground, he rose to kneel, feeling embarrassed at having not always prayed twice each day as Mr. Kreutzer taught. Reciting the evening prayer tripped him up the most. Far too often he was so tired to let his head hit the pillow first, thinking he'd do it laying down.

"*Shema Yisrael, Adonai Eloheinu, Adonai echad*," he began, "Hear, O Israel, the L-rd is our G-d, the L-rd is one." While softly chanting the prayer, the meaning of the words filled and renewed his body with energy.

Mind and soul purged and fortified, Manny still found stepping into public ten minutes later a struggle. Bugs Bunny hidden beneath the short, leather kilt was not the concern. He knew everyone would be looking at him. Self-consciousness was a troubling affliction. He hated being the center of attention. The shirt, a V-neck open to the breast-bone, fit loosely. He was grateful for that, disliking tight-fitting clothes. The sandals were simple pieces of thick leather laced over his feet and up, around the calves, obviously new, soft, and pliable, and easily walked in. Taking a deep breath, he stepped out of the tent.

"You look very handsome, My Lord," Naahmah remarked softly in a grandmotherly tone, an affectionate twinkle in her dark eyes.

"Please," Manny replied as softly to her and Bilnah standing at her side, "just call me Manny. And thank you. The clothes are very nice and each fits perfectly."

Following morning family prayers, Manny loaded up on a breakfast of goat's milk and something resembling Cream-O-Wheat. Afterwards Japheth's jaunty gait lead the work detail up the hill where the lions had wandered the night before, passing through the saddle toward the Ark. Although attired the same as the other men, Manny still hung the sword down his back. He wasn't going to leave it in camp, despite the suggestion. Ham would have to find another way to get his hands on it.

Chapter 8

Once cresting the saddle overlooking the Ark, the small company continued down into a lush, green valley bisected by the meanderings of a wide, but shallow stream. Other than the trees surrounding the camp, this was the most life Manny had seen since arriving. His heart pumped with excitement. There it was. The Ark. Of all the stories in the Bible, this had been one of the most enthralling to the impressionable child. Every so often Mr. Kreutzer would ask his little band of impromptu Yeshiva students if there was a favorite story they'd like to hear. Manny invariably asked for the one about the man with the animals and the boat, and then eagerly sit on the deli's glazed tile floor as the old man tirelessly related the story of Noah and the Ark. The boy unashamedly admitted to having a fascination with boats and the wild things in zoos. Both were here, except there were no walls and fences. All around, resting on hillsides, wandering among the stores of building materials were the animals, completely unconcerned with natural enemies, prey, or human presence

As the others set to work, Manny took a few moments to run his hand over the long rough, wooden hull. He knew the dimensions by heart—three-hundred cubits long by fifty cubits wide, and thirty cubits high. Of course, a cubit hadn't really made much sense when listening to the story. Now he saw it. The Ark was huge, easily filling one and half football fields reaching up so that if set next to his fourth floor apartment he would have easy stepped out the window onto the upper deck. He felt like the time seeing Disneyland for the very first time.

"What do you think?" Shem asked, putting a gentle hand on the young man's shoulder.

"Wow! It's just like the pictures only so, so big."

"Pictures?"

"Oh, shoot!" Manny rebuke himself once more. "Ah-h-h drawings, I mean . . ."

"My apologies Manny, I forget. Of course you would know about the Ark's design."

"You're not going to shake this angel identity thing if you keep slipping up with the big mouth," he silently kicked himself.

"Guess I better get to work." Manny stopped abruptly. "Shem?"

"Yes, My Lord."

He heaved a sigh. They just weren't going to give up on the formality. "Please . . ."

"I am sorry," Shem responded. "Manny."

"The first time you showed me the Ark it wasn't just the grape juice that caused me to pass out. There was something else . . . someone else was talking . . . wasn't there."

"Yes," Shem replied smiling broadly.

"What I mean, who was it?"

"Jehovah, blessed be His name."

"Jesus the Christ! Are you telling me that Jesus . . . ah, ah, blessed be His name . . . was speaking to me?"

"Yes."

"What did He say?" Manny shuddered, anxiously waiting for the reply.

"Do you not remember?"

Manny turned away embarrassed. "Not really. Something about precept upon precept. Was there more?"

"There was a great deal more, but I am admonished not to say."

"Last night, before I went to sleep I asked Him," Manny continued trying to draw out an answer.

"And did He who is our creator speak?"

"I remembered coming here and a voice that

said "Blessed art thou, My Cherub, above all my children save one." That's all"

Shem's dark complexion lightened as eyes and mouth open wide, obviously surprised by something in the statement, but what?

"What'd I say?"

Shem recovered his facial expression, but remained silent. "I cannot say."

"What's a Cherub?" Manny pushed

"Cherub is not a what, but a who."

"Hey, angel," Ham shouted from atop the Ark. "Bring me up some planks from that small pile over by those lazy ducks."

Manny turned to look up at Ham, and upon turning back, Shem was already several paces away and departing rapidly. Sensing it would be futile to press the issue he cast a glance toward the irritating brother, issued a casual, left-handed, military salute, and hefted the top board. It was moderately heavy.

"How many do you need?" He called back.

"I need the whole pile before I'm through. They're heavy. Try bringing them up one at a time if you can."

Manny popped three onto his shoulder and started for the gangplank as Japheth, who was standing on the upward-slanting entrance, winked, smiled broadly, and went off to his job. Stopping at the entrance the young man stared into the dark interior. A puff of cool air swirled around his body and into the sun-bathed pasture. He wasn't sure which way to go until Miriam came up from behind, arms embracing a large sheath of grass, and pointed out the proper route through the interior.

Most of the upper deck contained partially built stalls for various small creatures, but those finished were much more elaborate than the ones further down as if intended for some very special passengers. It was here Ham needed the planks so Manny laid the load down.

"Those are heavy," he remarked open-mouthed.

"Well, can't have you losing time for the lack of materials. Guess I'll just have to work harder to keep up with you, huh? That ladder go up top?"

"Yes."

"Well, if you don't mind, I'd just like to take a peek from up there," Manny stated, not really caring if Ham objected or not.

Ascending to the very top, Manny cautiously tread some loose deck planking to the rail and gazed out over the valley. Unlike the tortured, scrub-covered region he had traveled with Noah, this side of the mountain was luxuriant; a rich palette of colors from the smallest flower to the towering pines fringed the valley like a muffler. Throughout, animals roamed about freely, a virtual, living zoological garden without barriers. It was difficult to pull away, but Ham's call for more lumber was annoyingly incessant.

It was hard work and the sun's heat intense, but invigorating as Manny shifted between the heat outside and cool inside. The clothes Bilnah and Miriam altered for him consisted of a couple long nightshirts or burnooses like Shem and Ham wore, and some shirts and skirts like Japheth favored, when he wore anything at all, preferring to mostly traipse about in a diaper. Manny favored the shirt and skirt because they were cool and practical for work. Although his feet were pretty tough, the leather sandals prevented collecting splinters from the rough-sawn lumber.

As the work progressed and sweat spilled from every pour, Manny eventually shed the shirt after Miriam provided a piece of leather to pad his shoulder. Bilnah's task was to keep the men well watered and after receiving a long drought of cool, sweet water from her leather bucket, he poured a bowl over his head, and then grinned as a spring slipped into his step. Whistling softly, "Whistle While You Work," he increased the volume to nettle Ham.

Noah's youngest son was irritated because he had thought to give this angel person one of the hardest, most insufferable jobs he could think of. Instead, the boy relentlessly carried three and four times the timbers while making music. Even more infuriating, seeing Ham getting behind because he tended to dawdle, Manny pitched in, forcing him to work faster.

"Gotta get this boat ship shape before it rains," Manny taunt.

His endearing attitude increased Japheth's

admiration. Shem, too, but for another reason he would not disclose. The two wives paid particular attention to his needs. Miriam was more motherly while Bilnah was like an older sister with a whimsical flare for teasing.

When he didn't pour a bowl of water over his head that afternoon, but turned away, Bilnah said, "You forgot something, My Lord," and dumped a generous amount over his shoulders. The cold shock elicited a surprised yelped after which the two had a great laugh. At their tasks both Shem and Japheth looked up and laughed as well. Ham, staring from the top deck, glowered.

As the construction crew quit for the day Japheth had to remark, "You worked late, Brother Ham."

He usually stopped and bathed well ahead of the others and would be lounging under his awning when the others arrived. Today, he staggered back just ahead of the troupe, continuing alone when the men stopped to bathe.

"I think you worked him too hard, Manny," Japheth whispered in his ear.

"I'm sorry." Of course, he wasn't and silently prayed forgiveness for the lie.

Japheth chuckled discreetly, a rare occurrence. When they arrived at camp a half hour later they found him collapsed on his mat needing to be awaken for the meal.

From before dawn until night fall for nearly five weeks Manny labored with the sons of Noah to complete the last of the inner decks and seal it from all light with the completion of the top deck. It was only then they began framing the cabins where the human passengers would live out the deluge. Meanwhile, the prophet continued giving directions and working just as hard as the boys while Naahmah cared for the animals as new ones arrived daily.

Manny's physique filled out and hardened as skin turned a deep, rich, golden brown, becoming a slightly smaller, mirror image of the always-jolly Japheth. Although difficult at first, he always took time during the long noon break to keep his martial skills honed by practicing katas, the martial arts routines Roger had taught. "Dance of the angels," Japheth called them.

By week's end, Ham convinced Japheth he didn't need Manny's help and could finish alone. Manny had carted all the timber Ham needed and prodded him to get ahead of schedule. Japheth then commandeered him to help harvest trees and cut more timber. This suited him just fine. He enjoyed working with the jovial rascal who was full of whimsical stories and surprise pranks.

"You don't get angry as easily as Ham," Japheth said after kicking a prop out from a log and sending Manny into a heap of sawdust.

"A good friend once said, he who can laugh at himself will spend a lifetime well amused," Manny replied, a great grin splitting his face while accepting the athlete's outstretch hand up. Of course he had something in mind for Japheth when least expected it.

Sawing and shaping the timbers did not provide the cool respite, as did the trips through the boat's interior. In time, practicality won out over self-consciousness. Being around the carefree titan, Manny's bashfulness waned until he too, slipped off a thoroughly sweat-soaked kilt to work in nothing more than his Bugs Bunny drawers. The first time Bilnah came by with a water jug, he felt the rush of embarrassment, wanting in the worst way to run to the branch where his kilt hung to dry and put it on, but she paid little notice. Although unusual in design such simple work attire was practical, and around Japheth nothing out of the ordinary.

The strangeness of Bugs' pictures quickly wore off. Of course, when Egyptus happened to stroll by it was a different story. He could feel her eyes devouring every inch of his exposed body. She was obviously physically stimulated, but that only heightened Manny's sense of revenge, as it were.

"Take a good look," he snickered under his breath, remembering how difficult it felt to want something so badly, yet unable to have it, as when he used to stand at the window of a candy shop as a small child.

However, a problem began to evolve by the end of the second week. Frayed and torn, Bugs was dying. One evening in a private ceremony, deep in Noah's forest, Manny laid the boxers to permanent rest. Feeling a bit sad, he still chuckled to himself while returning to camp.

"What if some future archaeologists finds them? Explain that. Unlikely, but still . . .." He laughed to himself, visualizing some befuddled scientist trying to explain the astonishing discovery.

From that point, Manny had to wear a loin-wrap similar to Japheth. Coming to terms with that took time until again realizing no one really cared. That's the way working men dressed in the heat.

Another reason Manny enjoyed working with Japheth was the gentle giant's easy-going behavior. That first day Manny cut timbers with him, Japheth eventually looked skyward, and announced it time for the noon break.

As sweat welled from every pore to cut great rivulets down his torso and legs between sticky layers of sawdust, Manny watched with usual jocularity as Japheth gave his loincloth a haphazard toss and jumped feet first into the cold water. Manny wasn't as brave and kept his garment on, following with abandonment and demonstrating a perfect cannonball. Once buried in the water he felt easier about removing the covering to rinse out the sawdust and grit that had been collecting during the morning's labors, and then fasten it back on.

Each day as the sun slipped behind the hill separating the Ark and camp, the women left, returning to camp by way of the forest trail skirting the edge of the hill. Japheth explained they went to a more private bathing place to refresh themselves before returning to camp, and help finish meal preparations. As the sun light faded, Shem joined the two sawyers at the stream for one last plunge to wash off the day's labors. No longer held to the job, Ham resumed quit much earlier, washed, and was gone.

When the trio arrived in camp, the routine continued as Naahmah, Miriam, and Bilnah quickly washed and anointed their husband's feet with fragrant oils. Noah's wife then cared for Manny's feet while either Miriam or Bilnah combed his hair. It had grown. Maintaining his original style, after removing tangles, they tied it into a ponytail that arced high off the crown of his head to trail off, now ending between the shoulder blades.

Those first days Manny felt very discomfited by this special attention as the husbands looked on approvingly. Gradually becoming accustomed to the practice, he let himself enjoy the ministering. It was also another annoyance to Ham, who had trouble seeing the newcomer showered with so much attention.

Following each evening meal, Manny eagerly listened as Noah or Shem read from the journals of Adam, Enos, Mahalaleel, Jared, and Enoch. Afterward he sometimes wrestled Shem, but Japheth loved the sport with passion. A quick study, the man rapidly became a good Judoka. Unfortunately, Ham always had something else to do. As Manny's physique continued to develop so did his mental skills as Ham continued trying to get his hands on the sword, and Egyptus, her hands on his body; it became a game of wits he played well, never losing sight of the costs if he lost. However, his favorite past time was the music.

The first, impromptu jam session happened the third night when Manny asked about the lyre leaning in one corner of Japheth's porch. He would not have surmised the big, rough and tumble prankster could play that instrument so well until the first chord was struck. Shem quickly retrieved a drum to add a tantalizing beat. Bilnah joined with a tambourine while Miriam contributed a melodious warble. It wasn't long before the beat increased and Egyptus began dancing. Though fully covered, her alluring, sensual moves were stimulating—and obviously directed toward Manny.

Then, the most amazing thing happened. Naahmah brought her husband a long flute. A reverent silence came over the musicians when he lifted it to his lips and began a melodiously song, something Father Adam had composed, he explained.

Manny reveled in the music, his long hair bouncing, and swaying with the rhythm until Shem noticed him keeping beat with two, wooden spoons. When Bilnah slid a drum in front of him, he joined in. Once learning the words, Manny added his voice to that of Shem, Japheth, Miriam, and Bilnah, who he fondly referred to as the Flintstone-Rubble family quartet plus one.

One night, as Egyptus performed a very suggestive dance, Japheth and Shem slyly exchanged glances. Shem winked and gradually increased the tempo. Ham, who never participated except to sway in time, was oblivious to the prank. The finale ended incredibly fast causing her to fall to the ground in a panting heap.

This was also the night ever-watchful Calēb warmed to Manny's presence. Unexpectedly, the dog plopped down by his leg, and shoved a wet mussel into his hand for an ear scratching. The visitor had become fully accepted.

Work was well underway the day after Sabbath of the sixth week when Manny suddenly found Calēb at his side, but no Noah.

"Father Noah went to the mountain a while ago," Miriam replied to Manny's question. "The L-rd desired to talk to him."

He gazed at the area Noah always used for such conversations, but did not see him. "I've got an uneasy feeling. I need to check on something."

"When the spirit speaks one needs listen. Peace be with you and safe journey."

Manny trotted up the mountain to where Noah usually knelt in prayer just in case he was somewhere else. Not spotting the prophet, he continued toward camp where Bilnah calmly sat mending a shirt for Japheth. Calēb squatted close to her side staring mournfully toward the distant hills to the west, whimpering softly, unappeased by any ear scratching.

"Where's Father Noah?"

"The L-rd, reminded father that he was anointed Teacher of Righteousness and commanded him to resume his cry unto the people," she replied to his anxious question.

"And he didn't tell me?"

"The Great One will protect him."

"I thought I was sent here to do that?"

"Egyptus was sent to tell you."

"I haven't seen her. She wasn't on the crest trail."

"She probably took the lower trail. It is longer, but less tiring."

"Which way did he go?"

"Walk west along the edge of the trees," she directed. "They follow a shallow ravine downward. Where the trees end, you shall see a trail that follows the stream. Turn right. That will take you to a point where the water disappears into the ground. Cross over the hill and you will see the city. You should find father along the way."

Quickly ducking into the tent, he scooped up his gi. Pulling it on, he wished there was time to sponge off the layers of annoying sawdust glued to his skin by sweat. While tying off the belt he ducked into Shem's tent to retrieve his sword. Wearing it every day was impractical and the only secure place was in Shem's tent, the least likely place Ham or Egyptus would consider looking. Flipping the strap over his shoulder to span his broadened shoulders, he exited right into Shem.

"I'm sorry, Shem," he apologized helping him up. "I've got to catch up with Father Noah. He's gone to the city."

"Yes, I know. Shall I go with you?"

"No. G-d called me to this. You've important work to do here. Finish the boat."

"Oh, the boat is basically finished. One more Sabbath cycle should see all in place."

"So soon?" Manny stuttered, overcome by a sudden anxiety attack. "When does it start to rain?" he asked, shielding his eyes and peering into the spotless, azure blue sky.

"The flood shall come when father's work is done, but G-d commanded him to cry repentance 120 years. This is the end of that time, and the boat is nearly finished, but not all the animals have arrived, nor have we been requested to retrieve the special cargo that is to accompany us, so surely not before tomorrow," Shem replied with a smile aimed at calming Noah's guardian.

"Oh, good," was Manny's sarcastic response.

"Manny?" Shem called after him. "Do not forget this," and tossed him the staff fashioned from the giant's spear. Then with a smile and wink said, "Trust in Adom Olam . . ."

Before Shem could finish Manny shouted back, "Barukh Hu, Blessed be He," waiving farewell and breaking into a trot along the trail.

Chapter 9

Wearing shoes never appealed Manny as if some of his genetic makeup defaulted to primal instincts. As soon as convenient, he shed them like a snake with itchy skin. Mr. Kreutzer caught him more than once working behind the deli counter shoeless.

"Manny, what if the Health Department people visit? They will be very upset."

"I wash my feet, and I scrub this floor. They can eat off it."

"I know that, but they are very narrow-minded about such things."

"Then I will remind them that I serve with my hands, not my feet."

"Manny!"

"Oh, alright."

He resumed sneakers, but not for long after his friend went upstairs for a nap. He felt a kinship with Albert Einstein who also disliked shoes. The issue was resolved when his surrogate grandfather bought slippers in Israel that were thin and natural enough to appease both men. As a result, the soles of his feet were tough before arriving in this time, and became tougher over the preceding weeks. Still, he was grateful for the leather sandals at this moment. Although not very thick, they beat negotiating the rocky portions of the trail barefoot, which lead him to wonder how he had gotten to the camp with such little difficulty the first time. He remembered the trail as a lot softer. He began to question if this were the same one, although confident, it headed in the general direction he needed to go.

That resolved, the only problem now was that every so often a tiny grain of sand jumped up to lodge between foot and sandal. It felt like a boulder. The only recourse was to stop and jiggle it out and wonder how the others seem to ignore such problems, "Unless they've lost all feeling below the ankle," he thought.

The trail wound steadily downward mostly following along a stream that had carved its channel deep below otherwise level ground. After a while, a gnawing feeling began to fester that he made a wrong turn despite Bilnah's directions being simple and straightforward. His doubts cleared as ears picked up the sound of cascading water, and then the trail dropped steeply to cross the stream below the small waterfall where he and Noah stopped to refresh themselves. Less than a hundred feet downstream, the water entered a jumble of melon-size rocks and disappeared. Despite not appearing to be much, the water pouring off the slate outcrop was as much as from any showerhead back home.

Leaving camp so quickly had not allowed time to wash and by this time the sawdust began feeling like large grit sandpaper beneath his clothes. Quickly tossing the garments aside, he ducked under the cool water to rinse off, and then shook and brushed the gi to dislodge most of the irritants before redressing. The whole time took about ten minutes.

Cresting the hill Bilnah mentioned, he looked down a long decline toward a city set on the east side of a river running the length of the plain from south to north. A band of green bordered the river, but the plain itself was a dismal tan attesting to the drought afflicting the earth. With Noah nowhere in sight, Manny wordlessly grumbled about Egyptus' delay in carrying the message. The elderly man obviously had a longer head start or took a shortcut. Undoubtedly, he'd already reached the city, and from accounts told at the campfire, in danger.

If Manny thought it hot in the mountains, descending the steep, narrow trail into the broad plain was like stepping into a blast furnace. With each step the heat became more intense and oppressive. Sweat saturated the heavy jacket; he pulled it apart to allow the anemic breeze to cool him.

As the trail joined a wide road extending away from the city, he noticed a rock marking the junction, the only such rock in sight, the top half of a large beach ball and just as smooth. Glancing down, he noticed a peculiar mark on the side facing away from the main road, which appeared to be similar to the emblem on his headband, a flying crane, a moment's curiosity as his thoughts refocused on Noah. It was here he began encountering people coming from the city, a less than friendly lot. Approaching, they shuffled to the opposite side of the dusty road, clutching belongings closer to their bodies, and with heads lowered, quicken their pace to scurry pass.

Small bands of sheep dotted the brown prairie in all directions trying to scrounge whatever morsel of grass might provide relief from hunger. Nearer the city, groups of black or dark gray colored tents huddled in isolated pockets within easy access of the high, protective wall surrounding the city. Some distance from the city, away from the river, was a jumble of rocks and a large, dishpan-shaped hole inhabited by large, black birds circling about, landing, and taking off as if it were an aviary airport.

From a distance, the city appeared to be a motley jumble of brown, tan, and beige buildings jammed within the stone fortification. At the northwest corner was a large pyramid structure. The sight didn't improve as one drew closer. He rightly guessed the material for the wall came from the avian hole. The houses were mud brick plastered over with mud, stucco-like. Two giants guarding the large, gated entry eyed him carefully. One took a step forward, appearing to contemplate a challenge, but his companion reached out, grabbing his arm and whispering something. Continuing to watch Manny closely, the two backed into the shadows. Mindful of what he had done to one of their kind, Manny kept watch over his shoulder while passing silently through the heavy, wooden doors.

Once inside, he was plunged into a maze of narrow, dusty streets weaving between two story living quarters, a planning engineer's nightmare. The little breeze outside the city was completely lost intensifying the heat into a great, oppressive weight causing sweat to ooze from his body like a squeezed sponge, completely soaking his clothes and trapping body heat, a vicious, deadly, cycle that tore at his mind for relief. The few people encountered scurried away or ducked into buildings, slamming doors as if seeming to say, "Go away."

Manny wandered the maze for some time in search of a place he might find Noah. Coming to another nondescript intersection, frustration mounted. Every building, every street seemed like the one before. While trying to decide which way to proceed, he looked up and realized he had been going in circles. People hung their laundry on overhead lines stretched between the second stories of opposing buildings. Mostly a dirty white color there was one piece he remembered because of its gaudy combination of red and green stripes. It hung near where he started searching the city. It hung overhead as if mocking his predicament.

Forging ahead, he tried to negotiate a different route. Thinking back to the descent into the plain, he remembered the huge, pyramid-like building at the northwestern corner of the city on the riverside and an open area next to it. In one of Mr. Kreutzer's impromptu lessons, he learned agrarian settlements had market places, which could be that open area. Understanding

Noah had come to preach, wherever people congregated is where he would find the prophet. Instead of repeating his steps, Manny delved into his memory and tried to take turns that would only lead toward that pyramid.

The silence of the alley-streets was reminiscent of the Catholic Church he occasionally ducked into to cool off during a hot, summer day. The silence felt like a heavy weight occasionally broken by the distant cry of a child or bark of a dog. Then a swelling pandemonium reached his ears until arriving at a wide, open area overshadowed by the pyramid. He had been right. It was a public market. It was also the place he began to understand G-d's reason to terminate that which He had so lovingly created.

Leaning a right shoulder against the corner of a building facing the market place, he lifted a foot to finger out an imaginary boulder lodged in the sandal as an excuse to casually survey the raucous herd of humanity. Almost directly across from his viewpoint was a massive, squared entry of round timbers behind which a wide, paved avenue lined with towering statues lead toward the pyramid looming sentinel-like over the city. The charcoal gray and black stone structure rose up steeply to an impressive height with a small, squared house on top.

Several people strolled by staring nervously while arcing away from him. Still leaning against the building he turned and sniffed his armpit wondering if that could be the problem, although the disgustingly rancid smell of this sea of people might suggest another issue. Looking at himself more closely, a thick layer of dirt caked his feet, the salmon-colored stuff continuing up to stain his gi to the knees. Face coated with sweat-streaked dirt, he was generally a mess, but then, most of these people didn't look too impressive, either. Actually, he fit in.

Just then an argument to his immediate right erupted between two women of complete opposites—one disheveled, greasy, and sweating, the other a well-trimmed flower—screaming the foulest profanities at each other as a disgusting clutch of bystanders cheered them on. It reminded him of two streetwalkers back home arguing over a corner, just before erupting into a real, knockdown altercation. Small children stood passive, seeming more interested in sucking their thumbs or an exposed breast that momentarily transfixed his adolescent attention. Sure, he'd see pictures of naked women, but this was his first live experience. Shaking his mind free, Manny turned left down the length of the open area, concentrating on finding Noah.

The path of least resistance through the area was to hug the wall of houses facing the market, but others used this as well so that it took on the appearance of the fast lane of an Interstate highway. Still, it was far better than trying to battle his way between shoppers and vendors haggling over price, quantity, and quality.

He hadn't gone very far when he looked up to see a sizable, hairy-chested guy brandishing a spear coming toward him. Wearing sandals laced to the knee and a leather kilt, the only other adornment was a thick, leather helmet sporting a pair of horns and a colored, strip of cloth sprouting from the peak to trail down the back. If not for the threatening way he pushed people aside, Manny would have chuckled. The dark, hairy face added to the helmet giving him the appearance of an ill-tempered buffalo.

Behind the guy plowing the road was a much more slender, almost gaunt, man with a burnt brown complexion. Decked out in a long, white robe trimmed with gold designs, he was obviously someone important. People lucky enough to step out of the way stood stiffly and bowed their heads until he passed. On either side and behind of this man were three more guards.

Not wanting to draw attention, Manny stepped into a space between vendor stalls, but at that moment, a toddler waddled into the path of the oncoming parade and tripped. Sitting on the ground, it cried. Manny could see no one was going to remove the child and whoever was so important wasn't going to veer from his path. In an instant, Manny lurched forward, grabbed up the tiny child, and stepped back just as the train passed.

Unlike the others around him, he did not bow, but glared at the men as they passed at expressway speed. The side guard nearest Manny turned his head to look at him, obviously considering a challenge, but had to keep up as the others continued. When they were gone, a woman stepped up and snatched the child away without so much as a thank you, unless her snort was supposed to be a representation of such in this culture.

The highway clear of any more express trains, he continued on, looking for Noah in the crowds to his right. That's when he spotted a man who instantly drew his attention. Taller than anyone around and only slightly taller than Manny, what made him stand out were his clothes.

Japheth had said that the material of his Bugs

Bunny boxers was much finer than anything here. Certainly, the white robe conductor of the train that almost trampled the child was made of fine material, but this man wore fabric far richer in color and texture than seen even in his world, except for the robes worn by the Parish Priest. Of deep purple and reds with pure white trim, it shimmered in the bright sunlight with the appearance of flowing water when it moved.

He couldn't see his face as he was in conversation with a young girl, his voice deep resonated clearly above the tumult. He was holding a baby and trying to play with it, but it wasn't having anything to do with the man's advances, instead looking longingly at the girl who appeared to be about the same age as Manny.

"Ishiah, a beautiful name for such a child, a child that needs the security of knowing it is a part of a family," he heard the man say."

Manny couldn't agree more as he slowed in order to eavesdrop.

"These espousal agreements are nonsense and invariably lead to such children."

"My betrothed and I will marry, but my father insists we wait out the time of the agreement."

"Then it is more important than ever that you make sacrifice to Onuava, the goddess of fertility, for blessing you with this child, but you must also make sacrifice to Enlil to seek forgiveness for violating your espousal agreement."

Manny quickly changed his favorable opinion. Pagan salesmen like him were part of the reason the world was about to die.

"But my betrothed does not believe in the pagan gods or their priests. He insists that we be married under the covenant of the Father of Adam."

"I should speak with him as well. Such belief is archaic and meaningless. Enlil is the god of this time."

Manny quickened his pace, leaving the two behind. If not for feeling the urgency to find Noah, he would stay and put that pompous fool straight.

The whole of the market was jammed with people from the scant few well dressed to others barely covered, everyone bartering at an unbelievable level of intensity over a department store selection of goods. Threatening fists, sometimes weapons, amid an appalling use of profanity seemed the mainstay of any transaction. At one point two vendors exploded upon one another, the smaller of the two brandishing a long, wicked-looking knife. It didn't appear to faze the other as he grappled him to the ground and pummeled him with fists. No one paid attention to the altercation except those in the immediate area who merely made room by backing away and ignoring it. Others picked the brawlers' stalls clean while they were homicidally distracted. Manny tried to slip unnoticed through this thieving, uncaring sea of humanity jammed into a fetid sauna.

Toward the middle of the market, near a gated entrance facing the river was a raised platform. A large gathering of people stood in front as one by one, a man or woman was put on display. Encouraged by a fat man, various on-lookers began casting bids for the individual. Manny couldn't believe such debasing behavior. Sure, he'd read about how American slaves were bought and sold, but the stories had been sanitized by time. To actually see it, to hear the descriptions, and the crowd's response turned his stomach.

The auctioneer, attired in a garish, red and green striped robe with a silver and gold tasseled rope belt, hawked each individual using loathsome and debasing descriptions with unmistakable sexual implications. Watching for a moment, Manny noticed that women vied with men in the bidding war. Whether the individual was male or female, it made no difference to the women, but the men seemed only to want males. Moving a bit closer he came alongside a well-dressed, middle-aged woman clutching a pouch in a death grip close to her bosom.

"What's going on?" Manny asked as the woman craned her neck to see over or around the taller people standing in front.

"What part of the world do you live that does not know a slave auction?" she shot back, frustrated at not being able to see.

"We did away with them a couple hundred years ago."

"So how do you find someone to fill your bed?"

Taken back, Manny swallowed hard before he could ask, "Who are they?"

"Mostly folk who need money or their parents do."

"Where I come from such people just stand on a street corner and wait for someone to come along."

"No auctioneer?"

"No."

"Good heavens! No exorbitant commission fees?"

"No."

"Where is this paradise you are from?"

"America."

"Never heard of it," she snapped back while stretching on tiptoes.

"Of course we don't have ..." he stopped himself.

Manny was going to say that in his city there weren't many men or children selling themselves, but then, that wouldn't be entirely true. Suddenly the woman began to quiver with excitement. A boy not much older than he stepped onto a side platform dressed in nothing more than a dirty loincloth.

"O-o-o-oh," the woman frothed excitedly. "There is just the one that will do. He'll be next. I hope he sells cheap, but if not I will at least make the purchaser pay dearly," she commented, hefting her purse.

"You are a sizable lad. Help me get closer to the front," she said, grabbing Manny's wrist and pulling him forward.

He wondered why she needed his help until a couple men took exception to the woman's crowding through. Turning to confront her all they saw was a tall, white-clad youth with a very large sword strapped to his back and a hefty staff. They stepped aside without argument.

"Oh, good. This will be perfect," she said, stopping near the front.

"So why don't you just find a man and get married," Manny asked naively.

"Are you joking? I did that five times. A horrible path to boredom. Besides, they were always working the other side of the river anyway. Bore the ninth child when the last one up and left. I vowed not to make any more such mistakes. Besides, it is cheaper this way. Do you think he could service six?"

"Huh?"

"I have three daughters and two sons and me, of course. Would you say he looks fit enough to handle that many and do chores around a farm?"

"I guess," Manny replied, anxiously looking to find a way out through the densely packed crowd and away from this obvious nut case.

"Mar-rim," a man's voice called out. "You buying another? What happened to the last one? Wear him out so quickly?" Crude laughter accompanied the comment.

"I had him for four moons," she corrected, "and he started whining."

"So, where is he? I will buy him."

"Oh, that stupid one went to slaughter a pig and ended up slicing his leg open and bled out himself. Ended up feeding him to the pigs."

Manny wondered if this was the reason for the prohibition against eating pork?

Just then, the boy she had fixed her lecherous eyes upon stepped onto the dais. Silky, straight, black hair framed refined facial features. Smooth, dark skin glistened with sweat from the heat. The sight of him brought a twinge to Manny's stomach. It was a feeling he had desperately fought over the years since puberty. The boy was physically stimulating.

Bidding began at a feverish pace with the auctioneer inciting the crowd to more ardent offers until one by one the bidders fell silent. The woman next to

Manny waited for the bids to slow before jumping in. Soon it came down to her and a young man in his mid-twenties toward the back. Her response to each increase came slower as she bit her lower lip nervously, obviously coming near the end of her purse. She cast a final bid. The man in back bowed out. Grinning, she turned back to look longingly at the boy. Unexpectedly another raised the bid. The auctioneer looked at her. With a groan, the woman lowered her head and shook it sideways to indicate it was finished.

"One never stands a chance when those from the temple bid. They wear more braided in their side locks than all us have combined," the woman complained, then arching one eyebrow asked, "Come to find a companion for the night?" while examining him with a lustful leer.

Shaken, Manny quickly responded, "No. No. Just watching. Already gotta date. What about the guy who was bidding against you?"

"Nephtal? Hum-m." Mir-rim looked over at her rival bidder who was already engaged in what appeared to be a transaction with another man. She began working her way to where they stood.

The younger man shook his head at Nephtal, turned, and departed. With Mir-rim's arrival, Nephtal faced her, his eyes scrutinizing Manny closely. He suddenly felt as if occupying the only seat in a game of musical chairs.

"Looking for brief companionship," Mir-rim asked pointedly, "Or something a bit longer?"

"If you are offering, I'm not interested. I like my men," Nephtal answered coarsely.

"I had in mind that we join purses, buy a strong, handsome stud that could . . ."

Manny took several steps back and beat a hasty departure as the two negotiated a merger. He suddenly felt like a pimp.

Moving briskly away, he shot a glance over his shoulder toward the auction dais. The boy who purchased was walking behind a young man whose ebony skin was in sharp contrast to the shiny, white kilt he wore. He must indeed be rich judging by the skirt festooned with gold thread and chain, even the thin straps of his sandals were similarly adorned, and his bluish-black hair sported a side braid implanted with red, blue, and green jewels.

Something about the purchaser brought up a sour taste that slithered about Manny's mouth as he regained the highway. He was pleased when the dense throng thinned, but again conscious of occasional whispers and secretive glances in his direction. Amid disgust, a modicum of fear crept over him, not wanting to speculate about the promptings for such behavior.

"Hey," a voice called out.

Manny turned to face the young man who had initially been bidding against the woman. A bit winded as he approached he said, "Are you with the old woman who was bidding against me?"

"No," Manny replied warily.

"Oh, good. I'm looking for a sleeping companion. I have a generous kitchen and pay well."

Being propositioned right in front of a number of people keyed in on the conversation took him completely off-guard.

"Sorry," Manny said. "Already have an engagement."

The stranger looked crestfallen, but determined.

"How much is he paying you?"

"Enough," Manny replied, looking for an escape route.

"I'll double it."

"I can guarantee you don't have that much. Besides, I thought you were making a deal with the old woman."

"I would not profit from it."

Manny said nothing in reply, but turned away and drove into a crowd of people, leaving the young man behind.

Approaching one of several, alley-like streets feeding into the market area he noticed several men come out of one looking into a leather pouch before hurrying off to melt into the throng. Glancing down the narrow canyon he spotted someone on the ground a ways back in a dark shadows. It was not unlike his ghetto with its alleys of drunks. Drawn by curiosity, he walked toward the prone figure and was almost on top of him before noticing a dark stain on the ground. Rolling him over with the tip of his staff caused a wave of nausea to seize his stomach.

Δ Δ Δ

Manny was all of nine with nothing much to do as usual except roam the streets in search of diversion.

Opting to take a shortcut to the next street, he entered an alley. Almost immediately, the tall, dark buildings created a cool, cavern-like atmosphere where less street clamor penetrated. The crunch of gravel beneath his feet echoed off the stained and weathered brick walls.

Passing a rusting steel dumpster, a horrendous stench savaged his nose, turning his stomach upside down. He hurried on, but the smell seemed locked in his nostrils. Just then two older boys entered the alley and walked pass whispering secretively until well away. Scavengers, they were kids with no real home except a piece of cardboard in some alley alcove, the next meal coming from handouts, garbage cans, or from the little money earned granting "favors." Manny considered himself lucky. If not for Benny in the old, abandoned hotel and Mr. Kreutzer he might have found himself living from garbage can to garbage can, too.

Suddenly a loud bang shot through the narrow canyon joined by the high, piercing scream from one of the boys. Wheeling around, Manny squinted to pierce the dark shadows. Both boys were violently backing away from the smelly dumpster until slamming into the opposite wall. As one of them bent over to puke, the other ran toward Manny screaming hysterically. The noise brought several people to a halt as the kid careened into Officer Moody.

"What's got into you?" he growled. "Can't you watch where you're . . ." He broke off upon seeing the other boy staggering toward him still gagging.

"In the trash can . . .," the first boy stammered, about to lose what he had scrounged to eat earlier.

Officer Moody went to check as more curious folk gathered around the alley entrance along with Manny. When the cop opened the green top he let it slam back down and reeled away, too, covering his face with one big hand.

Regaining the street, he reached to his radio. "Dispatch this is Foot 9-4-1. I got us a dead body in the alley off Palmer between 91st and 92nd. It's in a dumpster. It's beyond ripe."

Δ Δ Δ

"Rough neighborhood," Manny joked to himself, trying to grab control of jangled nerves as the memory of long ago flooded back. He remembered how the men who pulled the body from the dumpster wore oxygen masks to fend off the stench. It didn't work too well or maybe it was the maggots. A couple of them tossed their stomachs.

A clattering sound barely registered over the noise of the marketplace as two kids, maybe twelve or thirteen, trotted through the unconcerned masses, and drop the tongue of their rickety, wooden cart at the entrance to the alley. Barely breaking stride, they move into the alley toward Manny. Hearing their feet slapping on the hard-packed ground Manny anticipated an attack. Spinning around to face the new arrivals, he whipped the staff up into a horizontal position in front of his chest. Seeing him poised over the body, the boys planted their dirty, bare feet and literally came to a dusty, sliding stop.

At first, they appeared startled and frightened, and

then the smaller one broke into a wide smile and seemed about to say something. Whatever it might have been was cut off as the larger boy jabbed an elbow into his companion's ribs and shot a warning look at him. The smile disappeared as they bent to one knee and bowed their heads.

"Who are you?" he said.

"We have come for the body M'Lord," the slightly taller of the two answered as they remained kneeling, heads down.

Manny slowly stepped backward over the dead man's legs and a few yards beyond. The older boy glanced up. When Manny nodded, he poked the smaller companion. Rising slowly, they inched forward, grabbed the victim's feet, and began dragging him toward the cart, not once taking their eyes off Manny.

"Where are you taking him?" Manny said, breaking the heavy silence with a dry, scratchy voice that seemed like rumbling thunder in the confines of the enclosed alley.

The boys flinched at the sound, but retained hold of the dead man. "To the pit outside the city walls," the larger boy said. "That is where all earthly remains are taken."

Manny acknowledge the answer by simply tilting his head forward sharply and then watched as the two seemingly malnourished youth wrestled with their chore. He wondered when it came time to put the body in the cart how they would manage. They struggled greatly. He hadn't been a particularly big man, but the dead weight created problems for them. As Manny walked up to the cart, the boys dropped their load and backed away.

Stretching out the staff vertically with the left hand, indicating for the smaller boy to hold it, he grabbed the corpse under the armpits and tossed it head first onto the cart to join another. For Manny, it wasn't much of a lift, but knew it made him appear to have great strength. Reclaiming the staff, he stood back, giving his head a slight jerk sideways. Understanding the gesture, the boys grabbed the cart handle and sped away, their cargoes' legs dangling off the end.

He recalled the flock of large, black birds circling the area off to one side of the city—the avian airport. Then, it was a curiosity, now he understood. Vultures— feeding. Suddenly his mind began intoning a refrain, "Feed the birds. Tuppence a bag. Tuppence, tuppence, tuppence a bag."

"Oh, cripes, Mary Poppins! In the middle of all this, Mary Poppins! You're losing it Guzman. Get the heck out of here! Stupid song!" he groaned, desperately trying to weed the morbid refrain from his head. "Why do you always come up with some moronic, asinine thing during serious stuff like this? Oh, G-d, help me find Noah."

Unexpectedly the tune vaporized and was gone. It happened so fast he felt dazed and off balance, and at the southern end of the market behind a loud, jeering crowd shouting epithets at someone standing on a stone bench. He'd found Noah.

As the prophet preached what sounded like a fine hell, damnation, and repentance sermon, a particularly vocal group of youths hanging toward the back attempted to drown out his words. Circling to come up from behind Noah, Manny noticed one specific individual on the edge of the crowd whose rich, silk robes of purple, red and blue made him conspicuous next to the much more coarsely clothed mob. The individual he'd see earlier.

Overhearing the man's comments to the girl was a turn-off, but now, the way he stood, arms folded across his chest, a sneering smile etched on an aquiline face, a total display of arrogant satisfaction, caused Manny to harbor an complete dislike of the man. But, there was something more.

A thin scar angled down the man's left cheek from the edge of the eye to near the mouth disrupting other-wise handsome, male model features. Something about that scar tickled Manny's memory, but he had no time to dwell upon it.

Again, his timing was near perfect. Just as he strode up to Noah, a rock came hurtling toward the old man from the back row. Manny's well-honed reflexes came to play as his hand shot upward to intercept the projectile. He even surprised himself, but displaying a bit of showmanship Roger encouraged, he held the rock in the air where he caught it for a long moment.

"May the force be with you." The words echoed triumphantly in his mind before opening his fingers to let the missile drop harmlessly to the ground.

An unearthly hush moved over the crowd. Out of the corner of his eye, he saw the rich man lower his arms. The leer changed to animosity as he began slowly moving through the crowd toward them. Noah continued his sermon seemingly oblivious to what happened directly beneath his hooked nose.

"The L-rd your G-d has ceased to dwell with the sons of Adam. He cries unto you, repent of your evil. Return to the laws he has given unto us for the day has come that he will destroy the world and only the righteous shall be saved."

Noah was in good form as strength radiated from his voice and carried over the background of market noises. The now silent crowd couldn't help but hear although their questioning eyes were fixed on the new arrival.

"Well, the so called creator of this world is going to destroy it," the rich man spoke. "The so called father of all living is going to destroy his children just because they disagree with some of his outrageous demands? What kind of loving parent would do that?"

Some of the crowd, their bravery rekindled by virtue of being in the back and mostly unnoticed, and the presence of this new heckler, raised their voices in accord to their leader's rebuke.

"And how is this loving father going to destroy his children? We are immortal," an invisible voice challenged from the back.

As he began working his way through the crowd, they cheered and he gestured for them to continue haranguing Noah. Manny began to wonder if this guy may have inspired the crowd's venom. He shifted to stand between Noah and the approaching figure.

"I don't think I know you." the rich man's voice was intimidating.

Unexpectedly Manny felt something in his breast,

like cold fingers searching around inside. One of the ancient Japanese mentors Roger had him train with warned of people with the skill to reach into a man's body as a way to search for weakness. Manny instinctively closed his eyes, focused his mind on grasping the fingers, and pulling them back out while passing an open hand in a circular motion from hip to shoulder to opposite hip. He could feel the fingers draw back. Opening his eyes, there was an expression of questioning surprise on the adversary's face.

When he took a step closer, Manny consciously decided on a significant show of force and reaching across his left shoulder wrapped his fingers about the hilt of his sword and began drawing it out. There was a distant rumble of thunder. The stranger stopped. For a fleeting moment Manny detected actual fear in his eyes, which vaporized as he quickly regained control, however, his attitude was markedly different and more subdued. Manny took the initiative.

"If you don't like what Noah's saying, fine, go about your business of robbing, cheating, and killing each other, but I'm getting tired of having to catch spears and rocks intended to hurt him. And I'm suddenly getting tired of arrogant, stuffed shirts who only have the guts to provoke people into violence while standing in the back so they don't get their peacock feathers soiled." Manny directed the last toward the fancy-robed man whose black eyes blazed with anger. "The next time someone tries a stupid thing like trying to hurt this old man, I'm will put this sword to use. Folks may live a long time around here, but you're not invincible despite what you think."

Finished, Manny was surprised at how forceful his own voice had been, and even swore it had lowered a whole octave so that it rang with power and authority. Certainly, there was none of that embarrassing, teenage cracking frequently occurring when excited.

The crowd went deathly silent once more followed by movement in the back as people began moving away. Those in front, feeling their support vanish, sheepishly back peddled to evaporate like wisps of smoke, while Noah continued his appeal to conclusion.

"This is not the end my young friend. We shall meet again," the rich man threatened, fingering his scar lightly.

"Any time dude. I'll be sure to watch for you over my shoulder," Manny shot back.

The stranger snapped his cloak about his left shoulder and stomped off. With his departure, the audience was gone, but Noah continued speaking until his message was finished, then using his staff and Manny's shoulder for support, he climbed down from the bench.

"They refuse to believe."

"No, they won't," Manny replied, "and that's why the flood will come."

"After preaching all these long years, I hoped. I'm tired, Manny. It has been a long day. Let us find rest."

Leaving the market place, the two entered another narrow alley as dark eyes of hate followed their departure from the shadows of a vacant stall. The confines of the alley-like streets, and what he'd seen earlier made Manny nervous, but nothing happened as they wound their way through the city.

"Say, Noah. You know that guy back there?"

"Which one?" Noah asked continuing to walk a brisk pace for someone professing to being tired.

"The guy in the fancy clothes."

"Oh, him. Amalekiel," Noah replied. "He's Lucifer's arch-lieutenant."

Manny stopped cold, staring blankly at the back of the old man's head as he continued walking, and discoursing. His whole body seemed to fill with helium and float, and then pivot to slam its back into a wall. Mouth agape, he felt knees buckle. Breathe vanished except for short, shallow gulps.

"Manny," he heard Noah's voice shout at him. "You can rest when we get to my house."

Manny turned mechanically to follow, senses numbed. All he could think was, "I just called out the Devil's own. You stupid punk! You just . . ."

"Manny, come on. I need to sooth a dry throat."

Chapter 10

With no particular rhyme or reason to the serpentine streets, this, house or that door in haphazard fashion, they all seemed alike. How Noah knew which was his seemed incredible, but upon arriving at a particular door he stopped and knocked with his staff. After a moment, there came a muffled inquiry to which Noah responded, followed by a scraping sound before it opened. Manny glanced up and down the street for any sign of trouble. Seeing it deserted, he followed Noah beyond the thick, wood door that closed behind him and a heavy plank slid in place from frame to frame to secure it. The whole entrance seemed grossly over built for stout.

From outside the overall structure appeared

larger in width than its neighbors, but his first surprise was that the actual house occupied less than two-thirds the area. The entry emitted him into an L-shaped courtyard. To the left a shaded porch off the main structure faced a small, square, stone well. Straight ahead a narrow ramp hugged the right and rear walls gently rising to the second story. He would learn that the back room contained large, earthen jars filled with food stores. Immediately below that room, a stable housed a couple newborn lambs being bottle-fed, some chickens, and a donkey.

His second surprise was the person who had admitted them and secured the heavy door. Walking around from behind to hustle after Noah who had made straight for a clay jug set beneath the wood-latticed awning was the most gorgeous person he'd ever seen and Manny made no bones about it as his jaw dropped open. In return, the sprightly girl glanced into his eyes before quickly bowing her head to look at the ground, but the smile upon her full, red lips sent his heart pounding as if he'd just sprinted a hundred meter dash.

Once Noah filled a wooden bowl from the jar, he sat in the cool shade of a tree to take a long, uninterrupted draft, sigh, hiccup, and belch. Following the girl, Manny eyed every inch of her delicate body and the graceful way it floated across the hard-packed ground. He felt a bit embarrassed knowing she had to hear his heart pounding like a jackhammer.

"Sit my faithful champion and rest your weary feet," Noah croaked cheerfully somewhat to Manny's surprise. The elderly gentleman was seldom this jovial except . . . he quickly glanced into the prophet's bowl. Sure enough, it was reddish-colored water.

"It's so good to see you again, Uncle. Who's our guest?" She asked while handing Manny a deep bowl of liquid as he looked at her slender, smooth hands before eyeing the contents suspiciously; sure enough it had a reddish cast.

"Do you have any plain water?"

"Water?" she replied incongruously.

"Wine and angels do not seem to be compatible, my dear," Noah responded cheerfully.

"Oh, I am terribly sorry, My Lord," she responded quickly fetching some water.

The voice was soft and sweet with the smoothness of youth, each word coming like the singing of a choir of birds, distracting him to the point he forgot to protest the angel reference. His gaze met the girl's soft, brown eyes, which once more quickly diverted downward as she blushed.

"This is Manny," Noah said jovially although his voice was still raspy from the long sermon.

"Hello, Manny," she replied. "My name is Sher'i. You're not from around here are you?"

"No," he sputtered as his tongue felt as if tripping over a sand dune.

"Manny came to my rescue some time ago when a gang of giants attacked me."

"So, this is the one. Everyone's heard about the angel who dropped from the skies and attacked some poor shepherds without provocation."

"Without provocation!" Manny fumed indignation

peaked. "They tried to kill him. I intercepted a giant's spear, and fought off four regular sized guys who wouldn't know a sheep if they tripped over it, and I'm no angel."

"Oh, really," she replied, a soft giggle crossing her lips.

"They have thrown camel dung many times, but that time they were really trying to do me great physical harm," Noah responded plunging his bowl into the clay jar to refresh it. "That was a new experience for me."

"No kidding," Manny responded sarcastically.

"The people are becoming very anxious, Uncle. The time you have prophesied is at hand. They really have been listening, they just will not heed how to stop the waters from coming. You have been really fortunate not to have been hurt before this."

"The Holy One promised I would be protected, and I have," Noah responded with a wave of his hand.

"Well, I for one am happy you appeared when you did," she said to Manny. "Perhaps, Uncle, what these people need is some visible proof of your divine calling. Maybe then they will listen."

"Don't count on it. My being here didn't have much effect a little while ago," Manny replied starting to feel depressed.

"Nonsense. It had a great deal of effect."

"What happened?"

"Oh, someone threw a rock, and Manny caught it, and then he exchanged words with Amalekiel," Noah explained nonchalantly as if it were something that happened routinely. Manny was a bit surprised. Noah was more aware of what had happened than he surmised.

"I don't know how you can take having one of the devil's own in your face so lightly, Father Noah." Manny responded feeling his anxiety level rise substantially so that he grabbed the table to steady himself.

"Oh, he's always around, especially when Uncle Noah is preaching." Sher'i responded, her voice trying to sooth Manny's consternation. "This violence is something new, though. That must be why G-d sent you. I'm really glad you came." Quickly putting a hand in front of her mouth, she chucked softly. "I think I said that."

The way she quietly laughed sent Manny's heart into another spasm of pounding as a tingling sensation shot through his body stimulating a shiver.

"Are you cold?" she asked. "Forgive me, of course. It is terribly hot and you have been sweating. My goodness, your cloak is soaked. Here, take it off so it can dry in the sun," she said as her delicate fingers reached casually for the knotted belt, nimbly untying it before he had sense to object.

"You will have to remove the sword."

Manny automatically lifted it over his head and placed it on the table at which point she stood behind him and began sliding the jacket off his shoulders.

"The material of your coat is very strange. It is so heavy and very wet," she continued, hanging it over the back of a chair in a sunny spot. "It may take the whole night to dry even as hot as it is."

Taking up a piece of cloth she began toweling off his shoulders and back. If it hadn't been for such attention given over the past weeks by Noah's wife and daughters-in-law he would have come unglued. The cloth material was very soft and pleasing and when she worked it down his spine to the small of his back, he was greatly relieved. It had felt like a veritable river running down that area. The shivering began to dissipate.

"Thank you," he said nervously, holding himself rigid as minute aftershocks rippled through his body.

"Your trousers are soaked, too. I have something of father's that will fit," Sher'i said, laying the drying towel over the back of another chair before disappearing behind a tapestry covering the door leading into the house.

Manny stood staring at the tapestry.

"She is every bit the dotting, motherly type," Noah chuckled while watching closely through partially closed eyes. "She will make a fine mother . . . and wife."

Sher'i reappeared cradling a bundle of cloth.

"I brought fresh garments, too," she said, handing him the bundle.

"Ah-h, thanks," Manny replied, and then just stood silently.

"Do you not wish to change?"

"Well, not exactly here," he squeaked nervously.

"Oh, men!" she said with mock disgust. "All so modest and bashful, but get a little excited and they cannot remove their clothes fast enough."

Noah's belly bounced as he laughed. Manny was speechless, until realizing the girl was teasing.

"You can change in the house," she said.

Feeling sheepish, Manny slipped through the

door into a dark, cool room wondering if someone had permanently taped a sign to his back saying "Tease Me." A couple girls at school back home, Mrs. Elam, Bilnah, Miriam, now Sher'i, women seemed to like picking on him, not that he didn't secretly enjoy it—afterward.

Compared to the heat outside, the interior was quite cool accentuating his chill. After a quick look around to be sure no one else was in the house, he slipped out of his trousers and garment and quickly put on the clean linen wrap. He'd become adept at "diapering." With one end of the long cloth tucked under the chin, he tossed the rest to hang over the shoulder and down the back. Grabbing the soft material at his hip, he wound it around his waist one and half times before stuffing the end underneath. Releasing the end hanging over his shoulder, he reached between his legs, pulled it forward, and tucked it into the belt. Quick, practical, and comfortable.

After slipping the long gown over his head, Manny stepped out where the girl grabbed his clothes and skipped up the outside walkway to the back of the house and disappeared. Presently her humming flowed softly from the roof like a refreshing waterfall as Manny helped himself to another bowl of cool water, sipping slowly.

Upon her return she said, 'That was my father's favorite robe.

"Was?"

"He died when I was quite young, may the Giver of Life provide him comfort."

"Actually you look very much like him," Noah

mumbled more soberly with a quizzical expression. "His hair was quite white at an early age, too."

Gliding behind her uncle, Sher'i began to massage the elderly man's hunched shoulders. Manny wished she'd do that for him. Anxiety had every muscle taunt as an over-wound watch spring.

"Manny. That is an unusual name," she commented.

"It's short for Emanuel."

"That is a beautiful name. Indeed angelic."

"I'm no angel," Manny retorted politely, but had the feeling he wasn't gaining much ground keeping the record straight. "Noah said this was his house and you call him Uncle?"

"Yes. My mother died in child birth, and then father was killed by bandits," She replied, continuing Noah's massage. "My father's brother came . . . to care for us." Her voice trailed off. "He was not a nice man."

"He was an evil, wicked man. He deserved to break his neck," Noah pronounced.

"One night he got drunk, more than usual and . . . and fell from the roof." Sher'i removed her hands from Noah's shoulders and hung her head in a shameful attitude. "Anyway, Uncle Noah came and has seen to our needs ever since. It has works well. He needs a place to lay his weary head after exhorting the people all day. I am sorry we see him so infrequently, though. He travels the wilderness so often. We remain here while he is off," She finished, moving to Noah's side to hug him.

"Couldn't have them living on the streets," Noah said.

"Yeah. And I thought my ghetto was bad. So, if you are Sher'i's uncle, then her mother was your sister?"

"Yes. My father had nine children, seven boys and two girls. I am afraid my brothers have followed father's example," Noah answered.

"I need to go to the market," she said, retrieving a shawl from a peg on the outer wall of the house and draping it over her head while heading toward the door.

"Will it be safe? I mean for you to go alone, in this city?" Manny asked.

"Go with her, Manny. I shall be fine right here," Noah said, helping himself to more wine.

Once outside Manny quickly scanned both directions of the alley-street, but there wasn't so much as a child within its cavern-like confines.

"You have seen the Ark?" Sher'i asked as they headed back toward the marketplace.

"I've helped some with it," he replied, wondering at the question. If she'd been with Noah this long, certainly she would have seen it, and then detected a nervousness in the tone of her voice, deciding this bit of small talk was to help relieve it.

"I have never seen it. From what Uncle Noah has told me it is very large."

"Huge. All of the animals will easily fit inside."

"Has he gathered any of them, yet?"

"There are many. They come on their own, arriving every day. I don't know how."

"G-d guides them."

"Yeah, I suppose. You've never seen the Ark?"

"No. I do not leave the city. Uncle Noah says that

it is not wise for a single girl to be in the countryside. Well, I do sometimes, to visit my brother while he tends our sheep. There is a man who has goats that run with our sheep, and occasionally I accompany him to the flocks when they are near the city."

"How old is he? Your brother."

Sixteen."

"Are there others, or just the two of you?"

"Just the two of us.

Manny kept glancing sideways at the girl with the small, bobbin-like nose, long, wavy black hair, and smooth, olive complexion. He couldn't explain it, but there was something about her eyes, dark, liquid pools that kept drawing his eyes toward her like a powerful magnet. When she glanced up, their eyes meet for a brief moment before both diverted them away. At those times he focused on his feet or scanned the street while sensing her furtive glances at him. He glanced toward the girl and caught her looking at him. They both turn away. So went the game until turning a corner to enter the marketplace. At that moment his whole demeanor rocketed to a state of paranoia as he focused on potential trouble.

"Must be tough not having friends, being cooped up in the house all the time."

"There are other girls my age who come to visit. Occasionally their mothers come, too. Sometimes I go to their homes."

"No guys. Doesn't anyone ask you out to . . . a . . . a dance or something?"

"No." She smiled so innocently that his heart felt

it was beginning a meltdown.

"How old are you?" She asked.

"Sixteen. Almost seventeen."

"You seem much older than that."

"How old are you? I'm sorry. I shouldn't have asked."

"I will be nineteen in five months."

Manny felt a little let down that she was so much older.

Exiting the street they were instantly absorbed into the throng of people still playing out their games of barbarous commerce. As Sher'i went about gathering up staples for the evening meal, a few men considered approaching her until seeing a man with a heavy staff in hand and sword strapped to his back obviously in her company. They quickly diverted lecherous eyes and moved on. Manny kept vigilant, ever-anticipating trouble, that's when he spotted him—Amalekiel. He hadn't moved far from the place of their first encounter. A chill rippled through Manny's soul upon noticing the dark, foreboding stare thrust at him, but took stock of what happened during their first encounter. Lucifer's lieutenant had backed down, actually backed down, which offered some comfort. Still, he knew that wouldn't be the end of it.

"Amalekiel, you're a wuss," Manny said under his breath, staring back defiantly. He was startled when the adversary seemed to react as if he had heard the derisive remark.

"We are finished," Sher'i said after concluding a vigorously successful, but civil bartering session. Her words jolted his attention away from the antagonist. "Is there anything you would like?"

Manny had the greatest urge to hold her hand, but didn't exactly know how to approach the issue. His mouth went dry as he looked into the ebony pools of her eyes. "You're beautiful," he blurted.

Sher'i lowered her head, smiling faintly, her dark cheeks catching a crimson blush.

"Oh, cripes! I mean . . . ah, I meant . . . I'm sorry." It was the worst moment in his life as once again his mouth preceded his brain.

"I think you are very beautiful, too," she responded softly, reaching out to take his hand.

They walked back to the house without another word, anything needing said felt through their clasped hands. Entering the courtyard they found Noah still seated at the round table, head upon folded arms, snoring loudly. Above came the noise of someone rummaging about. Manny's hand reached up and clasped the hilt of the sword.

"Oh, Aran is home," she squealed.

"Who's Aran?" he asked, still partially absorbed in a dreamy world.

"My brother, the one I told you about. Aran. Aran," she called out as they entered the house.

"Where have you been?" a voice said from within the house.

"At the market."

"I told you I would do that . . ." A boy suddenly appeared from behind another tapestry covering an interior door and stopped abruptly. "Who is that?" he glowered as they stood facing one another in the front room.

"This is Manny. He is Uncle Noah's guardian."

"So this is the one? You're not very old for such a mighty warrior," he commented, a hint of sarcasm in his voice.

"Manny escorted me to the market. I will have the meal prepared soon." Sheri's tone was firmly remonstrative.

"That's okay. Since Uncle Noah is here I will stay the night with Abigail."

"Oh," she replied, obviously disappointed. "Give my love to Abigail. Oh, here, before I forget. I made this for her baby," she continued, her voice returning to its light bounciness as she gathered something from a dark corner.

In the dim light Manny could see that Aran was dark skinned, probably from being outdoors he thought. Certainly, Manny loved the outdoors as a child and spent much of his time roaming in the sunshine when it wasn't foggy, but never had become as dark as in the past weeks. No one needed to say the boy was a shepherd. He looked as if stepping from a church picture book—a woolly, sheepskin kilt barely reached mid-thigh, and sandals similar to what Manny wore. A thin, rope wound around his waist. A leather sack dangled off one hip. Undoubtedly a slingshot.

Aran was handsome in a rugged way. A rope headband held long, curly hair off his brow as it cascaded to his shoulders, framing a face marked by wide cheekbones divided by a slightly rounded nose. He was only three or four inches shorter than Manny's almost six foot height, tall compared to others seen around town including Noah and his sons, except for Japheth of course. His frame was smooth, well defined. Obviously, Aran wasn't a shepherd that sat around much. Taking a cloth bundle from Sher'i, his thin lips parted to reveal pearly-white teeth that seem to glow against his dark complexion.

"Thank you. She will love it," he replied touching her cheek tenderly, then turning toward Manny said, "Thank you for protecting Uncle Noah and my sister. I will sleep better tonight knowing they are safe." His voice was more conciliatory as he turned toward the rear door, picking up a long staff leaning against the wall, and disappearing into the waning sunlight.

"It has been a strain on him. Things seem to be getting worse. He spends days shepherding our sheep and another man's goats insisting I stay locked in here until the animals are penned for the night. He stays with me many times when I know he wants so badly to be with Abigail and the baby."

"Who's Abigail?"

"She is the youngest daughter of the baker, Dan."

"She's his sweetheart?"

"They have been espoused for nearly a year now."

"What does that mean—espoused?"

"When two people plan to marry they consecrate themselves to each other for the first year or so to be sure the union will work."

"Oh, like an engagement, they spend all their

time together."

"Yes, only in this case Aran only has nights."

"The gift is for Dan's baby?"

"Abigail gave Aran his first child a month ago, little Ishiah. It happens sometimes."

"He's a father! But he's only . . ."

"It is true that some men wait until they are much older, but they are the righteous ones. Now men father children indiscriminately and leave. It is not unusual for individuals Aran's age to have fathered several children. At least in a way he is not violating G-d's law. Well, not too seriously. It will all be made right with the wedding in a few months," she defended.

"Doesn't seem like much has changed over the last 5000 years," he mumbled to himself.

"Do you have someone?"

"No," Manny responded brusquely, and then more subdued added, "Just my ol' man and me."

Her lips parted in a big smile that fanned the embers smoldering in his soul while at the same time something she said began to bother him as well.

Chapter 11

Later that evening Manny accompanied Noah to his sleeping room on the first floor. After prayers he sat on the floor next to the cot, holding the aged hand long after the prophet drifted off to sleep. Eventually venturing back to the courtyard, he met Sher'i who took his hand to lead him up the ramp, through the storage room, and then up another ladder to the roof. She had prepared a sleeping mat for him under the stars as if somehow knowing that was his most favorite place to sleep. She then left to curl up on her own cot on the opposite side of the roof, under a latticed awning. Slipping the burnoose over his head, Manny folded it carefully, laying it next to him before stretching out on the mat, hands tucked under his head. From deep within the house, Noah's snores rumbled like a continuous string of freight trains. From across the rooftop, Manny's ears also detected the soft, almost purring sound of the sleeping girl.

Sher'i hadn't said a word. He was glad. Emotionally, he felt as empty as a consumed water glass. It had been a very long day and his body was tired, but his mind wasn't ready for sleep, not just yet, so stared at the delicate, multicolored lights twinkling in the heavens. Here, in this world they seemed incredibly bright and colorful. There were few stars over the city in which he had been born. Their rhythmic pulsing helped him to relax. Vaguely his mind registered a bluish-green-yellow meteor flash across the sky ushering in the dream. It had come many times before in different surrealistic images. This time it seemed more life-like—incredibly life-like.

He slips quietly through a door—the front door of his apartment. His father is seated in front of the TV as usual, a mix of empty and partially con-sumed beer cans on the small table next to his elbow. The TV suddenly goes blank. His father has activated the remote's off switch, and then raises his left arm. Usually snapping fingers means Manny is to present himself front and center immediately. However, this time two fingers slowly gestured for him to come to him. The boy lays his judo gi on the cluttered dinette and walks around to face his father.

The man is slouched in the broken down lounger his expression pitifully blank. As Manny stares down at the woeful lump, he sees the man's left hand rise. The first blows always come that way, but not this time. It moves in slow motion, palm open. The man is crying as he reaches to caress his son's face. In the past, Manny's anger ruthlessly slaps the hand away, but this time there is no anger. He bends forward, feeling his father's strong, pudgy fingers gently caress his cheek. He drops to his knees as the man leans forward and buries his face on the boy's shoulder.

It's over. The frustration, the fear, the hate, the anger all evaporate. Manny understands. He is seeking forgiveness for all the hurt. The boy's heart turns to his father and in return seeks forgiveness for the terrible thoughts and feelings secretly harbored within his own breast. He is enveloped and filled with a powerful sense of love.

As the dream of his father slowly fades, a new dimension enters as Manny gently glides into a new vision eventually joined by the faint shuffle of bare feet and a soft, ethereal serenade suddenly overridden by Noah's voice sounding far in the distance. Manny kept his eyes closed so to linger with the new dream until the prophet's heavy steps upon the ladder seemed to shake the whole floor and jostle him fully awake. The sun was breaking the horizon.

By mid-day, Noah spoke to numerous groups of people at the western gate and others from atop the stone bench at the market place. He pleaded with several merchants outside the north gate as well, and dozens of individuals scattered in between. Unlike yesterday, response was less vehement. Mostly people just ducked their heads and moved rapidly away. A couple citizens appeared to listen while casting anxious glances toward Manny hovering nearby. As long as they remained civil, he ignored the burning glares and whispered conversations from the periphery. Instead, he watched for one particular individual who remained absent, and that was bothersome.

Approaching the flesh market, as Sher'i called it, he spotted a man in gold and jewel-encrusted white robes, and so did Noah who couldn't resist an opportunity to deride the pagan priests. Almost immediately, the old man's pace quickened as he headed straight for him like a bear to a honey log. Cutting off the priest's retreat, he engaged him in a duel of words causing the priest to become uncomfortable and annoyed, but there was no way to escape except force his way past the old man. As one of the guards moved to push Noah aside, another reached out to grab his arm and hold him in check, whispering something in the gorilla's ear. Both looked at Manny and backed up.

Suddenly, a boy in a dusty tunic ran up, tugged at the prophet's sleeve until he bent over so the child could whisper something in his ear. Immediately, Noah had another objective in mind and terminated the harangue much to the priest's delight. Making for the eastern gate, it appeared the prophet had suddenly decided to leave the city. Had he received a message to return to the Ark? If the waters were coming, and he had been summoned to board the animals, what about Sher'i? Manny couldn't just leave her here, but neither could he leave Noah.

Hustling pass the gate guards still lurking in the cool shadows, Noah kept to the road taking them to the rock marking the trail back to the Ark. As it loomed closer, his heart beat faster with anxiety until Noah peeled off to the right and head toward a large cluster of roundish, black tents. Without hesitation, he bore down on one stately figure who was talking to a half circle of men, each well-armed and well-conditioned. He hoped the prophet wasn't going to create a problem because Manny doubted he could take on this lot alone.

The man's back was to Noah, but a signal from one of the group alerted him. Turning to face Noah his jet-black, bearded face split into a wide, ivory smile. "Brother Noah! Greetings to the prophet of the Holy One, praise be His name," he said, spreading arms wide in greeting.

"Hamor, my friend, it is good to see you."

The two men griped forearms and hugged one another, kissing each cheek, a custom Manny was still uncomfortable seeing men do let alone practice himself.

"I acquired what you asked for."

"You are a good man, Hamor. Here is your

pay," Noah replied producing a bag of gold from his girdle.

Manny was dismayed that Noah had been carrying that much money around oblivious to the constant flock of thieves and robbers hovering about waiting to mercilessly descend upon such a treasure.

"How soon can you take it to Japheth?"

"I was making arrangements for my men to do just that. They will leave shortly."

"May the one almighty G-d bless you, my friend. Here is additional for your efforts."

The man happily took the second bag and stuck it with the other in his wide sash. Manny was even more concerned. How much money was he carrying?

"Now, my friend," Hamor said more seriously. "You must accept my hospitality so we may talk."

For the first time Noah ignored Manny, which was okay. He didn't relish explaining his status again. While the two men sat in the shade of a canopy sipping a hot drink and talking, Manny squat nearby, silently keeping an eye on all the activity.

Meanwhile, those Hamor had been talking with began leading twenty-three caravan animals toward the mountain. The remaining animals were unloaded and their burdens spread out on blankets as city merchants began to assemble. An impromptu satellite market was about to commence whenever

Hamor and Noah concluded their discussion.

"That is an unusual sword," one of Hamor's guards said, approaching from the side. "My name is Ru'el, Captain of lord Hamor's personal guard," joining Manny on the ground where he now sat.

"Hi. I'm Manny, Noah's bodyguard."

"In all our travels I have never seen a sword shaped like that."

"It was made in a land a long ways from here. I doubt you would have traveled that far."

Ru'el appeared to be in his mid to late twenties, but in this time of the earth who could tell. What Manny could tell was that he was every bit as muscular as Japheth with similar finely chiseled features, but darker colored. There was something in his eyes and smile Manny instantly liked, and a strange sensation they had met before. Manny's mind instantly began thumbing through its Rolodex of people he had come into contact with over the years until the connection came up. Ru'el looked a great deal like a Judo competitor at a Fresno, California meet who he learned later was named Roland. They didn't compete against one another, but the Judoka stood out in Manny's memory for the big brother way he treated the younger boys of his club. One in particular landed hard and was hurting physically as well as emotionally. Roland gently tended both pains. The meeting was less than momentary, but left an impression.

"May I look at it?"

"Sure," Manny replied, feeling he could trust Ru'el and anxious to relieve the boredom. Reaching over his shoulder he withdrew it slowly, cradling it in both hands, and handed it over, relieved there was no thunder.

Ru'el took the sword in both hands, inspected it closely, and then standing, swung it. "It has a very good balance, but why is the handle so long?"

"It is designed to be held in both hands."

Ru'el placed both hands on the hilt and swung it again. "Very interesting. Very interesting, indeed. And the workmanship is far superior to anything I have ever seen. How did you come by such a fine weapon?"

"It once belonged to a warrior."

"Did you kill him?"

"No. I sort of inherited it."

Returning it to the scabbard, he resumed sitting and said, "Lord Noah has never had soldiers before. Have things become so bad?"

"Yeah, they've tried killing him a couple times."

Suddenly Noah whisked by heading back to the city. Manny jumped up, waived a quick good-bye, and fell in behind him. As they approached the gate, the two boys with the death wagon trot pass, their cargo's legs dangling off the back. Manny suddenly stopped.

"Noah," he yelled. "Wait up." Noah turned around as Manny shouted at the two boys, "Stop!"

Unnoticed by Manny, when the boys recognized the man from the alley they slowed, shifting their course so to come close. When Manny yelled at them they dropped the yoke, stepped away, and dropped to one knee, heads bowed. Manny looked inside.

"Noah. This is the kid I told you about," he said staring at the body, "the one at the slave sale yesterday. His throat's been cut!"

Noah looked inside the wagon. "I am truly sorry. You, there, where did you find this man?"

"At the temple," the larger boy answered."

"Alright. Go about your grizzly work and G-d be with you."

"What happened, Noah?" Manny asked while watching the boys lift the yoke and depart.

"The religion of idol worshipers!" Noah spit out. "When Adam was cast from the garden, our Creator commanded him to make sacrifice in similitude to the coming of the Messiah. These followers of Lucifer have perverted that sacred practice, not by sacrificing hallowed animals, but human beings."

Manny's stomach churned violently as a seething rage welled up into his throat and radiated throughout his body. "He was sacrificed?"

"It is past time to pay these despoilers of humanity a visit," Noah announced as he headed under the squared entrance, negotiating the serpentine streets at an incredible pace unerringly straight for the street lined with statues Manny had seen when first arriving.

The street known as Avenue to Heavenly Wisdom was a broad, paved thoroughfare—the only one in the city—lined with large statues, a menagerie of human and animal combinations. The street terminated at a tall stockade behind which rose the gray, pyramid-shaped structure Noah identified as the pagan temple. To the side of the entrance to this street were several businesses selling stone replicas of their god. Standing some distance back, Noah raised his voice over the collective market bedlam. Manny thought it sounded stronger and louder than usual. He was right. Heads turned from all directions as everything went unusually quiet.

"Oh, you perverted generation. You are an abomination before Avinu Malkeinu, our Father, our King. He has commanded us from the days of Father Adam to have no other gods before Him, yet look at the blasphemy soiling your hands. He has commanded that we make no graven image or any likeness of any of the things that is in the heavens above, or that is on the earth, or that is in the waters of the earth. See how you have violated this, but worse, the blood of innocence is upon your hands. His anger is kindled against you and unless you repent He shall destroy everything from off the face of the earth."

"Shut up you old fool and leave us to worship that which has true meaning in our lives," a voice shouted from somewhere in the congregating crowd.

Manny's attention peaked. The voice sounded familiar.

"Go away and take your phony G-d with you," a woman's voice joined in.

More voices added to the swelling chorus as their inspired anger began to intensify. Noah could preach and condemn to his heart's delight, but not at the very throat to the abomination that the Lord had found among these people. It was a deliberate assault and Noah struck a nerve. He was provoking a confrontation.

"Go away and take that creature with you," another woman's voice shouted from within the group.

"Today, the blood of your human sacrifice cries out for justice."

"And our gods cry out for your blood."

Manny's disgust and anger foamed to the surface. This was no longer something in the past or some dream world aberration. It had become very personal and something came over him. It wasn't a voice, or vision, or anything one could tangibly explain, just a feeling that he must do something.

Silently he prayed, "G-d, I'm your servant. Whatever you want, let's do it." A sudden rush of strength filled his body. For the first, time Manny stepped between Noah and the crowd, not as a protector, but as a speaker.

"What's wrong with you people? What does

G-d have to do so you'll listen? You're going to die because of the evil you've allowed in your midst. G-d's had it with you. He'll tolerate no more."

"Take your weak G-d and go to . . ."

"Weak? You dare call the person who created everything from nothing including your pitiful souls, weak? Maybe we should see who's weak," Manny fired back staring directly into their eyes. Then he remembered something from Sunday school at Roger's church. Mr. Filburton had related a story about how Abraham handled a problem with idols.

Turning to one of the big statues in front of an idol vendor's stall he asked, "Who's this? Looks like a four-legged duck with a pimple on his nose. Is this one of your great, powerful gods? Come on carbuncle beak, I've just insulted you. What are you going to do? Go ahead. Show all these idiots how mighty you are. Strike me down. Go ahead you pot-bellied excuse for a paperweight. Kill me."

The crowd went deathly silent—watching intently, waiting.

"Hey, maybe this thing doesn't have ears. Yeah, that's it. It's deaf as well as stupid." With a blinding twist, the end of his staff crashed against the stone idol creating a shower of pieces.

The crowd squealed and gasped. A woman fainted, but no one noticed.

"Hey, zit face," he shouted skyward, "I just broke your look alike down here. What are you going to do about it?"

The crowd looked toward the sky and waited.

"Maybe that one's on vacation. Yeah, that's it. Went to Disneyland for the weekend. Well, maybe this guy's home," he continued, insulting the next idol, and when nothing happened, smashed it, too.

Again the crowd collectively gasped.

"Appears nobody's home there either." Manny felt in good form as the third stone deity exploded into a pile of dust, and then approaching the last figurine asked, "Well how about this one? What's this grotesque thing supposed to be?"

"That's the great and all-powerful Enlil, king of all the gods and lion of the world," someone shrieked.

Manny looked at the statue. It had the head of a man with four human-like arms outstretched from the body of pot-bellied donkey. He smiled.

"Well, well, well. So this is the big Kahuna. Nice chin whiskers, all in piggy tails. Looks like a deranged pig with a mouth full of alum. Naw, with that belly porky looks like a pregnant girlie-pig. Bet he's got a voice that squeals like one, too."

Stretching out his arms, Manny turned his face heavenward while keeping an eye on the crowd, and yelled, "Hey, girlie-pig. You're supposed to be so great and powerful, strike me with lightning." He waited a moment, but nothing happened. "Okay, then open a great hole in the earth and swallow me up." Still nothing happened.

"How about causing me to go blind and stupid like all these morons? Come on, don't just set on your big, fat donkey butt. Do something to show all these devoted idiots how powerful you are."

Resting hands on hips and turning his head from side to side as if appearing to study the thing up close, occasionally looking heavenward, he waited for a response. "I'm waiting pig face or are you out to lunch, too?" Suddenly his right hand swung out and clipped an arm off the idol. "Oops. So sorry," he said amidst anguished wails.

"Oops," he clipped another arm off. "How clumsy of me." Then wheeling to face the terrified crowd he said, "Do you really think this junk has any power? You want to see power?" With a roundhouse kick he knocked the head off to roll awkwardly in the dirt.

"Kill the infidel," that familiar voice rose above the wails of the crowd attempting to rally a charge, but the only respondent was the priest who purchased the now dead boy yesterday. Manny's eyes narrowed as building anger and hostility greeted the charge with a vicious upward swing of his staff into man's groin. The charge halted in mid-stride as his feet briefly left the ground. Face frozen into a grotesque contortion of pain he hunched over, turned around, dropping to his knees before crumpling unconsciousness in front of everyone.

"He's only one. He can't get us all," that familiar voice cried out again.

As the assembly collected for an assault a

child's voice yelled out, "Here come the temple guards. They'll do it."

Manny glanced over to see the two death cart boys casually leaning against a booth, a mischievous smile etched on their faces. Looking over his shoulder, he spotted a squad of temple guards, the size of bull elephants rumbling down the paved avenue.

"Oh, geez, Noah. I think I pushed this a little too far," Manny moaned.

With a wizen smile the prophet said calmly, "Not at all. The L-rd provides an army."

At that moment nearly three dozen of Hamor's soldiers circled in. The young man Manny had chatted with earlier moved to his side, sword drawn. The crowd faltered. One old, defenseless man and one boy would have been nothing in their hands, but all these well-armed reinforcements were another matter. The temple guards also faltered, apparently deciding the situation not serious enough to risk becoming permanent pincushions at the hands of a dozen archers. The crowd dispersed with such rapidity that only one individual was left standing alone.

Manny's eyes locked onto him, but taking a step forward, Amalekiel swirled his cloak in a great show of bravado and stormed away.

Noah and Manny accompanied Hamor's soldiers back to the merchant's tents where the prophet resumed his teaching to more willing ears while Manny and the young captain spent time together within sight of their respective charges.

"Noah says we must repent of our sins and be baptized to be saved from G-d's wrath," Ru'el said.

"Have you done that?"

"No. Do you think the great flood of waters will really come?"

"Yeah."

"Hamor is our master. Whatever he desires will be done."

"He's not convinced?"

"He believes, but we are very busy. We leave on the morrow for cities to the south. Perhaps after that we will have time enough to do this baptism."

"You can't put it off much longer. There really isn't that much time left. The L-rd, gave Noah 120 years to do his preaching before sending the waters. This is the year. It will happen any day now."

The young man silently stared at Manny, real concern shadowing in his dark brown eyes. "When my master gives the word we will respond."

Late that afternoon Noah gathered himself and slowly return to the city. With Hamor's consent, Ru'el accompanied them. The two young men followed several steps behind Noah, talking quietly. They had just passed into the shadowed recesses of the gate with its two glowering guards when a sudden movement from the darkest shadow caught Manny's eye. It was swift and he chastised himself for not being more alert as his hair-trigger reflexes responded as a group of men leaped upon them.

The staff flew from his hand in the initial assault. Countering with a flurry of feet and fists, Manny tried to spot Noah, but the old man had disappeared. Ru'el was on the ground with two big men pummeling him with fists. Manny successfully knocked them loose with one roundhouse kick, before everything went black.

Manny blinked. The sky was a soft, pastel blue streaked with a few wispy, pink clouds. Turning his head he recognized the familiar environ of Sher'i's roof, as he lay stretched out on a pallet, a blanket laid over him. Rising very slowly into a cross-legged sitting position, he rubbed a knot on the back of his head while trying to control the throb of a nasty headache.

"Hello," Sher'i's voice sang softly as she knelt next to him and applied a cool, wet cloth to the knot.

"Where's Noah? Is he alright?"

"He's fine."

"What happened?"

"Some men jumped you. They seemed intent on you so Uncle Noah was able to duck into a darkened doorway."

"What about the guy that was with me? Ru'el."

"He's fine. A bit bruised. He said you knocked some of the men off him just before one of them struck you from behind. That gave him an opportunity to draw his sword. He struck down three of them. Several of his soldiers happened to be leaving the city and joined the fight. Those attackers that could, fled. He and Noah then brought you here."

"Where are they now? Noah and Ru'el that is."

"Uncle Noah is in the courtyard eating. Ru'el and his men returned to his master as soon as it was known you would be alright."

Manny slowly sank back onto the pallet.

"Do you not wish to get up?"

"Why? This whole thing is pointless. The world is going to die and doesn't give a flip. Noah should just pack his bags, get on the Ark, close the door, and to heck with the rest of the world."

"He will not do that. There is still work to be done."

"Yeah, I know," Manny replied while staring into the sky wishing he could join the three white cranes circling overhead.

Sher'i remained kneeling, looking into his eyes.

"Where do you think G-d lives?" Manny asked after a long silence.

Placing a soft hand over his heart, she replied, "Here."

"I wish it were true. That He could be that close."

"But He is that close. Whenever we need him he's right there ready to help."

"I sure could have used his help a few times before I got here. Where was He then?"

"Maybe he was waiting to be asked."

"If He loves us that much why does He wait to be asked?"

"So that we will know from where the help comes."

"Yeah," he almost growled then looking at the girl said softly, "Do you know what I did yesterday?"

"Saved Noah from a rock?"

"Yeah, that and something really stupid. Lucifer's lieutenant was stirring up trouble again, today."

"That's not unusual. He has followed Uncle Noah from city to city, but seems to have become more active recently."

"He came up and we got into this argument, and I threaten him. All this is my fault because I had to be a show-off. For crying out loud I threatened a devil."

Sher'i giggled. "So you threatened a devil? And how did he take it?"

"Not well. Not well at all," he replied, pulling knees to his chest.

"So? What happened?"

"Today, when Noah chastised the people about their idol worship and human sacrifice, he was there trying to incite the crowd. Since no one was listening to Noah I decided to do something that Abraham did and break their idols to show

how worthless they really are."

"Who is Abraham?"

"Never mind, that's not important. What's important is that Amalekiel was obviously responsible for the attack at the gate, and it won't be the last. I've made one heck of an enemy, and I'm not that all-powerful. I've brought more danger to Noah than before."

"You've had a very full life since arriving here Emanuel Guzman," she replied ever so softly. Running her fingers through his hair and down his cheek, she leaned forward and kissed him gently on the forehead. The gloom and foreboding was instantly swept aside. Feeling better, his stomach rumbled a complaint.

"I shall bring you food," she giggled in response.

"That's okay. I can eat beneath the shade cover, but would you mind getting my clothes?"

Sher'i jumped up and disappeared below, returning with a length of cloth and another kilt.

"I washed your garments. They were badly soiled. I hope you don't mind. The material is so heavy and slow to dry. This will cover your nakedness."

Manny blushed at the girl's openness and took the cloth, then looked up at her eyes. They were so large and warm.

"Ah-h, mind looking the other way while I put this on," he said softly, embarrassment flushing his dark face.

The girl's face also darkened as she smiled and turned away, going to the kitchen.

Dressed in her father's kilt he sat on a stool beneath the latticework cover and watched as she finished preparing a meal. Presently Noah joined them for a bowl of a creamy concoction best described as thick soup. He never asked what it was, but Manny had grown quite fond of it.

Migrating to the shade of the tree by the well, the two sat talking quietly as Noah retired to his room to pray. His Judo gi lay neatly on a large blanket in the sun, now minus the sweat and blood stains.

"Are your clothes alright?"

"Yes. Thank you. I need washing, too. Up in the mountain it was easy to slip into the stream, but where do you city folks bathe around here? Not in that muddy river, I hope."

"Oh, no. I can prepare a bath on the roof."

"Yeah, but that's a bit . . . you know."

"There is a public bathhouse near the western gate. It has hot water from a well."

"Is everything around here public?"

"Hello," Aran called from outside the front door.

"Aran," Sher'i shrieked happily, sprinting to open the door, giving the boy a quick kiss on the cheek has he stepped in. "Manny was just asking about the baths. The two of you should go there while I prepare the evening meal." Noting her brother's wrinkled expression as if he'd just eaten something sour she added, "Abigail would much rather nestle in the arms of a man who smelled of something like wild balsam than old sheep."

Lifting his left arm Aran sniffed gingerly.

"Maybe you're right. Do you need anything from the market before we go?"

"No. The meal will be ready by sunset so don't fall asleep like the last time."

"Women! They never forget. That was a long time ago, sister. Okay, come on angel, let us prepare ourselves for the night."

As they walked the opposite direction from the market, Aran sighed. "If Sher'i even suspected I would never hear the end of it."

"End of what?"

"Can you keep a secret?"

"Depends."

"True. Well, revealing it would only embarrass Abigail and do none other any harm."

"Then it may be something I can keep quiet," Manny replied with growing curiosity.

"As part of the espousal contract, Abigail's father insists I live with them. It is like living together in full marriage except we do not share the same bed. There is always several smaller brothers and sisters between us. The most we can do is hold hands or sneak a kiss. Someone is always around.

"We tried very hard to abide the commandments Uncle Noah teaches, but the pressures grew too great. One afternoon Sher'i desired that we sup with her. We had not seen her for over a week and she was lonely. Coming in from the flock, I was dirty and tired from the shearing. She suggested I go to the baths while Abigail did some laundry. Well, the washing did not take but a short time and I convinced Abigail to join me. It was the first time we had been alone . . . just the two of us. There wasn't even anyone else in the pools. I chose a spot well back. It was dark and very quiet. Well . . . that is where our child was created." Aran's dark, reddish-amber face darkened even more. Manny could feel his own face burning, too.

"I . . ., we . . . never told Sher'i how it happened."

"What about Dan?"

"Oh, he was delighted. The more I consider it, the more I think he planned it to happen. We violated one of G-d's commandments. We really didn't mean to. We tried not to. It just happened."

Aran turned his head away secretly swiping at a tear. Manny's heart sank. He then remembered something either Roger or Mr. Kreutzer said. Maybe both. "Aran it may not be all that bad. G-d is also forgiving. If you go to Him with a broken heart and contrite spirit, He will forgive you."

"We have prayed for such, but . . . well, He hasn't spoken. Dan says it is proof that there is no such G-d as Noah preaches and forgiveness can only come by sacrifice to the fertility god. I cannot do that. Neither can Abigail.

"Manny! Manny! Are you alright?"

"Huh? What?"

"We were talking and you suddenly stopped and fell against the wall. What's wrong? Do you not feel well?"

"I'm fine . . . now. It's just that I saw something . . . a picture. It happened several weeks ago when I was with Shem. He said it was a vision from . . . from Heaven."

"Are you also a prophet like Uncle Noah?"

"Huh? No," Manny replied quickly, and then more contemplatively, "I don't think so. No. Prophets are old guys. And I'm not an angel either."

"What did you see?"

Manny's knees still felt like soft jelly so he continued to use the dried mud wall for support, took a deep breath, then closed his eyes to refresh what he had just envisioned.

"It was in . . . I think it was a throne room. It had beautiful white marble columns and floor, and steps that rose up to a platform. A man in a white robe was standing at the top near a golden chair. I was kneeling in front of him. His hands were on my head."

"What did he look like?"

Manny stopped to focus his mind on the person he had seen, "He's tall. I think he's kinda thin. It's hard to tell. Everything is so white it's hard to see. I think, yes, he's thin and has a beard just like Father Noah, but shorter and whiter."

"Did this person say anything?"

Manny thought hard. It seemed easy to revisualize the scene, but to recapture the words was difficult. Concentrating hard he began to sweat, until his lips began to move.

"Blessed are you my precious child. Because of your bravery you have helped defeat the Son of the Morning Star. Ever more shall your name, my Cherubim, be known as our faithful champion."

Aran silently stared at Manny for a long time as he struggled to regain his strength, then came more.

"The man poured something on my head, and placed his hands on my head, and said something, but I can't remember . . . Wait!" he said as more unfolded before his mind's eye. "I'm somewhere else. The light is not so bright. I can hear water. I'm standing with my hands on someone's head. He is kneeling in front of me. We are both wet as if we just came out of water." The scene disappeared. "That's it. It's gone," Manny ended completely spent, slipped into a sitting position as his legs now felt as if turned to warm Jell-O.

Aran stood transfixed, mouth agape, staring at Manny who was sweating profusely and breathing heavily, feeling as if having just gone three exhausting rounds on the judo mat with Roger. With the passage of time, Manny regained enough strength to stand on rubbery legs and continue on, but the two young men did so in silence, each trying to make sense of the visions. Presently they came to the bathhouse, not much more than four walls with a latticework roof to provide shade. Manny wasn't too sure about a public bath, but more than ready to surrender his modesty out of need. Washing stalls surrounded a number of tub-sized pools reserved for long, hot soaks that he desperately needed after what had just happened. Because it was the meal hour, only three other men were bathing. Quietly muttering eternal gratitude that there were no women, he guided Aran toward a back corner where it was even more private.

"Why do you choose this particular spot?" Aran asked.

"I'm a little modest, okay? I mean if a woman were to come in . . . Why?"

"This is the very place Abigail and I . . ."

"Probably coincidence. It's the most private area here, but then you know that."

Suddenly Manny thought, "I know this place," and feeling a little spooked. "But how could I. I've never been here before. It just reminds me of some place I've been."

Shrugging off the strange thought, he quickly disrobed. Using a container filled with something like soapy water, each used a piece of cloth to wash and then dumped several containers of clean water over each other to rinse off before slipping into the Jacuzzi-sized pool. With discreet pleasure Manny slithered into hot water for the first time since arriving, took a deep breathe, and relaxed.

Sprawled along one rocked side of the hot

bath Aran ignored the visions for the moment, delighting in talking about his new son and the virtues of his wife-to-be, until abruptly asking, "What do you think of my sister?'

Manny was surprised. Stammering and sputtering in search of a response he finally verbalized in total honesty, "I like her . . . very much."

"So what do plan to do?"

"How do you mean?"

"Angels come to earth all the time, see the beauty of our women, and take them. That's how we are blessed to have these giants among us," he answered sarcastically. "Angels take anything they want."

"I'd never do anything like that to Sher'i."

"Do you love her?"

Manny fell silent before answering, "I don't know. I like being near her. I get all tingly inside, and at other times feel so at peace."

"Oh, you are in love my friend." Aran laughed, and then more soberly said, "I would like having you for a brother."

"Yeah, but I can't. I've got a job to do, first."

"After that you can get married. You have my blessing, but you need ask Uncle Noah. I think he will say yes."

"Whoa. Not so fast. Sher'i has a say in this, doesn't she?"

"Not really, but she will anyway. Always does, but she will not object. She told me so."

Manny was sure from the heat that his face

was turning every shade of a cooked beet.

"We better get back before she thinks we fell asleep," Manny said as he climbed out.

Having nothing to towel off with he fastened the kilt while water ran down his legs. That's when the vision came again as clear as if watching a TV show. He was standing next to a pool, this pool, watching the steam rising lazily into the air as Aran wrapped a kilt about his loins. Manny wore the very kilt that now girded his loins, and dripping water. Then Aran knelt before him. Manny laid his hands on the boy's wet hair.

A voice he recognized said as clearly as if standing next to him, "Peter Emanuel Guzman, having been anointed by my son, Jehovah, the time has come for you to exercise your authority. Lay your hands upon Aran's head so that he may receive My blessing."

Startled, Manny said, "Aran. It happened again. The vision. The one of me with my hands on someone's head, but clearer. It's here, and the other person is you! I think that you are supposed to kneel in front of me."

"Then it shall be so," the boy said, lowering himself before Manny who instinctively placed both hands on the damp head and closed his eyes despite feeling self-conscious.

Almost immediately, an exhilarating feeling entered the top of Manny's head, coursed down his neck to spread across the shoulders, and down each arm until each finger tingled. Fascinated by the unusual sensation Manny focused on the feeling as it continued for several minutes before moving back up his arms, and out where it had entered. Mystified, he opened his eyes and blinked repeatedly before looking down at Aran face turned up to meet his eyes. Two great rivers of tears poured down each cheek as he sobbed.

"Blessed be the name of the L-rd!" Aran finally managed to exclaim hoarsely as he sprang to his feet and threw arms around a puzzled Manny. "Blessed be the name of the L-rd," he whispered again in Manny's ear. "Come! We must tell Sher'i."

"Tell her what?" Manny shouted at a rapidly disappearing Aran who didn't seem to care his not quite fastened kilt flopped in the wind.

Grabbing up the sword, Manny sprinted after him.

For All Time and Eternity:
waters from the deep

Chapter 12

Not that there was much to see, but what there was became blurred as the two young men careened through the narrow streets, forcing people to leap aside, and barking dogs to join in the run. Coming to Sher'i's door, Aran pounded wildly, shouting for her to open up. Once inside, Manny slipped into a quiet corner trying to be inconspicuous as Aran attempted to explain what happened, but spoke so rapidly his tongue kept tripping over itself.

"Aran, slow down," Noah finally said in frustration to understand.

"As we walked to the public baths Manny had a vision. He was kneeling before someone who anointed him, and then he saw someone kneeling in front of him. When we finally got to the baths, he recognized the place of his vision. It was the exact place where Abigail and I . . ." He stopped short and looked at Sher'i, took a deep breath then continued. "Where Abigail and I conceived our Ishiah."

"Aran! In the public bath?"

"Well, it just happened, Sher'i."

"Never mind that," Noah interrupted. "Go on."

As we finished bathing Manny's vision returned, and he was told I should kneel before him. When he placed his hands upon my head, a great peace came upon me. Then a voice spoke, a beautiful voice that filled every part of my body. It was not Manny's voice."

"What did this voice say?" Noah continued to quiz.

"Aran my son, peace be upon you. I have heard your supplications. The honesty of your heart is more pleasing unto me than all the sacrifices of men. Peace upon you and upon your espoused wife, for when you submit to the law through my servant Noah, your transgressions shall be forgiven."

"Praise be to G-d!" Noah shouted, lifting his hands into the air and doing a little dance.

"What does this mean . . .?"

Ending the dance abruptly, Noah took Aran by both arms and said, "The L-rd has heard your prayers and granted repentance if you obey his commandment to be married."

"I must tell Abigail," Aran cried joyfully turning for the door.

"Wait!" Noah called out sharply. "Tell no one except Abigail. No one else must know what has happened this day. No one. Do you understand?"

"Yes, uncle," Aran replied, a little bewildered.

During this exchange, Manny stood off, not knowing if the prophet of G-d would sanction what he had done, but as Aran excitedly slammed the heavy door behind him for Sher'i to latch and raced toward his beloved's home, Noah turned and faced him. His serious countenance softened as he reached out a hand and gently stroked Manny's cheek.

"G-d's blessings pour out upon us. Praise be His Holy name. Thank you my elohim."

Turning away, he walked toward the house, arms stretched heavenward, lips moving in a silent prayer. Sher'i stood in dumbfounded silence by the gate. Manny was more confused than ever.

"Father Noah!" he called out, running after the elderly man as he disappeared into the house. "Father Noah!"

"What is it, my son?" he answered, turning to meet Manny in the middle of the first room.

"What's going on? Why is this happening to me? I know you know."

Noah smiled, was about to speak, but something distracted him as he looked heavenward, before replying, "Yes, my son. The knowledge is given to me, but I am forbidden to say at this time. However, know that in the Lord's time you will come to understand."

"Why am I seeing these things? Why am I doing things like that to Aran? Should I have done what I did?" he pressed.

"It is time to explain a few things, but only a few. You are here in part to fulfill a special commission. You are very close to our Heavenly Father, blessed be His name. You do have certain authority to act in His holy name. What you did with Aran is within that authority. More I cannot say."

"Am I some kind of prophet?"

"A prophet is a person who is on a high level of communication with our L-rd. He may tell the people those things he is privileged to know, or be commanded to remain silent. You have the position and ability to communicate with G-d. Cherish it, but know it can also be a great burden on your heart."

"What is a Cherubim?"

"Why do you ask?"

"In one of the visions, I was standing in front of this tall man who had his hands on my head. He called me a Cherubim. I asked Shem. He said they are a who, not a what, but never elaborated."

"What did this man look like you saw in the vision?"

"Tall, thin, with a really brilliant, white beard. The light too bright. It was impossible to see much, but I was in a long room of marble columns, at the top of stairs leading to a throne of gold. I couldn't really see much, just the beard and his eyes. They were so gentle and filled with love."

Noah's eyes lit up like twin beams from a lighthouse as he replied, "As Shem said, Cherubim are not a what, but a who. They are Heavenly beings assigned to guard Holy things."

"Then I really am . . ."

"An angel? Only you ever doubted."

"But . . ."

"You have heard G-d's voice, Manny. You know what it sounds like. Listen closely and do as instructed. Now, I must retire to my apartment to pray," he replied, turning to disappeared into his sleeping quarters leaving the young man dumbfounded as ever.

Long shadows crept across the roof as evening descended upon the walled city. Sher'i settled cross-legged leaning against the outer ledge. Manny, stretched out on his back, nestling his head on her lap as they listened to Noah describe the great patriarchs. Much of it he had already heard since arriving. It was obvious Sher'i had heard the stories many more times, but each attended closely to what the prophet had to say. Manny loved listening to Noah's raspy, baritone voice, having come to love him as he loved Mr. Kreutzer and Roger.

Suddenly Noah said, "One by one the L-rd has taken the righteous unto His bosom; Lamech, and now Methuselah."

Sher'i startled, almost causing Manny's head to drop on the floor.

"Great grandfather is gone!"

"Yes, my daughter. The L-rd in His infinite wisdom translated our venerable patriarch two days ago."

"Sincerest pardons, Father Noah," Manny said, sitting up, desiring to clarify something. "What does it mean to translate someone?"

"That is when a living person is taken into heaven without tasting death."

"But, I've heard that this world was created as a place for His spirit children to obtain bodies, and by how they use their agency, prove themselves worthy of returning into His Holy presence. When we die, our spirits leave these earthly bodies to return home to the Father. That is what Father Adam brought to the world when he ate the forbidden fruit—death. It is necessary for the return to our Father in Heaven. "

"That is correct, but under certain circumstances the process of dying is not an essential element to our return, at least not in this time of the earth. That will change with the coming of the Messiah and full implementation of the plan of salvation. What is important is while here that we affirm through our deeds and words that the creator of all life is, as you say, Hashem, the one called Jehovah, praise be to His Holy name. During our time on this earth we must affirm that it is He who created the heavens and the earth, and that

He is the son of the great Elohim, praise be His Holy name. It is only through repentance of our sins, accepting Jehovah as the Messiah, baptism by immersion, and receiving the Holy Ghost in His name can we be assured of returning to our rightful place with the true Father of us all."

"But there are still good people left on earth, I've seen them. You and your family will ride out the flood in the Ark, but what about people like Aran and his family, and Sher'i, and Ru'el, and Hamor? What about them?"

"Yes, you are quite right. They are good people, and there are others, but none have accep-ted the waters of baptism, and their cries mingle with the wicked. Those are the voices I hear every night in my dreams, and my excuse for drinking too much wine. The difference will be in their judgment when they appear before the bar of the Holy One, praise be His name. Certainly, they will enjoy eternal life although at a lesser degree of glory, but there is no guarantee any will enjoy the eternal companion-ship of their loved ones. That special privilege is for those who have been united for time and all eternity over the holy altar while still on this earth."

Manny turned to look at Sher'i. He felt panic-stricken. Then something came to mind. Something he heard in the church Roger attended.

"It will not always be so, Father Noah. There will come a day when a man and woman will kneel across a Holy altar in one of G-d's Temples to be sealed for all time and eternity, and they will do it for people who have already died."

"Really? I should not be surprised. The L-rd will provide a way for the righteous in all dispensations."

A long silence fell over the rooftop before Noah slowly rose, stiffly using his staff for balance, and bid them good night. After a while, Manny turned and looked into the moonlight reflected in Sher'i's eyes.

"What are you thinking, Manny?"

"All my life I heard bits and pieces of this religion stuff, mostly from Mr. Kreutzer, and when I lived with Roger's family, and now from Father Noah. It's all coming together. I think I'm beginning to understand."

"Who are Roger and Mr. Kreutzer?"

"My teachers, where I come from." Manny took a deep breath and expelled it quickly. "At the bath Aran asked if I loved you." Even in the moonlight he saw Sher'i's cheeks take on a warm glow. "I never really understood the feeling of love that a man can have for a woman, but maybe now . . . When we are apart it's like a hole inside me, and when we're together that hole is filled. When you are near I feel warm and alive and at the same time at peace deep down."

Sher'i slowly reached her hand to his cheek. The touch was like that of a butterfly, delicate, yet spoke loudly of her feelings. Slowly they drew together, tentative at first, but once Manny tasted her lips an electrical current surged through his body so that every inch tingled with excitement. They embraced as her hands caressed his head, untying the ponytail so that the long platinum locks cascaded over his shoulders. Her fingers slowly combed through the silky strands causing them to shimmer like rivulets of water, then plied her hands across his wide, muscular shoulder blades, moving up and down his back pressing him closer as they became one with the current floating through a dreamlike world of infinite time. At that moment, he heard a voice in his mind, one he was familiar with. The radio announcer was broadcasting again, his words encouraging Manny to follow his body's desires set off deafening alarms. Abruptly he pulled back, halting her hands.

"What's wrong?" she asked.

"I love you Sher'i and want you very much, but I'll not violate you or the laws Noah has spoken of. Not for the sake of a few moments of sensuous pleasure."

"But what difference does it make now? The flood is coming. You even said we will all die, except Uncle Noah and his family."

"What Noah has been saying, is that we have to make a commitment to ourselves and to G-d, and to stand firm in defense of that commitment. The way I feel right now I'd like nothing better than jump in bed with you. That's the way of world—in this time and in mine—but that's not right. It's not the way G-d wants it. When He first gave Adam and Eve the commandment to multiply and replenish the earth they had no idea what he was talking about, but when they became conscious of each other the first thing He did was seal them in marriage. We are to have sex to provide bodies for the spirit children to inhabit when they come to earth, then love them, and teach them G-d's laws, and why they are important, otherwise they end up like those people in the market place. What we do here on earth is important because it effects what our lives will be like tomorrow, and tomorrow's tomorrows, even a million of years from now."

Sher'i stared down at the floor, a heavy silence settling between them. Finally looking up she said, "Manny, you are the sweetest, dearest joy of my life. You are right. We cannot allow ourselves to become like the rest of the world."

Standing, they held hands, saying nothing as their eyes stared into the other's soul. Finally, Manny leaned forward and kissed her forehead. Sher'i turned away and disappeared below. Gathering up his sleeping pad, he rolled it out away from the latticed canopy so to face up at the gleaming vault of stars. They seemed even brighter.

Chapter 13

"Hearken and give heed unto the words of your true G-d." Noah was in good voice as his words carried above the tumult. "It was He who created man in His image. You are His children and dear unto Him. He has given seven laws to guide mankind's dealings with one another. Beware not to worship false gods for they have no power upon the earth; Use not His name to curse your brethren or your G-d for it is offensive. Have no sexual relations with any but thy lawful spouse to whom you are joined by the powers of Heaven for the powers of thy loins are closest to creation. Lay not thy hand upon another to do murder for as it was not given unto Cain it is not given unto you lest you suffer as Cain has suffered. Do not steal that which does not belong unto you, only by the sweat of your brow shall man find pleasure from his increase. Do not eat the limb of an animal before it is killed for you are not like the wild beasts. Set up courts and bring offenders to justice for it is by law and order that mankind is to live."

Manny instantly recognized these as the first laws G-d gave his children through His Antediluvian prophet. How often Mr. Kreutzer quoted them saying, "Jew or Gentile, the Noahide laws are the basics which should govern our behavior, but mankind just couldn't do it without requiring more specifics. The laws of Moses were the result. We went from seven to 620 and one million lawyers. We should have listened to Noah."

Noah's voice was so good Manny swore to hear an echo. "The L-rd your G-d has given us these laws so to live in peace and harmony, but you have trespassed them, transgressed them mightily. Yet, if you repent of your sins, and become baptized in the name of Jehovah, even as your fathers have done, you shall receive the gift of the Holy Ghost so that you may have all truth made known unto you. Then by the laws of repentance, you can have the stains of your sins washed from your garments, and find eternal peace both on earth and in G-d's presence. But, if you do not these things, when the flood comes you will be denied a place with Him and thus suffer eternal torment."

This day was not much different from the

others. Upon seeing the prophet, the people hastily turned away, turning heads down to stare at the ground or hide their faces within the hoods of their garments until he was once again the sole voice in a sea of inhumanity. The lone exception came when a notable absentee figure finally appeared.

"Why don't you just go back to your boat, Noah? These people are not interested in listening to your babble," Amalekiel called out.

Manny was standing in a vacant stall a few feet from Noah when the arrayed peacock stepped forward to gloat at the prophet's failure to attract an audience. As there didn't seem to be any eminent threat, Manny held back in the cool respite from the intensifying heat of a brilliant sun. For the next hour, he listened with fascination as Amalekiel challenged Noah on every imaginable issue of spiritual doctrine, much of which was way over his head. The old man not only held his own in the war of words, but also landed more than a few licks. If Amalekiel had thought to wear Noah down or confuse the aged prophet with a perfect command of the language that twisted G-d's words into a jumble of confusing expressions, he was sadly mistaken. Manny had never seen Noah so alert and alive, turning everything back with definitive power. Then, obviously tiring of the lopsided encounter, Amalekiel turned away, deliberately passing close to Manny.

"I thought you had left? Gone back where you came from. Too bad."

"You mean back to heaven since I wouldn't be welcome in . . . ah . . . hell?"

"How do you know anything about heaven? Ever been there?" Amalekiel challenged, slyly.

"I have been IN a hell and I have tasted OF heaven," Manny responded firmly, a bit surprised at the answer, and pleased with the way it was put because for a split moment Amalekiel looked perplexed before typically recovering.

"You want to know what I believe," Manny continued, enjoying throwing him off balance. "Well, I'll tell you anyway. I believe in G-d the eternal Father and in His son Jehovah who will become the Messiah, and stand as our advocate before the judgment bar, and I believe in the Holy Ghost. I believe that through the atonement of Jehovah, all mankind may be saved, by obedience to the laws and ordinances of the Gospel, and the first principals and ordinances of that Gospel are Faith in the L-rd Jehovah, repentance, baptism by immersion for the remission of sins, and laying on of hands for the gift of the Holy Ghost. I know your boss was the Shining Light, Son of the Morning. He could have had it, had it all, but because of his sniveling, arrogant pride, he lost it—lost . . . it . . . all. Oh, you guys will do fine on this earth for a while, but in the end you'll have nothing, nothing but a hopeless emptiness devoid of the one thing you've thirsted for, but never felt or can really comprehend—love."

Every time Manny used the name Jehovah,

Amalekiel actually winced as if stuck with a hat pin. And each time his contorted scowl intensified with a raging hate that could seemingly consumed body and soul. Manny had really hit a nerve standing toe to toe with this powerful adversary so he emphasized the Messiah's name by slow pronunciation. This time Manny had full knowledge of what he was challenging and didn't blink an eye while speaking with a strength he didn't even know existed within himself. To his amazement, he won, but wise enough not to openly gloat and revel in victory.

Later, Manny wondered why he hadn't become a smoldering pile of ash at the time except something protected him, something encircle him like a coat of medieval armor. Satan's general must have been aware of it, too, yet despite that invisible protection Manny decided to keep a watch over his shoulder more so now, as Amalekiel turned away with a great blustering wrath.

Noah's reassuring smile and, "Well put. Well put," fortified Manny's hope he had gotten it right.

Despite a long, hard day, the old man's footsteps back to the house seemed to have more spring than before. Manny even detected the faint notes of a song on the prophet's lips, as usual not quite on key.

Feeling empowered with confidence, he skipped alongside Noah and said, "Father Noah, with all due respect, I'd, well, I'd like permission to ask Sher'i to marry me," he stuttered with nervous apprehension, "When you don't need me."

Noah stopped short, turning to looked into Manny's eyes for a long time before replying, "Are you aware of what you ask? This is a very sacred commitment you are seeking."

"I know that I love her, and she loves me. We've discussed this very carefully over the last week, and we wouldn't want to share our lives with anyone else."

"Sharing this life is easy. Are you prepared to share your life with my niece for an eternity?"

"Yes, sir," Manny responded firmly well aware of what he was committing to. "With what's going to happen that seems all that's left to us."

Noah placed his hand on the young man's shoulder and squeezed. He had a firm grip—a very firm grip.

"I will propose the espousal."

"No, sir. Not espousal. Marriage."

"So quickly?"

"Well, it's not like we have a lot of time left around here, is there? You said yourself the waters will come any day. We love each other and we don't want that love to stop just because the world stops. We want this to be legal in His eyes, and we want it for all time and eternity. The only way that can happen is to be sealed by you while we are still alive."

Noah remained silent a long time, staring deeply into Manny's eyes as if searching for something before answering, "It will warm this old heart to seal the two of you. I will consult with the

L-rd. This is unusual. Angels have never asked permission before taking one of the daughters of man to wife."

"Hey, I'm not a . . ." Manny started to protest for the thousandth time, but suddenly found his tongue unable to form the word—angel.

"I'll need to baptize Sher'i first, though."

"And me."

"Do angels need to be baptized?"

For the first time, Manny understood something about the doctrine Noah seemed to have momentarily forgotten. "When the Messiah comes to earth he will ask to be baptized because it is an ordinance that can only occur on earth . . . for G-d, angels, and mortals."

Noah's smile radiated special warmth. Placing arms around the young man, he was drawn into a breath-taking hug after which Noah planted a kiss on both of Manny's cheeks, turned, and practically ran home with the intended groom floating behind in tow.

Three great knocks on the gate with his staff announced their arrival. Once inside the elderly gentleman headed for the wine jug, filled a bowl, and turned to face the young couple walking up hand in hand. Lifting the bowl to his lips, his eyes twinkled with a joy Manny had not seen. Sher'i looked bewildered at what she saw. Manny's gaze met his.

"Well, are you going to ask or not? You have my permission."

Sher'i's mouth dropped open, suddenly realizing what was coming.

"Sher'i," Manny said, turning to stare into her eyes, "will you be my wife?"

She stared first at Manny, then at Noah who winked. Looking back at the young man holding her hand, she squealed, "Yes!" and leaped into his arms nearly knocking him to the ground.

"A drink to the newly intendeds," Noah said, and raised the bowl above his head. "Barukh attah Adonai eleheinu melekh ha-olam, shenatan nes bamakom hazzeh. Blessed art thou LORD our god, King of the universe, who has given a miracle in this place, richly bless these two of your children in their days." Taking a sip from the bowl, he watched as the two kissed, and then said under his breath with a smile and wiggle of his bushy eyebrows, "And nights."

That evening Sher'i and Manny sat alone on the roof, cuddled in each other's arms. Staring at the brilliant display of meteors streaking through heavens he asked, "Sher'i, do you still think I'm an angel?"

"Yes."

"Would you be disappointed if I'm not?"

"No, but why do you ask?"

"Okay, here it goes. Father Noah thinks I am because of some things I've done. I think the jury is still out on that because they are just . . . well, I don't know. I'm confused, but what I do know is that before coming to this time and place, I lived far into the future. That's how I know some of the stuff that will happen. To me, this is all history. I felt trapped in a miserable life and was in the process of getting out of it, but at that moment, a bolt of lightning picked me up and dropped here. I don't know if I died in that world. In that life I learned special fighting skills and I guess G-d dropped me here to use those skills to protect Noah. I think I've gotten the better deal.

"In the world I left, there is a record of this event. It's called the Bible, a bunch of stuff recorded by G-d and His prophets. It says that the only persons on the Ark were Noah, his wife, his sons, and their wives. Our names aren't on the manifest. Maybe we'll be translated, or maybe we will drown with the rest of this inhumanity, but once we are sealed as man and wife, at least we'll be together afterward. And that I am looking forward to that very much."

The two embraced tenderly before snuggling closer, feeling each other's warmth, and love in the chilled night.

"Where I lived you really couldn't see the stars or meteors. They are beautiful. I didn't realize there could be so many."

"It is unusual to see this number of shooting stars," she replied.

At that moment, they heard Noah enter the front gate and set the heavy timber latch with a reassuring thud. The sound brought a sigh of relief to Manny's mind. Noah had been very insistent that his guardian not accompany him when he left the house.

"I am going to have a walk with G-d," he announced.

Initially, Manny wasn't going to allow the elderly man to be on the streets alone until a calming feeling passed through him, and all concerns vanished.

"Well, for cryin' out loud, who's going to harm anyone in the company of G-d?" he reassured himself.

Noah's walk took much longer than Manny anticipated which he really didn't mind, and it was well past the usual time the elderly man went to bed. Sher'i gave Manny a quick kiss before slipping quietly down the ladder to help her uncle.

Manny sat on his sleeping mat, knees pressed against his chest, a blanket laid over his shoulders. Alone, he contemplated the future, occasionally struck by a tremor of apprehension at the thought of what was about to happen. Back in his first life, the thought of dying hadn't frightened him. It had only seemed a curiosity, perhaps because he had been too nearsighted to see a future. Now, things had changed. The thought of death weighed heavily. After a long while, he decided to tip toe down the steps to see what was taking Sher'i so long to return.

A small, oil lamp set in one corner lit Noah's sleeping chamber, barely illuminating where he slumbered noisily. Looking down, Manny noticed

Noah's cover had slipped exposing the garment worn beneath the outer robe. About to replace the blanket, he hesitated. The piece of clothing was nothing like what he and the other men wore, but instead had the look of a modern, knee-length under garment.

"That is the garment of Father Adam," Sher'i whispered.

Manny jumped, staring across the room to pierce the darkest corner, relaxing upon seeing her eyes reflect the lamp light.

"It is the garment Jehovah, praise be His name, made for Father Adam upon discovering his nakedness in the Garden of Eden. It is passed from father to righteous son."

Manny said nothing. "Made by the hand of Jehovah?" he thought, before hesitantly reaching out to barely touch a seam with one finger. "Jesus sewed this for Adam," he thought, becoming overwhelmed. He never felt so close to G-d, to touch something He'd actually created. Then it dawned on him. He had. The way he looked at Sher'i, he would never look at her that way again. She was something vastly more than a sweet, beautiful woman. She had been carefully fashioned with G-d's own hands as carefully as He had fashioned Noah's garment.

Chapter 14

"You'd think a guy who'd just turned 600 years old would show some sign of slowing down," Manny mumbled to himself as the two once again traversed the countryside heading for yet another town. Each successive day Noah seemed increasingly driven to spread the appeal for repentance. That peaked his anxiety levels especially when reflecting on where he was at, what was going to happen, and if the Bible was correct, and he had no doubt about that, he and Sher'i were going to miss the boat.

Since leaving the Ark's completion in the hands of his sons and coming to the city, Noah maintained an incredible pace that pushed Manny's youth to near exhaustion. For a solid week, sunrise to sun set, he preached to the people in the city, which met with no success. Then before the sun began to touch the horizon with a faint glow, the day following Sabbath, Noah pulled the warm covers from Manny to announce a trip to neighboring towns. As he trotted alongside a donkey carrying the venerable prophet, they seemingly charged through the western gate, following the chocolate-brown river upstream to arrive at the first village by noon.

A nondescript cluster of mud and thatched huts, the inhabitants were no more interested in hearing Noah's words than those in the city. By mid-afternoon, they were once again on the trail arriving at the next community by dusk. Such went their travels day after day, moving from one unconcerned community to another often across rough and dangerous terrain, spending chilly nights huddled near a fire because there were no inns and no welcome mats extended to give them cover for the night. Although man and beast lurked in the shadows along the way, it seemed as if they didn't dare consider molesting them, delighting Manny to no end.

Days stretched into weeks until nearly two and a half months passed during which his knowledge and understanding expanded as Noah spent the travel time rehearsing all the oral works from Adam onward until his guardian could replay them by heart. After that, much of their conversation became a matter of Noah making an abstract remark to which Manny responded with the appropriate answer. He even found himself questioning or debating the great prophet, not that he won any arguments, but that was what Noah intended—knowledge, understanding, and most importantly, thought.

Those days away from Sher'i only seemed long at night as the two travelers lay beneath the stars. While Noah promptly fell asleep and contributed to the wild, night noises, Manny's rest came slowly as he thought of Sher'i before drifting through a fuzzy dream world filled with strange pictures of them together.

There was the dream of them standing next to a pile of rocks. He was dripping wet as if he had been swimming. Then the two were sitting upon a mountain in a rainstorm. The weirdest image was Sher'i in a military uniform driving a tank across the desert. That brought an audible chuckle that nearly woke him, but immediately came the scene of them kissing in Mr. Kreutzer's deli, a fanciful illusion to fill the void of separation.

However, there were other dreams, some of which had come several times before in bits and pieces. Many of these centered on a pyramid of white, marble stairs, a golden chair, and two men at the top surrounded by men in tunics with spears and swords. There is a crash as two tall doors at the end of a great hall burst open. People charge into the columned room, swords waiving wildly overhead, their blood-curdling screams filling the chamber. He can see their leader's face clearly, Amalekiel, an irregular smirk plastered across his face. His followers engage the warriors defending the steps and push them backwards up the stairs. Another noise crashes upon the scene, high-pitched cries, like a bunch of girls at a football game. It diverts Amalekiel's attention. The battle is joined by reinforcements. Amalekiel fights desperately, but is driven back. There is blood on his face. Despite being troubled at seeing him hurt, Manny is secretly pleased with that thought.

A scene at the top of the stairs always follows the battle. A man clad in a short, white, pleated skirt, his broad, brown back to Manny's view, is kneeling before a tall man in a silvery-white gown. Placing hands on the kneeling man's head, something is said about being a champion, and then a few drops of liquid from a small, white flask drop on his head. He is being anointed to something, but the words are disjointed and incoherent. The man at his side holds up a long strip of cloth of equally brilliant white. In the center of the cloth is a picture of a flying crane, its gold color glowing. He hands this to one of the men standing on a step just below who ties it about his head. That man vaguely looks like Noah.

Because these two dreams always come together, Manny came to feel that they must be connected somehow. He relished the thought of someone taking on Lucifer's lieutenant and beating the tar out of him. Whoever the dark skinned man being honored was, he had Manny's gratitude too.

After a particularly active night of dreams, Manny was awaken by a sudden noise. Grabbing his sword, he sprang to his feet poised for battle.

"I am sorry if I startled you," Noah said softly.

The light of a growing fire highlighted an aged face giving him a haggard appearance, something Manny had seen often of late, but never so much as now. The time and work was taking its toll. Manny slipped to his knees and gathered up the scabbard, hanging the sheathed sword over his back. That's when it suddenly dawned on him something different had happened.

"Something wrong my faithful servant?"

"When I drew the sword just now, there was no thunder."

"The thunder only comes when you use your sword in G-d's cause. That is when you draw on the powers of Heaven in righteousness."

"Oh," Manny replied, trying to clear the cobwebs from his mind. "You're up early."

"I have been instructed to return to the city."

No words could have been received with so much delight. He quickly snatched up the bedding.

"Food first, then travel anxious one."

"Yes, sir."

Although his footsteps struck the parched ground with a light spring, Manny was troubled. Only yesterday, Noah decided to visit a village several days journey to the north until this sudden change. The prophet wouldn't say more and became unusually quiet. Yet, all the young man could really think about was Sher'i, so it was with joy and surprise they entered the city that same day just before the great gate closed for the night. Arriving at the house, Manny pounded impatiently on the heavy door and fell immediately into her soft, strong arms as it opened. Noah smiled as he slipped pass the couple to lounge in his favorite chair near the grape juice jar.

"Did you have any success?" she asked while helping him remove the sword and the sweat-laden, cotton jacket.

"No. It's been like screaming into a windstorm. No body hears. Nobody wants to hear. This morning the L-rd told Noah to return. He says we'll spend some time here."

"I'm glad."

Slowly their lips came together for a lingering kiss before Manny pulled back.

"I haven't bathed in days. Weeks. I'm sorry. I must stink like an old goat."

"You smell just fine to me."

"Well, I'll run down to the bath . . ."

"There's hot water on the roof. The L-rd prompted me to prepare some for what purpose I did not understand until now."

"Okay. You take care of Noah. He's got to be exhausted. I'll tend to the donkey and take a quick bath."

Sher'i immediately set to washing Noah's feet as Manny lead the equally tired, gray donkey to the stall around back. After graining and insuring the faithful beast had plenty of water and a thick cushion of straw, he climbed to the roof.

He really wasn't interested returning to the public bathes, instead steeling himself to public bathing on the roof after dark. During this time, he moved the bathing area next to the canopy near the outer edge, and built a frame to hang cloth over the exposed sides. This provided sufficient privacy, not for himself, but more importantly for Sher'i. This alteration impressed Noah, and for the first time his niece could bathe any time she wanted instead of waiting until after dark.

"I think that would make a good addition to the Ark. I shall consult with the architect," he said.

Combining hot and cold water to a comfortable temperature in a large basin, he finished undressing, sat on the little wooden stool behind the curtain, and sponged the thick layers of dirt from his body. The fatigue of miles of endless walking literally melted away. Untying the ponytail, he thoroughly lathered down the long hair, and then poured several containers of water over his head to rinse away the soap. After toweling off, he took a favorite skirt Sher'i had specially made, wound it about his waist, and then tidied up. After leaning over the short wall overlooking the courtyard, he called to Sher'i. Coming up, she found him standing at the edge of the back wall looking out toward the river and distant plain. Taking his hand, she led him to a stool by the clay oven where she applied fragrant oil to his feet and lower legs. The lotion left an invigorating sensation, but not so much as the feel of her strong fingers kneading tired muscles.

"That feels good. I've never walked so much in my entire life," he said with a sigh.

The girl smiled, stepped to his back, and began massaging oil into his shoulders.

Tense muscles only slightly relaxed. She finished by taking another bottle to anoint his hair and rub it in before methodically combing out a few tangles. While she always combed and tied up the long, fine, strands into the customary arching ponytail every morning, but in the evenings she left them to hang over his shoulders. This was a ritual he looked forward to.

She had just finished when the voices of Aran and Abigail sounded below. Soon they appeared, Abigail carrying their baby, and Aran a basket of food. Their visits had become more frequent and welcomed, but from the first time Manny was introduced to Abigail, he did not mention that he had seen her in the marketplace talking to Amalekiel the first day he arrive.

While the two men talked, the women prepared the meal. Manny enjoyed these visits and holding their little boy in his arms. He had never held a baby before. At first, he was scared to death of dropping Ishiah or breaking something, but after a time really got a kick out of bouncing him on a knee to evoke squeals and giggles, or gently cradling him in his arms while tiny fingers played with his hair which seemed to fascinate the child.

"You will make a wonderful father, Manny," Abigail said, smiling coyly at Sher'i.

"Probably," Manny responded to her weakly veiled hint, thinking, "but that will have to wait."

As usual, Noah appeared in time for the meal after which the three men sat talking while the women cleaned up. Typically, the old gentleman would launch into a discourse about some theological topic while tenderly playing with the baby, or deliberately engage the two young men in a debate. Tonight was no different, but he broached a topic before sidestepped.

"When the L-rd gave our parents the commandment to multiply and fill the earth they were still children with no conception of what their creator meant. After transgressing the word they came to realize their differences; they became as adults. That is why the L-rd sealed them in the marriage covenant soon after the departure from the garden. Thus, the law, no man should know a woman or a woman know a man until they have been properly sealed over the holy altar by proper authority. Espousal contracts do not count," he said bluntly staring directly at Aran.

"It was not planned and we are very sorry, Father Noah. Abigail's father will not permit marriage until the contract is complete. It is a hold on me for servitude, as you well know. We want to do what is right, but . . ."

Noah rocked Ishiah gently. "That will be the baker's burden, correct little one?" Ishiah cooed as if responding, and then looking into Aran's eyes said, "This is your burden until all is made right."

After pronouncing a blessing upon the day, he handed the baby to Sher'i and hobbled to his bed leaving the two couples to talk softly into the night.

After a time Manny approached the subject. "So why don't you two go ahead and let Noah marry you?"

"The contract. Until that is fulfilled Dan will not permit it," Aran responded, trying to sound patient.

"He'll keep playing games to prolong that. You said so yourself."

"I am young. I have no trade. I have no way to provide for a family right now."

"And he wants you to become a baker?"

"Yes."

"Do you want to be a baker?"

"It is an honorable trade."

"But do you want to be baker?"

Aran was silent.

"So, what do you need to provide for a family? Huh?" Manny pressed. "Food?"

"Yes."

"Shelter?"

"Yes."

"Clothing?"

"Again, yes," Aran replied becoming vexed. "It is what I promised in the contract."

"Well, if I miss my guess, you can provide shelter. Doesn't this house belong to you, too? And as for food and clothing, what about all those sheep you own? Don't they provide meat, wool, leather . . . money? What more do you need? Nothing wrong with being a simple, wealthy sheepherder."

Aran looked startled. Why it hadn't dawned on him that he was really freer and probably wealthier than the baker was a mystery to Manny, and then remembered one of Mr. Hauptmann's stories.

"There were these two old horses pulling a wagon. They'd done it for years, and then one day the owner takes the blinders off one of the horses. The horse immediately sits down because he's in shock. The owner asked if he's alright and the horse answers, "You never said the horse next to me was a girl."

Although the conversation changed, he could tell the seeds of independence were taking root in Aran's mind.

Talking late into the night, it again became too late to safely venture the streets back to the baker's house. The first time that happened Manny suggested they spend the night, and suspected succeeding visits were deliberately delayed so they didn't have to leave. So, like all the other times, Aran and Abigail withdrew to his bedchamber on the second level. Sher'i also had a room on that level, however opted to lie upon a sleeping mat under the kitchen canopy while Manny nestled beneath a light cover at the opposite end of the roof. As usual sleep came slowly as he listened to the night sounds—an occasional dog bark, the screech of an owl, the muffled voices of Aran and Abigail, the soft purr of his beloved, and the volcanic rumblings of the prophet below.

When sleep came so did the dreams, except this night there were two additions; a battle with a giant and his band of humans, especially a wiry, hawk-nosed rogue, and a vision of standing by a tree, sword pointed heavenward. That dream was particularly disturbing because in it Manny saw himself crying and the tree he recognized as the one not far from the western gate where Aran kept his sheep.

For All Time and Eternity:
waters from the deep

Chapter 15

Whenever deeply troubled, requiring the need to think it through, Manny invariably ended up at the Japanese Gardens to sit under the vine-covered arbor. It set in a secluded area in the back where few if any people went except on the weekends. More than once, he spent the night there. No such place existed here. Besides, he needed to stay near Noah. When the dream of the tree occurred any hope of sleep vaporized. It was too disturbing. Knees pulled to his chest, back against the sunbaked brick roof ledge, he carefully reviewed his life before deposited in this time and place.

Really, it hadn't been so bad. Sure, his dad

reacted inappropriately, first to the loss of Manny's mom, then to his inability to keep a job and provide for his son—a son who reminded him too much of the wife lost, and too much of what he could be. In response, the man wallowed amid the hopes, desires, and dreams cruelly corroded by choices, angrily lashing out when reminded that he chose poorly.

Roaming the streets to stay away from his dad's rages often resulted in hunger. Even if he went home, there was little food. At one point he became desperate enough to search a garbage can like some of homeless wandering the neighborhood. He was lucky. Mr. Moretti's son, Dom, home on break from college, caught him and made him come into the kitchen.

"Sit over there," he said, pointing to a small table against a back wall.

Manny was both curious and scared as he watched the young, second-generation Italian prepare an order. When it went out, there was extra which he dished up and set in front of Manny.

"Who's that?" Mr. Moretti growled as he entered the kitchen.

"Just a kid looking in the garbage can."

Mr. Moretti stared at him for a time. There was anger in his black eyes. "*Pelle e ossa*. No kid should be skinny." Without further comment, he forked more spaghetti on a plate with meatball sauce and plopped in front of Manny, disappeared out front a moment, returning with two glasses of cold milk, served up a second plate and set across from Manny. "You eat. No good if gets cold."

Moretti's wasn't the only place he received a handout, just the best, but it was over a mile from where he lived. He didn't go that way often. That was when Mr. Kreutzer stepped into Manny's life. He had always been there, lurking in the shadows, as it were, until really needed. His firm, under-standing, caring nature provided a safe haven during the bad times and a meaningful way for Manny to provide for his own basic needs. Sitting at the feet of Noah was so like sitting on the deli floor listening to fascinating stories from the Bible brought to life by the elderly delicatesseneur.

Manny always thought of the stories as entertaining, secretly dismissing them as just stories. However, they were as much a learning experience as when man and boy sat each night at the well-used, rectangular, wooden table in the upstairs study to "learn Torah." Manny even had his own yarmulke to respectfully cover his head during those special times, and when he attended shul, the Friday evening services at the synagogue. He became good at chanting the prayers, and more than one person expressed how beautiful his voice sounded over the croaking grunts of the men and husky voices of the women.

Then there was Roger who put an arm around a skinny, battered kid, sheltered him in his own home, provided for his martial arts education, and encouraged him to pursue excellence in school and in himself. They treated him like one of the family, like something he was—special. Of course, being one of the family required donning a white shirt and tie and hauled off to a Christian church at 8 a.m. on the one day of the week he usually slept through.

That first visit to Roger's church held an air of nervousness mostly because he wanted to please his surrogate family. Actually, Manny had come to feel more Jewish than Christian so he entered the simple, brick building with a quiet, standoffish attitude. In that first encounter, he met Brother Filburton, the Sunday school teacher. Like Mr. Kreutzer, he was knowledgeable, didn't shy from questions, and really knew how to spin a story.

On the surface, it appeared to be a spur-of-the-moment, good-natured prank, but he wanted Mr. Kreutzer and Brother Filburton to meet. Secretly, he wanted to see them battle it out. He had heard so many different views on religion he wanted to know the truth. Who was right? Judaism or Christianity.

Manny really hadn't held out much hope such a meeting would ever transpire until one afternoon Brother Filburton stepped through the front door of the Deli. Manny was suddenly shot through with intoxicating elation at the prospect that his great desire was about to be fulfilled. However, the initial contact was cordial and somewhat boring. Mr. Filburton sat at the counter.

Mr. Kreutzer stood on the other side chatting about—of all things—the weather. Manny couldn't let that go on. He had set this up and out of frustration decided to prime the pump by asking what he knew was a derisive, theological question.

"So why did the Jews kill Jesus?"

Mr. Kreutzer's exasperation flashed from dark eyes like sparks from an exploding electrical transformer. In his culture, a person did not attack a guest's personal views, especially religion, unless they opened the subject. He was about to be roundly chastised for such a provocative remark when Brother Filburton replied quite easily, "They didn't. The Romans killed Jesus."

"But didn't the Jews demand his death because they objected to his teachings?" Manny shot back, trying desperately to get the debate going, ignoring the sub-frigid, arctic stare from his mentor.

"Not the people as a whole. Why would they? Jesus wasn't teaching anything not already in the Torah. He just stated things in a way the people would understand. Jesus was a Pharisee by his teachings. The Pharisees not only expounded the Law of Moses as given by G-d, but were intensely committed to that view as if it were life itself. Of all the sects at that time, they would be the only survivors of the Roman destruction to carry the remnants of Israel on their backs and become the Rabbis of today. No, it was not Jesus' teachings that resulted in his mortal death. He was very charismatic and that came to be a real negative. He drew huge crowds and political conditions were such that the Jewish leaders were paranoid with fear of reprisal from the Romans. Pilot had already shown himself to be a couple bricks short of a load in his violent treatment of their nation. No, Manny, the Jews as a whole did not object to what Jesus taught. They feared the throngs gathering around him might draw down the Roman wrath.

"The Sadducees were different. They were the aristocrats of that society by virtue of their wealth and status as priests, and the majority in the political body. That doesn't mean they were popular. On the contrary. Placing themselves above the people forced them to cooperate, especially with the Pharisees to implement public policy. Their religious views ran counter to what Jesus taught. They espoused only the principles, rituals, and sacrifices proscribed in the Books of Moses. They cared nothing of what the prophets wrote, therefore didn't believe in life after mortal death, and certainly not in the resurrection, judgment, or hell."

"Quite right," Mr. Kreutzer added. "To rein-force those beliefs, the Sadducees were open to the influences of Greek culture leading them to believe there was no eternal consequence for their behavior here on earth. The people of Israel fought to expel the Greeks, but that way of life was much easier than living the laws of Hashem."

"When anyone, including Jesus brought that

to their attention the people were ashamed and embarrassed because they were shown to be in violation of Torah law, and that is not what those like the Sadducees wanted to be publicly reminded about," Brother Filburton added.

For Manny, it had been downhill from the beginning. His plot had failed. He wanted to know which religion was right. What transpired before his eyes were mutual respect, understanding, and agreement. The goal for mankind was the same. They just espoused a different approach. Still, Manny wasn't giving up.

"But didn't they kill him for claiming he was the Messiah?"

Mr. Kreutzer heaved a small sigh, trying to be patient. "The people of that time didn't know what they were looking for, Manny. Under Greek persecution, they thought Mattathias or his son, Judah, might be the Messiah as the Maccabees revolt threw off that yoke. That only led to inviting the Romans onto the scene, an even worse predator."

Mr. Filburton added, "You see, Manny, the people were looking for a Messiah to come riding to their rescue on a white horse, not a white donkey. And, by the time of Jesus, some, like the Essene, began to think in terms of two Messiahs; one a priest and one a politician. They were becoming desperate," Brother Filburton chimed in.

"But the Jews never accepted Jesus as the Messiah," Manny said.

"No, we don't. Some of the less conservative sects believe he was a great teacher, but no, not the Messiah."

Manny mentally threw up his hands in despair. This was not going the way he intended as the two settled into a corner table for a spirited discussion about the Torah and the Book of Mormon for nearly two and a half hours. Manny tended to the incessant interruptions from curious customers, but caught pieces of conversation that led him to learn something unexpected. Both religions addressed the exact same things only to different cultures—love, respect toward one another, and obedience to G-d. Then the visit end.

"Mr. Filburton," Mr. Kreutzer said as he escorted his new friend to the street following the lengthy visit, "you'd make a good Jew."

"Why thank you. That's a great compliment. I'll bring that book I was telling you about next week."

"I will be interested in reading it."

Seeing his new friend to his car, Mr. Kreutzer stepped back through the Deli's double front doors, stopped, and placed a fist on each hip. "Well, are you satisfied?"

"What?" Manny answered sheepishly.

"That was a setup, young man. You were expecting, perhaps, an argument over our beliefs?"

The boy behind the counter turned white as his apron.

"I only . . . I wanted to know . . . I'm sorry,"

he said bowing his head.

"And what did you learn . . . if anything?"

"They aren't that much different–Judaism and Christianity."

"How so?"

"Except for believing in Jesus as the Messiah they pretty much teach the same things."

"Precisely. We travel a different road, but toward the same destination. You need not have sponsored a confrontation to find that out."

"I'm sorry, sir," Manny replied nearly breaking into tears, wanting to jump down the floor drain he was staring at, and disappear.

"I think you have learned a very valuable lesson, both theologically and socially, and I have made a friend worthy of thoughtful discussions. For that I thank you."

From that moment Manny attended even more carefully to whatever the two men taught.

Recalling the major encounter with Lucifer's adjutant, it was Brother Filburton's lessons he used to beat down the adversary so thoroughly. Without realizing it, Manny had quoted from the Articles of Faith, the essence of LDS belief. He smiled at the recollection of Amalekiel's distress bordering on physical pain and almost childish fury as the words tumbled from Manny's lips as if daggers stabbing the body of Lucifer's lieutenant.

No, life hadn't really been so bad in the other world. Curiously, just when he needed help someone always came forward with a hand and an important lesson. Yes, even Benny the recluse druggie, that time in the old hotel when a piece of wall collapsed pinning his tiny body beneath its rubble. He pulled the child free. Much later, Manny came to believe that act cost Benny his life.

Until this moment, he had chanted prepared prayers in Hebrew, offered formula-like prayers of thanks at Roger's dinner table, and knelt with Roger's children by their bed at night, but this time he felt a real need to do something not done for a long while. Rocking forward, he shifted to his knees, folded hands together, and bowed his head for personal prayer. As his lips parted to begin, he stopped, unsure what to say, or just how to say it. Not moving, he remained kneeling until remembering Mr. Kreutzer's words while strolling through the park one Sunday afternoon.

"Whenever you want to speak to Hashem, speak as you would to any other person. Then your words come from the heart."

Manny imagined the tall man in his dreams sitting on the empty stool in front of him, and began unloading his soul. Any personal prayer he'd heard or given couldn't have lasted more than 30 seconds, a minute tops, often feeling like an eternity, but this time each hour was like a minute as he became unconscious of time, absorbed in baring his soul, and declaring earnest gratitude, but mostly seeking forgiveness for taking his own life.

Slowly the blackness of night with its twinkling lights and meteors yielded as light inched its way into a clear, azure sky. When the warm rays of the sun crested the roof ledge, they lay over his back feeling every bit like Sher'i's gentle, messaging fingers, a comforting caress that penetrated and warmed him inside as well. He knew G-d had heard. A new strength entered every cell of his body, but it was the voice that startled him back to reality.

Standing quickly he looked around. He was alone, yet the voice had sounded as if the speaker were standing next to him. It was the voice he knew and he wondered how long G-d had been there, sitting on the stool, patiently listening. That simple statement, "I have always favored you, my son, and will be with you always," burned deeply into his soul ever ready for instant replay when he needed strength the most.

"Thank you, Father."

Hearing movement below, Manny bent over stiffly, gathered up the blanket meant to be a bed, and tightened it around his shoulders. Avoiding the chamber where Aran and Abigail still lay entwined in each other's arms, he slipped quietly to the lower level using the back ladder.

Noah was standing in the open gate talking to the boys who pulled the death cart. The larger one nodded, took something from the old man's hand, shot a fleeting glance at Manny, and disappeared. He thought that interesting. That brief glance appeared to have the look of . . . homage?

"Manny!" Sher'i exclaimed. "You look . . ."

"I didn't get much sleep. Had a lot on my mind," he replied while dismissing the momentary curiosity.

"Me, too," she replied a bit sheepishly.

"But you look beautiful."

"Love," Noah snorted good-naturally as he latched the gate and joined them. "She could look like a sheared lamb and you would still see her as the most beautiful thing on this world."

"For an eternity," Manny said.

"Well, my love struck friend, we must journey today. Get fed, and dressed, and do what lovers must when parting. I will gather some dried fruits and bread. We have a ways to travel."

"So soon? We just got here last night."

"Where are you going?" Sher'i asked.

"Adon Olam, praise be His Holy name, came last night and commanded that I should go to the cave of Adam-ondi-Ahman. There I am to gather the remains of Father Adam and take them to the Ark. After the world has been cleansed, I will bury him in a place holy unto Jehovah, blessed it be His name."

"I heard nothing last night," Sher'i remarked.

Manny's complexion paled. "I did."

At one time earlier in the night he had distinctly heard two voices rise up from Noah's sleeping chamber. One he recognized as the prophet's. The other was . . . the one who spoke to him upon awaking.

After returning to the roof to exchange the

sheepskin kilt for a freshly laundered judo uniform, he returned to the patio. There Sher'i combed and tied his long hair into an arching ponytail. Finished, she secured the headband with its gold emblem of a crane. While appreciative of the attention, he balked when she began lacing his sandals. She quietly prevailed.

"I have been meaning to ask. Do you know that symbol on your head band?" Noah said.

"It is the sign of my dojo, the place I learned my fighting skills."

"Interesting," Noah replied thoughtfully. "It is known to me as the sign of the archangels."

"Archangels!' Manny snorted, too tired to be in much humor. "You, not me."

"Me? An archangel?"

Noah's stomach bounced as his voice boomed a great laugh while turning to leave. Manny wondered how long it had been since the prophet laughed like that?

For All Time and Eternity:
waters from the deep

Chapter 16

Leaving through the northern gate adjacent to the flesh market, Noah lead Manny across the once wide river now shriveled by the protracted drought to a dark, ankle-deep flow. Manny was delighted sufficient rocks provided a dry path so he need not step in the foul-smelling, polluted water. Even better, the stench of animal urine and human sweat began to become dislodged from his nostrils, replaced by the smell of conifers hugging the far side of the river, their sweet scent borne on a light but hot breeze.

Noah stopped on the opposite bank to sit on a big rock as if walking the short distance across had tired him. Having traveled many miles over the past weeks with only a night's rest, Manny became silently concerned how they would manage the distance Noah mentioned, especially as they had left the donkey behind. But Noah was far from tired.

"So, you heard voices last night?" he remarked, shaking a pebble from his sandal.

"Yes, sir."

"He spoke to you, too."

"Yes, but how . . . ?"

"Your face . . . this morning when you came down from the roof. To Sher'i you looked haggard and pale, but I saw the light in your countenance. He speaks to His children all the time, only they have difficulty hearing. Too much noise."

"I heard," Manny said.

Noah smiled, stood up, cupped a hand behind Manny's neck to pull him close and plant a gentle kiss between the eyes just below the headband before turning to resume a brisk pace across the wilderness.

The country side was different from where they traveled before; a gently undulating plain scored by shallow, dry ravines, and clumps of trees, their leaves hard and brittle from the heat and lack of water. Late that afternoon, they traversed a ridge overlooking a broad, flat valley, overrun by a jungle of tinder-dry grass and low bushes with no leaves. Noah suddenly left the well-defined trail, crashing down a steep decline through heavy brush until emerging onto another trail almost obliterated by disuse and low, grass-like vegetation. This trail carried them across the wide, treeless valley. It was hot in the open sun and perspiration trickled down Manny's face, chest, and legs. The heat and humidity were dragging him down, forcing him to mentally plant one foot in front of the other. The one thing helping to drive him forward was the promise of cooling shade other side, drawing steadily closer with each step.

Noah didn't waste any time as he headed for a particular rock beneath a large, leafy tree and stopped, obviously tired as well. Manny immediately peeled off his jacket and hung it over a bush to let the breeze attempt to dry it some, and then plopped down on the cool grass before stretching out to rest. That's how he came to see a large, red object dangling directly over his head. Sitting up, he stretched forth his hand to grasp it when Noah broke his uncharacteristic silence.

"The devil's fruit."

Manny's hand froze just before locking his fingers around the shiny object.

Noah reached forward, wrapped a calloused hand around the apple, and plucked it from the branch. "Something similar to this got Eve and all of mankind into a great deal of trouble, or so some people would lead you to believe. The truth is that man must have agency to progress. He is the only one of His creations endowed with that gift, but without having knowledge of good and evil how could he possibly exercise it properly? Eve understood that," Noah continued, rolling the fruit around between his fingers before unexpectedly taking a bite that cracked like a dry branch in the wilderness silence. "A tasty lesson," he quipped with a sly smile and wink, plucking another, and tossing it to his companion who eagerly chomped into it.

It was so juicy the sweet liquid dribbled down the corners of his mouth, but Manny didn't care as he eagerly devoured it and several more before detecting the soft gurgle of water. A few feet behind the tree, a spring issued forth clean, drinkable water of which both men liberally partook. It was then he noticed a shadow lurking in the bushes a few yards beyond—a predator—but it didn't trouble him at all. Such would follow and circle as if seeking an opportunity to attack, but Manny felt that protective shield once again, like Roger's or Mr. Kreutzer's, or Japheth's strong arm encircling his shoulders.

"A lioness," Noah said, pointing his staff toward the creature buried within the dense growth. "We need not worry. Our G-d protects us on this sacred mission."

Manny wasn't, but did wonder why he was needed on this trip, unless to keep Noah company. Being little concerned, the two resumed their journey until very late in the day the dense canopy of vegetation opened like a movie curtain to reveal a light brown, sandstone cliff.

"Over there," Noah said, pointing toward the right side of the near vertical rock face. Without hesitation, the two began the slippery climb, helping one another over talus deposited by the decaying precipice until some minutes later they reached its base.

"Behind those bushes," Noah said, pointing to the cliff face. Winded from the climb, he sat to rest on a flat, table-sized boulder.

Pausing a moment, too, Manny once again shed the sweat-drenched gi and laid it across a sunbathed rock before approaching the bushes, curiosity peeking. He couldn't see anything through the profuse growth, but felt cool air chill his skin. Pulling some branches aside, he spotted the entrance to a cave. As he stepped to wade through the overgrowth, a hand latched onto his shoulder. Noah, still breathing hard, was at his side.

"We shall kneel in prayer before entering."

Kneeling next to the elderly Patriarch, Manny clasped his hands, and bowed his head preparatory to Noah's words.

"Manny, would you give thanks for our safe arrival?"

"But . . .," he sputtered.

"I have heard you pray many times when you thought no one was listening," Noah answered the hesitation.

Swallowing hard, Manny closed his eyes, took a deep breath, and let it out slowly. "Father Noah and I are grateful for your protection during the journey to this spot. I'm guessing this is the cave where Father Adam rests which Noah has often spoken of, and we are ready to do your will."

He stopped. The words had come easily, and then suddenly his mind went blank. He couldn't think of anything more to say so after a pause he concluded, "Amen."

"Amen," Noah agreed. "Short and to the point. That is what I like about you Manny, a man of few, but meaningful words."

The sunlight barely penetrated a few feet into the cave, but Noah obviously knew this place. Despite the claustrophobic terror welling up, Manny willed himself to battle the growing panic as the prophet's iron-like grip on his left arm dragged him deeper inside. Barely swallowed by the blackness Noah stopped abruptly. With youthful eyes, Manny could just make out something projecting from the left wall within arms' reach. Noah carefully removed the shaft and laid it on a table-size rock, and then using a flint from his sash, struck it against the rock.

Gentle blowing encouraged the sparks into a flame to life providing a modicum of light so that one could at least see the occasional rocks littering the smooth floor. It did little to relieve Manny's panic as they drove deeper into the cave, nausea welling up, fear wringing perspiration from his body, and generating spastic shivers. Desperately concentrating on the surroundings as an attempt to hold the attack at bay, a prayer entered his mind, *Shema Yisrael, Adonai Eloheinu, Adonai echad*. Mr. Kreutzer recited the Shema every day, the first words to pass his lips in the morning, and the last at night. It was the first Jewish prayer he learned and it provided comfort as he silently recited the words while remembering the love and warmth of his old mentor, and what the words meant. The diversion helped.

With each step Manny made out the marks of habitation. This had obviously been someone's home. Nearing the rear, an object came into view, seeming to hover about waist high reminiscent of something in a Sci-Fi movie, another distraction because of the spooky feeling it conjured. Drawing closer helped define it as a white, stone box set upon a dark stone dais.

"This estuary contains the bones of Father Adam," Noah said reverently.

Manny swallowed hard. "The Adam?"

"Yes. The first man."

"Father? Father? Are you in there?" a voice called out from the entrance. Already on edge, Manny startled so badly he spun around into a defensive posture.

"We are here, Shem," Noah answered quietly, his voice echoing easily to the front of the cave so that his eldest son promptly moved to their side. "The two of you prepare a litter so that we can fulfill G-d's commandment and take Father Adam's remains to the Ark."

Leaving the torch with Noah the young man carefully made for the entrance. With the thought of getting out of that confining place, Manny really didn't care how often he stubbed his toes. It didn't happen. He was a little amazed how easily his eyes picked out an obstacle in the near-total blackness, although often at the last second. Re-emerging into the world of sizzling brightness and heat he more than welcomed the discomfort and expelled a deep breath not realizing he had been holding it in.

"It's good to see you again," Shem said, putting a hand on the young man's shoulder and drawing him into a powerful hug. He obviously noted Manny's anxious departure from the cave, a near run, and the great beads of sweat on his brow, but said nothing.

Manny reciprocated eagerly, relishing the unique feeling that filled his breast, something he had grown to look forward to when around the future prophet.

"How'd you know we'd be here? Oh, never mind, I should know. The L-rd visited you too, last night?"

"In truth, no. Two boys carried a message from father this morning. They also told us briefly of your adventures. You have been busy."

"Not me. Father Noah has been busy. How far is it from here to the Ark?" Manny asked.

"If we leave immediately we should arrive by midnight, but I should think father will want to stay if for no other reason than to remember this place. Soon no man will know it for what it was—the home of our first parents."

Moving to the edge of the plateau, Shem

selected a tall, straight, oak sapling as a litter handle and began hacking at its base with a bronze ax. The hard wood resisted mightily as each stroke rang almost like a bell.

"Here, let me try," Manny said after a dozen strokes barely marred the trunk.

Slowly withdrawing his sword, he shot a glance heavenward and sighed slightly when no thunder sounded, then chided himself, "Silly. What'd you expect?"

Raising the blade overhead, he swung down, stiffening for the concussion. Little resistance occurred as the blade slipped through the entire diameter with little resistance.

"Sharp," Shem remarked. This was the first time he'd seen the young man use the beautiful weapon. "With that great tool we can fashion a litter very quickly."

As predicted, Noah decided to wait until morning. Although relatively spry for 600-years-old, he was still an old man, and the journey here had been at a strenuous pace. With the delay, Manny eagerly anticipated hearing more stories as they sat around a small campfire. He was not to be disappointed. As evening descended, Noah settled onto a large boulder near a crackling fire and began to reminisce about the days of his progenitors.

"And Seth, son of Adam, sat over there," Noah began, describing the great family reunion while pointing to a rock not far to Manny's left. "He returned to the presence our L-rd fourteen years before my birth, but Grandfather Methuselah, told me he was . . ."

One by one, the elderly prophet described each of the great patriarchs, from Adam down to himself, many with whom he had personally walked alongside, or sat at their feet as Manny now did. Shem must have heard these stories many times, yet sat cross-legged on the ground next to Manny, propped against a rock as enthralled as if it were for the first time. Perhaps it was because this wasn't a story that happened far away or a long time ago, but on this very spot within living memory.

As Noah continued well into the night, Shem encouraged the small fire to continue yielding a warm glow until Manny's mind simply slipped away from exhaustion.

"I think he's asleep, father," Shem whispered.

"Appropriately so. He has had a very long journey, and has further yet to go . . . as do we. Here, let me cover him. It will allow me return a kindness he did for me once."

The others appeared to have been up for some time as Manny awoke. He was stiff. The others had eaten and were making preparations for the solemn journey, but being late didn't prevent him from kneeling in prayer, chastising himself for having failed to pray last night and seeking the L-rd's forgiveness. While eating fruit Shem collected that morning, the icy tentacles of panic began to encroach upon his mind.

"Would you rather wait while I bring the body of Father Adam out?" Shem whispered just before they entered the cave for the last time, sensitive to the young man's problems with tightly enclosed places.

"No. I can do this. Thanks anyway," Manny replied, inhaling a deep breath before plunging into the cold darkness, filling his mind with distracting thoughts about how the end of the world was fast closing in and what would happen to Sher'i? Such thoughts readily diverted any anxiety.

In reverent silence, he and Shem carried the encased remains strapped atop two oak poles across the rolling countryside as lions and other predatory beasts stalked the periphery of their vision until suddenly disappearing just before entering the upstream end of the valley where the Ark rested. Only then did Manny privately sigh in relief.

Without hesitating, they made directly for the boat. The others were waiting. Following a solemn ceremony, Shem placed Adam's remains in a specially built niche in the topmost portion of the Ark. Impatient to return to the city and increasingly apprehensive, Manny had to wait for conclusion of the Sabbath after which Noah commenced a meticulous inspection of the Ark.

The evening of the following day, Noah and Caleb stepped down the wide gangplank. "It is finished," he said, the sound of sadness edging the declaration.

"You say the Ark is finished and Japheth reports all the animals accounted for. What is the L-rd waiting for?" Manny asked, wanting to leave.

"He awaits a sign," Noah said, looking into the clear, pale blue sky.

"What sign?"

"He has said only that it will be a final cry of righteous condemnation against these people."

"From you?"

"He would say no more, but I think not.

All along, Manny felt troubled about something, and suddenly that uneasiness descended upon him. Noah had preached about the end of the world, and the route to salvation that might stem the colossal destruction, but seemed to have an unspoken reservation. It stunned Manny when he conjectured that perhaps Noah had a secret wish born of frustration, that the flood would destroy an unrepentant world. Not once had he heard Noah solicit the L-rd to hold back the curse. But then why should he? Except for Sher'i, Aran, Abigail and their baby, and yes, a few like Ru'el and Hamor, there hadn't been any whom he had met worth redemption.

Returning to camp at noon on the fourth day after Sabbath, Manny noticed visitors had arrived which wasn't unusual. Sometimes people came to look and scoff, but rounding the corner of Japheth's tent he came face to face with Sher'i, Aran, Abigail, and Isiah. They immediately embraced, more so

Sher'i.

"I was afraid I wouldn't get back before . . . you know," he whispered in her ear as they hugged, finding it difficult to mouth the impending.

"Two boys appeared at our door very early this morning saying we must come to the Ark—all of us. Is the flood coming?"

"Not immediately," Noah interjected dolefully, "but I will not be returning to the city. The L-rd has told me to stay here. My days of preaching repentance are done."

Manny saw the fright in the others' eyes as his own heart begin pounding and a knot form in his stomach.

"We will now fulfill Heavenly Father's command. Japheth, Shem, we are to have baptisms and a wedding," he announced with great pomp.

As expected, Japheth's "Hooray," was loudest as he instantly led the others with excited congratulations.

"Enough of this espousal, Aran. The time has come," Noah said. Aran responded by bowing his head and nodding agreement, provoking another wave of merriment.

"Break out the wine jar," Japheth's big voice rang out.

"Water for me," Noah surprised everyone. "This is too sacred an occasion."

"Father Noah?" Manny said with apprehendsion. "What about Sher'i and me? Has the L-rd, turned his face against our union?"

"No, my son," Noah replied gently, putting a hand on the young man's shoulder. "He has smiled upon your espousal."

"But that typically takes a year to pass. Will we have time?"

"That is what I have been instructed."

Manny didn't think he could have felt lower. "But . . ."

"Manny," Noah interrupted, "our Eternal Father has given unto me to know that you have it in your power to save yourself and my beloved niece, and perhaps others when the flood comes upon us." He then tapped the hilt of the sword and winked.

Manny's heart immediately lifted as that sagacious smile filled him with renewed hope and confidence. "But how?"

"It has no power except through the righteous hands of he who commands it. Now," he called out loudly, "we have work to do before commencing all this celebration."

"Come, daughters," Naahmah said, "We need to prepare for two glorious events, a wedding, and an espousal."

"And you two come with me," Japheth announced stepping between Aran and Manny, gripping their arms in vice-like holds, and escort them bodily into his tent.

As preparations for the ceremonies proceeded, Noah called each of the young people separately to the tent of learning where they knelt in prayer. He then elicited their knowledge and acceptance of the laws of G-d. Satisfied with their understanding, and acceptance of those laws, he imparted a blessing upon Aran, Abigail, and Sher'i. He neither interviewed nor pronounced a blessing upon Manny.

Preparation was relatively simple. Retiring to the tent used for study, prayer, and other special religious rites, Shem washed Manny while Japheth did the same to Aran, and then each donned a simple, white, ankle-length tunic. When all was ready, they emerged and stopped. The young men were awestruck by the beauty of their sweethearts draped in similar, long, white gowns, a halo of white flowers upon their heads. To Manny, Sher'i looked more like an angel than any picture he ever seen. It took a gentle nudge on the back by Japheth to break the spell and head to the stream.

Beneath a multicolored canopy of forest leaves, the assembly gathered next to the waist-deep, bathing pool created by a rock dam, something Japheth put together after some more than subtle hints from Naahmah and her daughters about bathing. Another pool, further upstream, was the one Manny greatly appreciated at the end of hot, sweaty labors, shivering in its crystalline depths. However, there was an addition beside this lower pool. A somewhat circular pile of stones capped by a large, flat piece of slate set on the grassy bank.

At Noah's instruction, Shem took Manny by

the hand and slowly escorted him into the water. It was just as cold as ever, but the two men only flashed a silent grimace as they sucked in a deep breath when the water enveloped their loins.

Positioning the boy off his left side, Shem raised his right hand and began. "Peter Emanuel Guzman, having authority from our Almighty G-d, Jehovah, as a testimony that you willingly enter into this covenant with Him, I baptize your mortal body that you may be granted eternal life through the redemption of the Messiah, the plan which was established from the foundations of the world. And this I do in the Holy name of the Father, and of the Son, and of the Holy Ghost. Amen."

Manny bent his knees and leaned back as Shem laid him beneath the water then lifted him out. Facing his friend, water streaming from his face, he threw his arms around the stocky, spiritual giant. The cold feeling disappeared.

"Now it is time to fulfill the commandment I was given by the Holy One," Noah said softly as the pair exited the pool. "Manny, kneel before me." G-d's antediluvian prophet then placed his hands on the crown of Manny's head joined by Shem and Japheth.

"Peter Emanuel Guzman, by the authority of the priesthood after the order of the Son of G-d, we lay our hands upon your head and baptize you with the spirit of fire that you may receive the Holy Ghost unto your bosom that the Spirit of the L-rd may be poured out upon you."

Manny felt that familiar, warm sensation enter the top of his head through Noah's hands and fill his body to the tips of his toes. It was as if basking in warm sunlight, a feeling that, this time, did not leave as the three men lifted their hands from his head. However, without allowing Manny to stand, Noah stretched forth his right hand to secure a small, leather flask from Naahmah and poured some of its contents on the young man's head.

"Peter Emanuel Guzman, having previously been anointed to the lesser priesthood under the hands of Jehovah, I anoint you with this Holy oil consecrated under the hands of His holy servants, and confer upon you the priesthood after the Order of the Son of G-d with all its rights, privileges and responsibilities, and do so in His Holy Name, our God, even the great Jehovah."

By the muffled gasps it was obvious no one except Shem and Naahmah had expect the last ordinance, however the prophet wasn't finished and continued, "Peter, I now bestow upon you a father's blessing. You were sent here by our Heavenly Father for the purpose of fulfilling a promise made to His humble servant, Noah, and to provide for you an opportunity to begin receiving, understanding and accepting the true word of G-d, and to receive the precious ordinance of baptism. This is but the first of your continuing service to the L-rd. You were before the beginning of time a stalwart champion proving yourself worthy in all things. During that time with the great Father Elohim, you and Sher'i pledged to become eternal companions if you should meet in this world and were faithful to your G-d. That pledge is fulfilled. Your mission in this time is about to end, however, there is yet one act to complete which shall be made known unto you at a later time. For now, know that having no living parents you are adopted into the house of Noah with all the rights and privileges of a son. You shall attain the first estate on the day of the great resurrection if you continue your faithfulness unto our Heavenly Father. This blessing from the Lord Jehovah is now sealed upon you in His Holy name. Amen."

Rising very slowly, Manny felt overwhelmed, dazed, and uncertain exactly what had just happened.

"Father!" Ham protested. "Do you realize what you have done?"

"Yes. Emanuel has received the great priesthood, and is now a part of our family. For what purpose is known only unto Adon Olam, praise be to His holy name, but it has been done by His commandment. That could not please me more. Now, truly, my son, welcome," Noah said, stretching forth his arms to envelop the young man in that crushing bear hug Manny cherish.

With tears filling his eyes, Manny unashamedly kissed both of Noah's cheeks as

Japheth and Shem swarmed around the pair. Turning to them as well, he embraced and kissed their cheeks. Ham, acting friendly, but cool, discreetly joined the group hug from the periphery, as he had participated all along; however, there was no exchange of kisses.

"Now, my new son, having received the great priesthood it is the will of our Eternal Father that you now exercise that authority and baptize your beloved, her brother, and his espoused bride."

"But I don't know . . .," Manny began to protest, until Noah held up his hand.

"Shem will assist you," he interrupted softly with a knowing smile.

Manny was more nervous than any time before in his life, but Shem coached him through the ordinance—first Aran, then Abigail, and finally Sher'i. As she rose above the water's surface, it felt as if his whole body were beginning to float heavenward. It left any earthly orbit when she kissed him.

"What about our baby?" Aran asked.

"Children are protected by the love of Jehovah until the age of accountability," Manny said, recalling what Bro. Filburton had said, and then looked at Noah, suddenly wondering if that was truly right.

Noah's right eyebrow shot into a bushy arc as he smiled proudly, and nodded agreement. "Now let us confirm each one and bestow the power of the Holy Ghost," Noah said.

As each, newly baptized soul knelt, Noah placed his hands upon their head as he had done with Manny, was joined by Shem. At the prophet's direction, Manny laid his on top of Shem's hands. Noah confirmed the blessing.

During this, the young man was strongly impressed to pay particular attention to how this ordinance was done. Sher'i was last, and as she knelt, it was Manny's hands that first lay atop her silky hair. He remembered the words of the sealing, but what followed left him a bit shaken and amazed.

When it came time for the blessing, he paused, not knowing what to say, until feeling as if transported into another realm. In the distance he heard a strong, clear voice proclaim, "Sher'i, for this purpose have you been glorified in the palace of G-d and preordained to stand at the side of the L-rd's anointed champion as wife and mother to his children in this world, and for all time, and for all eternity."

Manny stopped. The sound had come from his lips, but the words were those of someone else, that familiar voice he had heard before, but could not put with a face. While it spoke, his eyes were blurred, and his mind filled with an intensely bright light. As his lips formed, "Amen," the world came back into focus and the light faded. Looking first at Noah then at Shem, wonder etched his counten-ance as they smiled proudly.

Shem then escorted Aran and Abigail to kneel on either side of the stone altar. Reaching across the top, they held hands as Noah stood at one end, flanked by Shem on the right and Manny on the left.

Leaning forward, he placed his hand upon theirs as a glow filled the old man's eyes and radiated over his wrinkled, brown face. Manny felt the warmth emanating from Noah. It was the same feeling the time he confronted Amalekiel. Someone was invisibly standing in their midst and although it was Noah's scratchy voice, they were not his words as Aran and Abigail were blessed and sealed as husband and wife for all time and eternity.

When Naahmah brought forth their infant, tears of incomprehensible joy streaked the young couple's face as Noah laid the infant in their hands between them and pronounced the words that sealed the three together as an eternal family. Manny looked toward Sher'i. Her cheeks beamed a rosy blush.

It became Manny and Sher'i's turn. With one hand, he led her to stand in front of Noah, now flanked by Shem and Japheth. Stretching forth his hand, Noah locked their hands together with his and began, "For all to know and recognize that this man and this woman have sought my permission to enter into the marriage covenant. As the great Jehovah, praise be His Holy name, has decreed, an espousal agreement is acceptable to

Him. From this moment forward until a time specified by the Father of all mankind, they shall be faithful to one another, sharing their time exclusive of all others, but in no way are released from the laws of chastity. This is a time to cherish one another, learn of each other's strengths, faults, and weaknesses, to love, and respect one another. You, Peter Emanuel Guzman ben Noah, now have the responsibility to protect and provide for your sweetheart, Sher'i, daughter of Molag ben Mahalaleel. All here witness that the authority of the Holy Priesthood of G-d condones this espousal until such time that you a sealed as husband and wife at His holy alter. Amen."

Manny leaned forward, kissing his espoused tenderly. In that short, intimate contact, he expressed his most profound passions to his bride-to-be while standing next to the altar of G-d.

Bride-to-be! Sure, he could protect, but provide? That thought suddenly struck him with the impact of a hammer. He had only recently turned seventeen years old! How could he support Sher'i? He hadn't graduated from high school, yet! He didn't even have a job, well not something that paid money. His work for Mr. Kreutzer only afforded a room and food not the cash to buy things she would need and deserve. All he knew were the Jujitsu arts and there wasn't much call for that in his world. His world? Was he even going back? If he did, how would Sher'i get there? Maybe he shouldn't worry about life in that world. Hadn't he tried to escape it? Maybe this was all that remained. Then a peaceful feeling settled over him. This world, that world, what difference did it make? He had accepted Sher'i as his bride-to-be no matter what or where.

Overhead three white cranes in an offset V circled several times, honking loudly.

Chapter 17

A slight breeze barely moderated the intensity of the sun until giving one final gasp and died, allowing it to really bear down to finish scorching the earth. Manny decided this must be how a Thanksgiving turkey felt in Mrs. Elam's oven. The only relief was the small waterfall where the earth swallowed the stream that once passed the Ark. The two couples were glad to splash cool water on their faces. At least three of them were.

"I am glad we stayed an extra day," Abigail said as she patted a damp cloth on Ishiah's face.

"I worry about our sheep." Aran said. His anxiousness had grown with each hour they remained at Noah's camp. Having tossed several handfuls of water in his face, he moved about nervously as the others lingered. His voice reflected building anxiety.

"They are fine," Sher'i tried to comfort him. "The shepherds in your group are good men. They have trusted you many times with their animals and have often expressed how difficult it is to repay your kindness. They will protect them from the others."

"Give the girls a chance to catch their breath, Aran. You've pushed them pretty hard," Manny chastised him privately.

Aran appeared mollified, but remained anxious.

"You have been very quiet," Sher'i remarked as they crested the hill overlooking the city.

"I've a lot on my mind."

"About our future?"

"Yeah. That's part of it."

"As I said, we own many sheep and their care takes much time. Aran really has needed help this past year."

"I never pictured myself as a shepherd."

"There's something else, isn't there?"

"Yeah."

"The flood?"

"Not really. Our lives are in G-d's hands. He will take care of us. Whatever comes, comes."

"Then what is wrong?"

"Since coming here my time has been spent with Noah. All of sudden I'm done. I just feel kind of empty."

"But you now have a greater assignment," Sher'i responded, taking his arm and pressing her head against his shoulder.

Turning, he kissed her forehead, acting comforted, but inside his breast, something continued to bubble. Something was to happen that he wasn't going to like, and it wasn't a tidal wave of water.

The evening meal hour rapidly approached as they entered the city gate and split up, each couple going their respective ways. Manny and Sher'i chose to take a circuitous route through the living quarters to reach their home, thus avoiding the market area. He remembered some of the streets from when he first arrived. In particular, he spotted the garish, red and green robe hanging across the narrow street between opposing, second stories. It was the only one of its kind he'd seen in the city, the signature robe of the egregious slave auctioneer.

Arriving home, he went through the place to be sure no unwelcomed visitors lurked in the shadows. Secured, Sher'i went to change into fresh clothes. Manny had just fetched some dried beans and flour from jars in the back storeroom and taken them to the roof kitchen when a knock came at the gate door.

"Aran! Abigail!" he heard Sher'i cry out in alarm.

Running to the front ledge he stared down at the courtyard. Abigail clutched their baby close to her bosom as Aran encircled her quaking shoulders with his arm. She was sobbing. Sprinting down the ramp, he saw that Aran sported a bruise under his left eye.

"What happened?"

"When we told my father that Noah baptized and sealed us as husband and wife he went into a horrible rage," Abigail struggled to explain as Aran held her tighter.

"Not to worry," Manny responded. "This is your house, too. Let's take a look at your face, Aran. He tagged you pretty good."

"I am afraid I hurt him more. I am sorry, Abigail."

"You had no choice. He had a knife."

"You didn't . . .?" Sher'i asked.

"No. At least I don't think so. I only struck him, but he didn't move after hitting the floor. I pray I didn't kill him. There was no time to check. His servants were coming.

"Too bad we don't have a steak or some ice," Manny said absently. Manny only saw the baker from a distance. He was a burly man, easily twice Aran's size. "What did you hit him with?"

"Like you taught me," the young man replied imitating the moves. "A left circling arm to deflect the knife hand, a right knuckle punch to the chest, a flat hand to the base of the throat, and a roundhouse kick to the side of the head.

"Well, that will certainly do it."

"Could I have . . .?"

"Killed him?" Manny finished the sentence. A vicious hammering came upon the gate as the baker screamed for them to open up. "That sounds pretty healthy. Let me handle this." Manny picked up his staff leaning against the gate wall and unlatched the door to face the baker and two other men of equal size.

"I suggest you leave," Manny warned with a soft, but firm voice.

"This is not your affair," Dan bellowed.

"Aran happens to be my brother-in-law now, and as kin that makes it my business."

The two men accompanying the baker took a step back, obviously intimidated by Manny's reputation. Dan stepped forward in a threatening manner reaching for a knife in his sash. The end of Manny's staff flipped up and smacked the man's wrist, eliciting a howl of pain and causing the weapon to drop to the ground. As he clutched his wrist, Manny put the end of the staff under the man's big, hooked nose and backed him against the wall on the opposite side of the street.

"Leave, baker," he ordered, his voice low with a menacing growl. "And don't entertain any ideas of coming back or I will visit destruction upon you and your house that will make the coming flood look like a simple rain shower."

From the horrified expression on Dan's face, it was obvious he got the message. Turning, he hurried off, still clutching his wrist, feet kicking up a trail of dust to mark his rapid retreat, the companions leading the way.

Coming back inside and securing the gate, Manny said, "I don't think there will be any more trouble. You might say I put the fear of G-d into him."

"I still need to check our flock," Aran said after they moved their meager possession into his room and Abigail and Ishiah were comfortable. "It will only take a little while. I must be sure they are penned safely for the night."

"Sher'i, you two should be alright. I'd like to go with Aran and see how this shepherd thing is done. I've got to start learning this new trade sometime."

"We have thirty seven ewes. We could double that by next spring," Aran dreamed aloud as they walked toward the southern gate.

Manny kept quiet. In all likelihood there wasn't going to be a next spring, for these people at least. It was amazing how people continue planning tomorrows in the face of pending radical change.

Finding the sheep safely penned for the night, they returned home. The two giant guards lurked in the shadows just like the ones at the other gates, but he could feel their dark eyes follow every movement. At the first intersection, Aran took a sharp left turn.

"Let's take a quick bath."

"Okay. I'd like to shake loose some of this dust, too," Manny agreed.

Still having a problem with public bathing,

he headed directly to the back-most booth where it was darkest, checked to be sure that no one might be looking, tossed off his garment, and quickly sponged down.

"How do you think we will die," Aran said softly, following suite.

"Why the change in heart?"

"What do you mean?"

"Well, just a while ago you were planning to double the flock by next spring like you didn't think the flood was coming."

"I know. Dying is not something a person my age thinks about . . . or wants to think about," Aran replied. "So, what do you think?"

"I don't know," Manny replied, dumping a jar of clean water over his brother-in-law.

"I pray the L-rd will not let Abigail and the baby suffer," Aran said, reciprocating by dumping water over Manny.

"He won't. Noah said the righteous will be taken pretty quickly. Translated, I guess."

Aran walked to the nearest Jacuzzi-sized pool filled with hot water and sat on an underwater stone bench. Manny wrapped a cloth around his waist, having to hold it until buried beneath the water. This was the only reason he would come to here.

As the hot water worked its magic, tired muscles relaxed, but neither spoke, each deep in their own thoughts. "How will they die?" A small child romped by sans clothes, squealing gleefully with another in hot pursuit. Manny looked out over the communal bath. There were men and women of all ages lounging or cavorting about, children splashing water or running around the edge, all completely oblivious to the future. "How would they die?"

Upon returning home, they found the girls had also bathed and started a delicious, hot meal. No sooner having climbed onto the roof, the girls took turns anointing their men's feet and legs with a fragrant oil, and combing frankincense into their hair. Once the last morsel of food disappeared, all eyes turned toward Manny.

"What?" he asked.

"It is now your place to say the blessing," Aran advised.

"Why me?"

"You hold the sacred priesthood," Sher'i reminded him.

Resting on their knees, Manny groped for the words, trying to remember what Shem and Noah had said during this sacred time. There was no rote prayer. Each time it had been different, yet the same.

"Oh G-d, our eternal Father, thank you for this food we just consumed. We are humbly grateful . . . grateful for our lives and your blessings upon us, especially the blessings of this day. May we always be mindful of what you have done for us, and may we always be a source of pride unto you. This is our prayer in the name of thy son,

Jehovah. Amen."

A long silence followed as each said, amen, and lift their head. When Noah was present, they settled for the evening to hear a story, but now a very large void existed. In his absence, eyes again turned toward Manny.

"You have been Uncle Noah's student for these many months," Aran prompted. "Surely you can tell us a story."

Manny was silent for a long time. He had never really felt comfortable telling stories because it put him in the spotlight. What could he say? Did he really know what to say? Then words began to pass over his lips as he told the story of Enoch and the city of righteousness, and its eventual translation.

"So may it be with us," Sher'i said softly, hugging his arm.

"That was wonderful, Manny," Abigail cooed.

"Uncle Noah could not have told it better," Aran added.

Manny felt more confident. Without realizing it, Noah had not only taught him the stories and lessons, he had taught the young man how to teach them as well.

When it came time for bed, Aran and Abigail curled up on their sleeping mats in his room. Manny lay on his mat listening to the usual night sounds— the bark of dogs, the screech of a hunting owl, and soft breathing. He also heard soft footsteps and a mat placed next to his as Sher'i lay next to him.

"I need to be near you," she whispered, taking his hand in hers.

He had never slept so near a woman as she cuddled close to him beneath her own cover. The espousal covenant weighed upon his mind. He had taken a vow of chastity and here he was lying next to the woman he deeply loved with little more than their two light covers separating them. However, as quickly as she had come, he heard the familiar purr of sleep. Lacing fingers behind his head, Manny stared at the stars. Several meteors shot overhead, one splitting in two. One piece plummet to earth a bright yellow ball, the other continued a bit further as a blue light. He heard Abigail's soft giggle. With a sigh, he could tell this was going to be one very long, sleepless night.

Δ   Δ   Δ

Each morning the two young men waited until hearing the heavy timber fall into place locking the gate behind them. Satisfied, they made their way through the southern gate and to the sheep pens, often arriving before the other shepherd boys. Just as the sun began to disappear over the distant hills, they secured the animals in pens to protect them against marauding animals.

Twice each week, the young men took their turn standing guard through the night. Although a sedate routine began to develop, Manny continually looked over his shoulder at the sky. It continued to be cloudless with only the pencil line contrails of meteors flourishing. At night, their sudden, colorful appearance was the closest thing to fireworks and a pleasant distraction, although from comments, Manny knew this was a very un-usual occurrence.

Once leading the sheep to a grazing area, there wasn't a lot to do except talk and watch that none of the creatures wandered too far from their protection. The second afternoon the sheep suddenly put up a nervous bleating. Aran's trained eye spotted the trouble, a lioness creeping on her belly through the grass, her tawny coat blending perfectly with the dry grass to make her almost invisible. Manny was all set to charge down the hill and run her off, but it was obvious she was too hungry, and he too far to be successful.

Aran unwound the sling from his waist, loaded a stone in the pouch, and swung it several times. The speed in which he drew and fired was like an old west gunslinger, but more accurate. The stone struck her hip. She spun around and snarled loudly sending the sheep on a panicked run. The stone no sooner struck her than Aran launched a second, striking the ground, and bouncing into her belly. Foiled, she had enough and turned to retreat. A third stone struck her rump, lending speed to her departure.

"You have got to teach me to use one of those," Manny said, "As soon as we round up the sheep."

Walking onto the plain, Aran approached the nearest creature, comforted it, and whistled. Immediately, the others began moving to him. They knew him, and he knew each of them. Wherever Aran went, they followed. As the evening shadows crept over the plain, he'd whistle and start walking toward the pens, and secure them for the night. Predators continually stalking the herd, but Manny quickly learned to use the sling, becoming a reasonably good shot, much to the dismay of those looking for an easy meal.

At the end of the fourth week, they came in early to speak with the man who would purchase the wool when shearing began. His home was conveniently located not far inside the wall, but as they approached the gate, a great tumult echoed from inside moving toward them.

"Where is he?" a giant roared, having to duck as he stomped through the gate. "Where is he who crippled my brother?" His thundering voice silenced even the light breeze that had been keeping the insufferable heat at bay.

"That is the brother of the giant you fought to protect Noah," Aran whispered nervously.

"Step back, Aran. Let me handle this," Manny replied, then to the giant, "I guess that would be me," and walked forward.

"You shall die! I will tear your arms from their joints, and squeeze your eyes from their sockets! I will tear out your liver, and eat it uncooked!"

"That seems like an awful lot of work on such a hot day. Sure you wouldn't want to have some cool wine in the shade of that canopy over there first."

"You insolent son of a lizard! I will twist your head from that scrawny body and kick it over the wall so that the vultures may feed as they fly."

Manny was cautious not to be over confident. He knew from his short tenure that giants were smart and endowed with great strength, but their bulk made them much less agile. He also knew his assailant had traveled some distance judging by the dust on his heavy leather armor, greatly reducing his stamina. To win, the giant had to make his victory quick.

"Well, if you refuse my invitation to hospitality and refresh yourself, then I must submit to your challenge. Do you wish to fight or simply scare me to death with threats?"

He realized such a statement would enrage the antagonist even further; rage diminished judgment and inspired recklessness. He was right. The giant reared back, and shaking a long, shaggy mane, bellowed like a wild beast. With sword already drawn, he raised the huge, bronze blade overhead and brought it crashing down. Manny moved easily sideways, countering with his staff, a sharp crack to the man's ribs. The giant cried again. Despite the layer of leather armor, it was a cry of pain.

Swipe after swipe the great sword rippled

the air, but each time its intended victim easily dodged to deliver a sting from his stick targeting the most vulnerable areas. The giant began to breathe hard. With each humiliation, he became more reckless.

Manny was cautious, watching his opponent's every movement from head to foot, but he also kept an eye on the gang of accomplices. As he circled the giant, a compatriot made a forward motion. Manny suddenly turned, did a cartwheel, and laid his staff along the man's ear dropping him like a watermelon. Within the same motion, he pelted the giant across the right shin, laid another sharp whack on the ribs, and spun a blow to the side of his head sending the leather helmet flying off. The giant reeled sideways, dropping to his knees, shaking his head. At that moment, Manny grew careless. The giant's sword swung sideways making a deep fluttering sound as it split the air, the point skimming across the young man's chest.

He felt the slice. Forcing himself to look down he was astonished to see no trace of a wound, but the strap of his sword sheath across his chest bore a slice half through the leather. He brought the staff down across the giant's wrist with such force to jar the weapon loose and elicit another painful howl. He didn't wait. With a twirling attack, he laid three more blows, one into his opponent's solar plexus, one across his throat, and the last to the back of his head. Each blow was devastating as he put as much force behind them as possible. The giant, already on his knees, fell onto his face unconscious.

However, that wasn't the end as a half dozen accomplices launched their attack, including a heavily pockmarked man with a broad hairy chest, by far the biggest, who assumed command. Manny also noticed a thin-faced rouge with a long, straight nose reminiscent of a sewer rat. This one began working his way around to his back.

"That's odd," Manny remarked to himself. "Where have I seen that one before?" There was something very unsettling about that particular one, something frightening he should remember, but there wasn't time.

Apprehension swelled into Manny's throat. Those he engaged upon first arriving were not fighters, ill-armed, and spread out. These men were well armed, obviously had training, and attacked as a group. As the hairy-chested man and another charged something whizzed past Manny's right ear striking the second man's head. He took one more step and dropped to the ground. Aran's sling greatly improved the immediate odds. Meeting the attack with staff and feet, he wreaked havoc upon the attackers as two more fell victim to Aran's sling. Within minutes, they lay scattered across the road painfully injured or unconscious. The hairy leader seemed the worse; blood oozed from one ear as he lay in a heap at Manny's feet. While staring at the carnage and regaining his breathe, a blood-chilling cry rose up from behind him.

Spinning around, he saw the sewer rat jerk a large knife from Aran's chest and back away. Manny loosed a scream of rage and charged. The man threw down his bloody knife and grabbed up a sword lying nearby and swung it diagonally sending Manny's staff flying, then with a sneering howl began flailing wildly. Manny dodged the first cuts, countering with a front kick to the mid-section that loosed his attacker's lungs with a heavy grunt. The smell of stale booze shot across the young man's face.

Unleashing a flurry of feet and fists, Manny's mind went blank until suddenly finding himself looking down at sewer rat lying in a crumpled pile. He couldn't remember how it happened. After all the years of intensive training, there was no need to think. The man's wrist and forearm were badly misshapen, the lower left leg didn't appear attached very straight to the knee, as blood oozed from his nose, mouth, and ears. His breath was heavily labored with a sporadic rattle.

"Manny," Aran groaned.

His mind clearing, Manny quickly surveyed the scene. The giant still lay unconscious. The others were moaning or staggering away, hampered by their injuries. Assured no more attacks were eminent he sprang to kneel next to Aran.

An ugly wound just below the point of his left rib cage flowed copious amounts of blood. Manny felt paralyzed. Murder and death in the ghetto was all too common, and he'd seen some people die. He remembered the dead man in the alley when he first arrived in this city, but he had never knelt next to someone and held their hand as they died. Maybe if Aran was in front of a hospital emergency room full of doctors they might have been able to save him. Not here. Not in this place. Not in this time.

"Oh, Aran, I'm sorry," he moaned. "I don't know how to help. Wait a minute! Noah said that the priesthood had the power to heal."

Moving to Aran's head, he placed his hands on the young man's clammy forehead. Taking a deep breath, he struggled to remember what Noah had taught him until Aran's bloody hand took hold of his and pulled them away.

"Please." He struggled with the word between gasps for air. "It is best. I . . . really . . . really do believe . . . about . . . the flood, but . . . I . . . just wouldn't . . . wouldn't admit it. Now . . . I need to . . . to go . . . and prepare a place . . . place for Abigail and . . ."

"No, Aran. You're wrong!"

"You said . . . the righteous . . . were taken quickly. Tell . . . Abigail I . . . love her. When . . . the flood . . . comes . . . do not . . . struggle. I . . . will . . . be . . . waiting." Aran's voice rattled more loudly as he talked until a cough forced more blood out the wound. "Please . . . comfort Abigail."

Aran stiffened, nearly sitting up as his glazed eyes widened before sinking back. His chest stopped heaving as the blood slowed to a trickle. Finally, his head rolled sideways, eyes fixed in death.

Manny's tears bathed Aran's shoulders as he pulled his brother against his chest, his own body convulsing with grief. Turning his face toward the heavens cried, "Damn these people! No-o-o."

Not since Adam found his son slain in the fields had such a cry wrenched the hearts of Heaven. Rising up over the walls, it spread across the city, carried unto the pagan priests atop their temple causing them to look skyward in wonder as a chill of fear entered their blackened hearts.

After holding Aran's lifeless body to his chest for a time, he gently laid him on the ground, and closed his eyes. Still sobbing he remained on his knees, tilted his head heavenward, and asked, "G-d, what am I to do now?"

Three shepherd boys they worked with came and stared. After a bit one asked tearfully, "We will take him away?"

He gazed at the boys blankly for a moment, and then at his brother before answering hoarsely, "Thank you."

The boys lifted Aran and began carrying him.

"Not the quarry," Manny called out.

"But only the wealthy can afford burial pits," one of the boys replied.

Now Manny remembered the dream about the hooked-nosed man. It had been a warning he hadn't understood. Or was it a warning. No, it had been a vision of what was to come. He understood now. The dreams were not only of things that happened, but also of things to come. Looking up he saw the object of one of those visions—the lone tree.

"Lay him beneath that tree. I'll get his wife."

Tears continued to stain his cheeks as he moved through the streets—streets filled with an unusually heavy silence. Not even dogs barked, but tucked their tails to cower away. It was as if all mankind and nature knew what had happened, and were ashamed.

Rounding the corner to their street, Manny spotted the heavy front door ajar. That wasn't right. Drawing closer he could see the entire frame dislodged.

Bursting through the broken door he cried out, "Sher'i! Sher'i! Where are you?"

There was only silence amid overturned and broken furniture and jars. Looking into the back room where Noah once slept, he stopped and stared with horror. There lay the bodies of Abigail and Ishiah.

"Oh, dear G-d! Sher'i, where are you?" he continued to shout, running from room to room.

"They took the woman away," a small, thin voice said when he returned to the front room.

Spinning around he saw the bony figure of one of the boys who pulled the death cart outlined in the doorway. His companion stood looking over his shoulder.

"Who took her? Where did they take her!"

"The temple priests took the woman after a

giant and some men tore down the door. They killed the woman and child, and the priests took your woman to the temple. She will be sacrificed to their heathen gods when the moon rises directly above the temple. They believe that will prevent the flood waters from coming."

Manny looked to where the moon was in the clear, blue sky, took a deep breath to calm himself, and tried to think. It wouldn't be in position for another two hours. He had time.

"Please. Carry the child and follow me," he said, cradling Abigail in his arms, and heading for the city gate.

As the three traversed the road outside the gate, the assailants were gone except the hook-nosed murderer, the hairy leader, and the giant, still alive, but incapacitated. If they didn't get inside the city wall when the gate closed, they would fall victim to the wild animals prowling about looking for an easy meal. Manny wasn't distressed about that prospect.

Making his way across the dry stubble grass he saw Aran's body laid beneath the lone Olive tree, the shepherd companions standing silent vigil. Laying Abigail's body next to him, Manny then laid the baby between them. Standing back, he was unsure what to do next.

Kneeling, he prayed aloud again asking, "Dear G-d, what would you have me do?"

"Peter," a voice answered only to him.

He looked around, but there was no one

there to fit the voice, yet he knew it.

"Peter."

"Yes, L-rd?" he answered the voice he was familiar with.

A chill raced through his body in anticipation of speaking directly to the G-d he had only heard. The shepherd boys stared in abject fear. To them Manny was talking to himself. The two death cart boys sank to their knees with bowed heads.

"There is no more to be done. By your cry of condemnation, I have released the waters of the deep by which all life on earth shall be destroyed. Take your sword from its sheath, and raise it to the heavens, and I shall take these unto me as I have taken the other righteous of this world. Then go to your espoused wife. I shall be with you."

"Stand back," he said to the boys and slowly withdrew the sword.

From above came the familiar clap of thunder, a deep, rolling sound. The shepherd boys broke into a panicked sprint toward the city. The two who pulled the death cart remained motionless on their knees in the attitude of prayer.

Δ   Δ   Δ

From their shaded porticoes, the two giants standing guard watched as their kinsman and his companions attacked the white haired youth. Eagerly anticipated hearing his bones grind under their brother's awesome strength, they were stun-

ned how easily a mere boy dispatched them–
defeated them all. Only a god could have done
such a thing, and they were afraid. Remaining
hidden, they watched the shepherd boys take the
god's fallen friend to the tree. Later the god brought
the body of a woman and child to join with his
friend. When the shepherd boys ran away, the
white-haired god lifted his sword amidst a peel of
thunder from a clear sky to summon a great bolt of
lightning, which devoured everything except the
god and two little boys at his side. They deserted
their post.

Unable to peer at the sun, no one saw the
black spot that appeared along its left rim, steadily
growing larger. Even in the early mornings, if they
had taken the time, it would have only been a
curiosity. When Manny's sword summoned the
chariot of light fewer still noticed the bright flash of
light far to the north. Moments later a deep, rolling
rumble passed over the city as the earth trembled.
The Angel of Death had sounded his trumpet.

For All Time and Eternity:
waters from the deep

Chapter 18

Raising the sword, he lifted his eyes toward the contrail-streaked sky. The spiral of light that had carried him to this time was coming. Whipping back and forth like a blazing tornado, gradually descending until wrapping its brilliant, blue-white light around him and the bodies of Aran, Abigail and the baby. White gowns, like those worn at their baptisms and marriage, replaced bloodstained clothes, and then the three began to move. Aran rose first, lifting the baby into his arms, and then helped Abigail to stand. Encircling an arm around his wife's shoulders, she snuggled their very alive baby to her bosom. Aran said nothing, but smiled as if saying thank you, and then they were gone with the light, leaving Manny standing by the lone tree in a vast field of dry grass with two boys kneeling nearby.

"Who are you?" he asked, but they only smiled, bowed, turned, and laughed happily as they skipped back to the city hand in hand.

Receiving no reply, Manny hurried back to the house. A number of people were shuffling in and out; those exiting had their arms filled with things. Looters. A man was leading the donkey down the ramp, a boy behind him carried a bottle lamb. Inside, people were rummaging through everything.

When he walked into the yard, everyone who saw him froze where they stood. He didn't care. Everything they coveted was soon to be destroyed and he had no need of any of it except one item. He kept his clothes in Sher'i's second story room. There were two women pawing through Sher'i's things and arguing. He stepped aside as they fled in panic, still clutching what they had grabbed. The sheepskin kilt he wore had been soaked with Aran's blood, and some had caked to his bare chest, hands, and arms, but that all disappeared with the departure of the chariot of light. Tossing the kilt, he quickly changed into his gi, deliberately preparing his mind for what was about to happen. Tying the headband with its golden crane about his head, he slipped the sword over his shoulder. The looters had fled, leaving the place unnaturally silent. Picking up the staff by the front door where he had dropped it earlier, he stepped onto the deserted street, and took a deep breath before turning toward his destiny unaware of an aura, a soft, white glow, surrounding him.

Those in the market area knew of the giant and his soldiers seeking out Noah's angel and cheered. When the priests carried the angel's woman away to the sacrificial alter, they shouted approval. However, as people living on that side of town streamed into the market place telling of the great battle at the southern gate, and the defeat of the giant, and then the sight of the gate guards in flight, the people became sorely afraid and ran to cower in their homes leaving a few vendors scram-bling to collect their wares.

The mysterious cry overshadowing the city, the flash of light and peel of thunder from a clear sky, and the sudden trembling of the ground deepened the peoples' dread, putting them on the verge of panic. When those lingering in the market place saw Noah's guardian suddenly appear, they knew there was to be trouble. Eyes blazing with anger, the determination in his stride, there was to be serious trouble. The angel of the L-rd's path headed straight for the temple. The stragglers dropped their wares and scattered.

Arriving at the mouth to the street leading to the temple, Manny ignored the hideous monstrosities lining the street, poor substitutes the people elected to honor over the real G-d. In the middle of the avenue were thirty armed temple guards blocking his way. Wondering how he could overcome this obstacle and save Sher'i, someone move to his side.

"Ru'el! What are you doing here?"

"My master is dead," he replied. "G-d visited him last night as he prayed and took him unto His bosom."

'I'm sorry. It would have been better had he been baptized."

"But he was. An angel visited him while praying and said that if he truly believed the words of Noah, then he should go to him and be baptized. We arrived two days ago and all those who so desired entered into the covenant."

"And you?"

"I as well had a visitation during my sleep, and it was confirmed that this was to be." Manny suddenly felt calm. "Before passing beyond the great veil, Master Hamor gave me leave with instructions to come to your side. It appears I am just in time."

"They killed Aran and his family. Sher'i is in there. They intend to sacrifice her to one of those so-called gods when the moon comes atop the temple. There will be blood on their filthy altar, but not that of my wife. I wasn't sure how to handle all these guys, but the odds are much better."

"True, there are not so many, but they may slow our travel, and there does not seem to be much time remaining before that happens," Ru'el said, looking up at the moon's position. "Lord Noah said that you have the power of G-d. This would seem a good time to use it?"

Manny glanced at the inlaid hilt of the sword protruding above his left shoulder, then at the staff. "You're right. If Moses worked miracles with a staff . . ." his voice trailed off.

Raising the rod over his head with both hands he called out, "By the authority of the priesthood and in the name of Jehovah I call forth the powers of Heaven to clear our path." Lowering the staff, he touched one end to the ground honestly having no notion what would happen. He didn't have long to wait.

Deep within the earth, a rumble began, first as a distant sound swelling into a grinding, shriek. The earth moved. The idols swayed. The heavily armed guards turned all directions in terror as the stone deities began to sway, rent, and crumble into piles of mushrooming dust. As the world reeled before them, the two warriors stood on stable ground until the avenue lay in dusty ruin littered by its stone guardians that had crushed the opposing force.

Suddenly Manny noticed the two death cart boys who standing nearby. For a moment, he was confused. They always seemed to be near when needed, and had remained unflinching when the chariot of G-d came for Aran and his family. He now perceived they were more than mere street urchins. The dullness that had masked their eyes was gone, replaced by a bright, almost flickering gleam as a feeling of some subliminal familiarity came over him. Manny motioned for them to approach.

"What are your names?" he asked.

"I am Kira'im. He is Ka'atibel," Kira'im, the larger of the two answered.

Handing the staff to Kira'im he said, "I won't need this for the time. Hold onto it and wait here until I return."

The boy smiled broadly, taking the staff in both hands, and bowed.

On the northwestern horizon, a thin, black line appeared sending forth a deep, rumbling boom to announce its ominous approach as both men entered the avenue. Weaving around the remains of the fallen idols at a trot, they quickly reached the main gate to the temple ground. Through a wide crack where the two huge, gold clad doors came together, they could see a heavy, metal-clad, wood bar securing them together. It was demoralizing. How could they possibly breach the entrance? As Manny considered the obstacle, Ru'el gasped.

"What's wrong?" Manny said, expecting more guards

on the attack, but his companion was staring at the ground and pointing. His eyes went down, but saw nothing to elicit any such reaction. "What?"

Ru'el simply pointed to Manny's feet. He looked again, but still didn't see anything wrong.

"No tracks!" Ru'el gasped.

"What?"

Manny turned and looked again. When the earthquake destroyed the avenue of idols, it laid down a thick layer of dust. Their feet were the first to disturb the powder, but there was only one set of footprints—Ru'el's!

"What the heck . . .!" Manny hissed.

"Angels leave no footprints," Ru'el answered in a hushed voice.

There was no denying it now. Manny had to admit what had always been lurking in the back of his mind. To his world, he was dead—really dead. The blinding light from the sky had been his Coach d'Bower—his death coach. All this had been some kind of punishment—trial—preparation. Whatever, Noah knew and Shem knew. He really had become an angel, and being one, he had the power, too.

Raising the sword with both hands over head, he swung down in a smooth arc, guiding the blade between the doors. The blade cut through the heavy bar without so much of a spark. Ru'el lifted a foot and shoved one of the gold plated doors inward. It swung wide with a groan.

Across the paved plaza, incredibly steep stairs rose up one side of the pyramid-like structure to the little house perched on top where priests encircled an altar beneath a huge statue of their pagan idol residing just within the portico of the house. Another cluster stood to one side.

Knowing his bride was up there tied to the altar, he charged up the steps. Seeing the intruders, four priests broke away and charged down the steps, waiving drawn swords. Eyes narrowed with resolve, Manny closed upon the onslaught.

Ru'el met the first priest who was at a disadvantage being too high. His swing meant to decapitate the intruder, went wide of its intended mark. Ru'el's sword struck him in the exposed side sending him screaming off the side of the steps to topple onto a terrace fifteen feet below. Manny met another attacker in a frightening collision as swords rang amid a shower of sparks. To injure someone had been an abhorrent nightmare, yet, what Manny had seen happen to the young man from the market, to his brother and family, and knowing what they intended for his beloved on their bloody alter, his soul filled with consuming wrath.

"I am with you," the familiar voice sounded clearly in his ears. Then the words of Noah came to mind, "You have it in your power to save yourself and my beloved niece, and perhaps others when the flood comes upon us." The ancient prophet had then tapped the hilt of Manny's sword. Determined strength flowed into his arms and breast as his sword sliced through the first attacker. To Manny's satisfaction, the second priest was the one who had taken the boy from the market place. Standing on the same level, his sword raised, the priest charged. Manny swung upward to deflect its lethal arc. To the man's surprise, his blade broke off near the hilt. In that moment, as he stared in disbelief, Manny's sword rounded up and then down, severing flesh and bone to the breastbone with lethal precision. As the priests toppled down the steps others joined the fray intensifying the battle, but even their numbers could not withstand the two warriors of vengeance as they relentlessly plowed toward the alter leaving a windrow of mangled bodies in their wake.

The chief priest, seeing the unrelenting approach, broke into a panicked sweat as he looked up. Enlil's silvery chariot was just beginning the approach his stone throne atop the temple. Just a few seconds, just a few more seconds, and the king of all the gods will have arrived to accept the sacrifice, and then surely intervene. Raising the sacrificial dagger over Sher'i, the timing had to be perfect. He looked up once more. Just as the moon settled over the concave throne's back, a massive, boiling, blackish gray cloud devoured the white orb, blotting it out, and the steel grip of a hand locked onto his wrist.

Turning, his eyes met those of the white-haired soldier of Noah's G-d. He struck out viciously to free himself, but there was no escape from the grip pulling the obsidian blade down and turning it inward. He felt a drop of rain splash on his face as the knife entered his own body.

Slumping to his knees, the priest crumpled onto his side in a writhing heap, fingers locked onto the dagger embedded in his torso. With dimming eyes, he watched the intruder sweep the girl from the altar and move to go down the steps. With maniacal determination, he pulled the blade from his body and began to rise up to meet them. Manny lashed out with a right foot catapulting the man down the long flight of steps until tumbling off the side and bounce down two terraces.

Manny found descending far more difficult than climbing. Besides the steepness of the stairs, the individual steps were narrow, littered with bodies, and made slippery with their blood. One miss-step spelled a fatal decent, yet with the approaching storm they had to hurry. Breathing a sigh of relief upon reaching flat ground, they made for the marketplace. However, as the trio passed through the huge gate, an imposing figure clad in black chain mail stepped from the shadows of one broken colossus to bar their way.

"Out of our way Amalekiel," Manny com-manded. "I've no time for you."

"This won't take long," the adversary replied slowly drawing a long, straight sword from the scabbard on his hip. In the increasing flashes of lightning, it reflected spots of amber and blue light.

Manny motioned for her and Ru'el to stand aside.

"Let me help," Ru'el said. "Together we can make short work of him."

"No, my friend. This is between the two of us. It has been from the very beginning."

Turning to face the man who had become his arch antagonist, Manny slowly drew his own sword. This time there was no distant rumble of thunder. Instead, a fearsome crack and deep, rol-ling peal wrenched a shudder from the earth.

Amalekiel struck first, coming overhead. Manny met the powerful blow showering both with sparks. Blow and strike, their swords met with frightful furry, the clang of steel upon steel like the clang of a hundred church bells.

In the last few hours, Manny had fought a battle with a giant and his henchman, suffered the heart-wrenching agony of losing three loved ones, battled his way up the incredibly steep temple steps to rescue his wife, and was now engaged in a life and death struggle with Lucifer's lieutenant. Despite his superior condition from years of exercise and working on the Ark, there was a limit. Amalekiel's power and seemingly endless energy began to take a toll as Manny's arms and shoulders felt the effects of each crushing blow. His reactions were slowing, realizing it was going to be impos-sible to resist much longer. Amalekiel knew it as well, evidenced by the wide grin baring glistening, white teeth.

Years of intense practice welled up so that the young warrior need not think of defense and counters. Move-ments came automatically allowing him to fight on longer than any normal human, but as physical strength obviously faded Amalekiel unexpectedly stepped back. Instantly the young man felt icy, cold fingers prod inside his breast. He tried to block the probe like before, but wasn't quick enough this time. A look of surprise spread over Amalekiel's gaunt face.

"So! It is you!" the lieutenant howled, lightly stroking the scar on his cheek. "I wondered. You are better than when we first met, but becoming mortal has put limits on your strength. I have no such encumbrance.

"When I heard that you had finally yielded to our enticing and accepted a very permanent solution to a very minor problem, I admit to being a little saddened. I had wanted to be the instru-ment of your defeat. What a delightful surprise Jehovah dropped you into this time, and how stu-pid of him. At first I thought you were just one the angels, but this brings me exquisite joy. I shall indeed relish my revenge."

"Well, I'd like to know if you intend to kill me with that sword or talk me to death," Manny retaliated, knowing that Amalekiel's chatter was not only intended to rattle him psychologically, but distract him as well.

"You don't know, do you? Well, no matter. You will in a few minutes as my sword slices through that pretty mortal body and divides you completely in half from the top of your head to the end of your bowels."

"You may kill me and the others, but you can't stop G-d's plan. Noah will sail the Ark, and mankind will go on to defeat you in the end."

"There's still time for a thing or two. I have not yet failed. Lucifer is lord of this earth and shall continue to rule with blood and vengeance against all those as foolish as you."

Manny knew there was no way to stop him. There was no strength to lift the beautiful sword. Whatever Amalekiel's plan, G-d's Cherubim was powerless to intervene. Silently he looked heaven-ward now engulfed by a continual blaze of lightning as Amalekiel savored his moment of glory before consummating victory.

"I'm sorry, L-rd. I've failed you. I tried."

Suddenly the world came to a standstill. There were no blinding flashes of light, no shattering thunder. Manny's victor stood motion-less. Overhead the boiling, black clouds ceased to move as a shaft of light sliced its way through the thick mass focusing on him like a spotlight. In that instant, the world of pending doom evaporated and within that literal blink Manny found himself moving down a long, narrow, white-marbled hall at a rapid rate. Looking down he saw his bare feet pounding on the gleaming surface, eating up dis-tance with incredible speed, driven by some inexplicable urge. Born in front by a dark brown hand was his sword, its slightly curved blade reflecting points of light as if encrusted with mil-lions of diamonds. To either side of the hall were mirrors. He turned to look.

It was him, slightly younger, clad in a white tunic from shoulders to just above the knees and tied at the waist by a silver cord. It was startlingly white next to his deep, burnt amber skin. Long, white hair flowed behind borne upon the wind created by his speed. A blue headband encircled his head. He wasn't alone. Others of his youthful age dressed and armed much as he, followed close upon his heels. But why were they running? Where were they going? Were they being chased? The boy didn't understand. Then he did.

Days before there had been a meeting. Everyone attended. Millions came. Manny was late as usual. He was late for everything except training practice. Well, it wasn't formal training, just a bunch of friends who liked to wrestle and fight like the older warriors they secretly watched in training. Then one who had become too old to participate came to teach them "a few things." He taught them a lot, and well.

Father stood before the massed congregation. On either side stood the council of twelve, the archangels. Father's two oldest sons were there, too. Son of the Morning was speaking, loud, long, and animated as usual. Lucifer was charismatic, drawing a large number of the crowd to applaud him. Manny didn't like him very much. He shouldn't feel that way, but Lucifer was so boastful and arrogant it set the boy's teeth on edge.

When Lucifer finished a great cheer arose. Manny wished he could hear everything that was said; something about a new world, the need for bodies so that we could find our way back to Father. They would have to leave? And find their way back? It didn't make sense. He regretted missing that other meeting a couple weeks earlier.

Then Father's other son stepped forth. Manny liked him. Always soft spoken with firm conviction. Some time back Jehovah had stepped in on one of their "play" sessions. Sitting to one side, he watched for a time before beckoning them to gather around. He spoke of peace, and love, and respect toward one another, and the dangers of playing so roughly. Manny loved listening to Jehovah. Every word came from deep within his being. He lived what he spoke, but the boys were determined to continue their play. Not long after that, they met the old warrior who agreed to teach them. Now he wondered at the coincidence.

In contrast to his brother, Jehovah spoke quietly to the gathering. Though unable to hear clearly, Manny could feel his words. It was necessary to gain a human body in order to be tested. Only the stalwart in the law could return, but Jehovah said that such strict obedience would be very difficult, and for some impossible, so volunteered himself as a sacrifice to purge the sins from man thus guaranteeing a way back to Heavenly Father's presence. This was diametrically opposed to Lucifer who wanted to order the world that man would not be allowed to sin. The difference was the exercise of agency—the opportunity to choose right from wrong. That was a foundation principal from the very beginning. Lucifer loathed agency. When it came to a vote, the grand council chose Elohim's plan to be carried out by Jehovah.

Lucifer's childish behavior got the better of him. He

ranted and screamed before storming away. Fully one third of Father's children followed. Within days sporadic arguments erupted, at first only amounting to heated exchanges of words. Then came blows, then war—full-blown fighting. Manny and his friends remained distanced from the arguments, spending their time in training until one day a commotion arose in the outer courtyard to the Great Council building.

Looking down from the balcony off the training room they saw a battle erupt. Lucifer's allies had shed their white robes for crimson bearing the gold emblem of the Morning Star. Like a great sea wave pouring into the courtyard they openly attacked. It was a highly uneven match as the attackers pushed the white-clad guards steadily backwards up the long stairs toward the council chamber doors. It was obvious the crimson army was winning. The boys had to do something as Lucifer's army headed for the council chamber.

Charging down the mirror-lined, marble corridor, he came to a certain door where his bare feet slid to a squealing stop. The others crowded in close. In the back were Kira'im and Ka'atibel. The youngest of Manny's warriors, they had the look of anxious concern etched on their faces as determination burned in their dark eyes. Holding a finger to his lips, the group fell silent. They had followed a forgotten, side corridor to the Council Chambers, forgotten except to inquisitive boys. Beyond the door, they could hear a commotion; yelling, the metallic ring of swords, a rhythmic thud shaking the floor. Manny slipped the latch and slowly opened the door.

Beyond lay a long, rectangular room lined three-deep by brilliant white columns. At one end silver mail-cloaked soldiers lay shoulders against a set of immensely tall, double doors, straining to keep it from opening as each heavy thud of something beyond began to bear fruit and overcome their efforts.

From that entry a long approach of highly polished marble flecked by thin veins of gold extended to the base of a wide set of stairs lifting to a dais. There, surrounding a beautiful gold throne a group of men in long robes stood ready, long swords at their sides. Manny instantly recognized them - Elohim and Jehovah either side of the throne, and on the lower steps the archangels.

Another grinding thud and the doors burst open throwing its valiant guards back, some to the ground. Immediately a hoard of crimson warriors poured through the rupture. The inner guard fought with determination, but there were just too many intruders. Relentlessly the defenders were pushed back toward the steps, then up, up toward the men waiting at the top. At the head of the attack was Amalekiel.

Manny cried a challenge and rushed for-ward, those behind following into the fray. His charge was so violent that feet slid on the slick floor as he crashed into Amalekiel, knocking him sideways. Without hesitation, the red-clad attacker blindly swung his sword.

"Amalekiel! What's wrong with you? Have you gone mad?" Manny cried out narrowly ducking the blade.

"Get out of my way."

"This is wrong. We've been friends too long."

Amalekiel swung his sword again. Manny dodged the silver blade, feeling the wind on his face as it passed by.

The intruder swung again at a different angle. Manny barely raised his sword in time to avert a fatal blow. Amalekiel's companions attempted to storm to his side, but Manny's friends engaged them in a furious battle. The boys were good, younger, stronger, and amazingly well trained, better than the older ones. Manny swung and parried with furious determination.

"You'll not rise up on this throne!" he screamed over the din of battle.

The intensity of Manny's attack took Amalekiel by surprise, obvious by his expression. Then eyes like coal-black pools narrowed and burned with hatred as he desperately defended against the furry of Manny's attack, attempting to counter, but able to muster no more than a defensive reaction. He was forced back one-step. Manny heartened. Amalekiel was several years older and had become a seasoned soldier since the two friends parted company. Digging down, Manny gathered up more strength, more determination. His sword blazed furiously. All the training he had undergone came into play. Amalekiel lost another step, then another, and another until pushed back onto the flat vestibule. He tried to counter, to regain that which had been lost, but he and his soldiers were slowly, steadily pushed back toward the broken doors.

Lucifer's lieutenant couldn't loose, not when victory was this close. He swung and parried with more determination, but something new had entered into the picture—fear. For the first time he envisioned defeat, defeat at the hands of a child! For all his skill and strength, Amalekiel was left to blocking and dodging that strangely shaped sword. Then it happened.

Manny initiated a two-handed cross swing that arced high from Amalekite's left. The older boy swung his sword up to defend, but the concussion pushed the blade aside. There was a sudden burning sensation on his face.

Staggering back, Amalekiel touched his cheek with the left hand. Drawing it aside, he looked down. It was covered with blood. The gleaming, razor-edge of Manny's blade had driven through. It barely touched his face, but opened a wound that angled across the prominent cheekbone from near the outside corner of his left eye toward the corner of his mouth. Blood cascade from the cut as water from a fountain.

Amalekiel staggered back, staring at his hand then at his one-time friend. A look of horror overshadowed his countenance. One sweep of his blade and Manny knocked Amalekiel's sword to the floor. Lucifer's leader turned to run, but there was no place to flee.

Δ Δ Δ

Understanding had come. Somewhere in the dimmed past Manny had led a victorious defense of G-d's throne. He had helped to win that battle, but not the war. That was still playing, no longer in Heaven, but on earth. Amalekiel was still leading the assault and he—Peter Emanuel Guzman, one time friend—had become this man's nemesis. And, Manny wasn't going to lose this time either.

Suddenly a bolt of lightning shot overhead, raising every hair on his head. It was as if touched by a live electrical wire and filled with a surge of renewed energy. The ear-splitting thunder, blinding flashes of light, and the boiling, black clouds of a dying world resumed.

Glaring down at the boy now in kneeling submission, as he had been forced to assume so long ago, Amalekiel wanted to roar out is long-awaited satisfaction, but held the outward emotions in check. Touching the scar on his face, he wanted to savor this victory, but as Manny turned his face upward, Lucifer's lieutenant saw something in the young man's eyes that became as a stake of fear in his heart. Those penetrating blue eyes, glazed from fatigue, and submission had suddenly change. As they narrowed, a new light blazed in their depths, a light of renewed strength.

With unforgiving ferocity, Amalekiel swung his sword down to extinguish that light. Manny brought his sword up. The two blades collided with a sound that rose above the thunder as a shower of sparks paled the lightening. Digging deep within, Manny pushed up to repulse the assault and launch an attack.

"I understand, now. You were robbed of victory once before, and shall be again," Manny said, unleashing a series of crushing blows.

Sher'i and Ru'el watched in awe at the violence of the conflict, and then with growing fear as Manny faltered. Their hearts sank when their friend drop exhausted to one knee. Ru'el tried stepping forward to intervene, but some unseen power held him in check. Amalekiel's final, murderous attack wrenched a cry from Sher'i's throat, but her fears were abrogated when Manny unexpectedly lifted his sword. It was as if a shimmering, blue shield of light had surrounded him. The collision of steel upon steel resounded over the intense thunder. Manny's strength seemed to grow with each of Amalekiel's strikes.

Blow after blow Manny swung his sword with renewed vigor forcing Lucifer's deputy backward, backward through the carnage of fallen idols, backward to the vacant market place. Then at the entrance to the avenue Amalekiel's heel struck the shattered body of a statue knocked from a vendor's booth. The devil's second toppled onto his back. Manny raised his sword high over his right shoulder preparatory to bringing it down onto his adversary.

"You can't do it," Amalekiel challenged. "You couldn't kill me then, and you can't do it now."

"Guess again," Manny shouted.

The deadly weapon slammed into the earth just as its intended victim rolled away and scrambled awkwardly to his feet. Amalekiel realized victory over his avowed enemy was no longer possible and G-d's angel indeed intended to kill him. Now fighting a desperate defense he was sorely pressed to avoid that shining blade as it inched ever closer to his body. It had come too close once before. He had never experienced pain before the Great War, but at the height of battle, just as he was to become the triumphant victor, that blade touched him. Amalekiel had always thought himself to be invincible as immortals were, but something had changed that day, and suddenly realized he could be hurt. He could be destroyed. That sword had the power. The same hands that wielded it then left the scar on his face, and the boy who grasped it now knew this. Moreover, his human-trained skills had enhanced the old ones. He was too much once again for the Son of the Morning Star's lieutenant.

Jumping back Amalekiel wheezed, "Another time we shall finish it," and flinging his arm, threw a handful of dirt toward Manny's face.

By luck, Manny's left arm was just above his forehead. Seeing the ploy, it was a simple matter to bring the arm down to shield his eyes from the potentially blinding assault, but by doing so, he covered them for just a moment. In that instant, Amalekiel was gone.

"Where'd he go?" Sher'i yelled above the deafening roar of the storm.

"I don't know, but we've got to get away from here, too," Manny shouted over the deafening roar of the storm.

As the trio began to run for the eastern gate, they found the two street urchins still standing as instructed, staff in hand. A light drizzle had begun.

"It's good to see you again, my friends. Thank you for your help," Manny said to them, "But I'm sorry." Then pointing at the approaching storm continued, "The flood that Noah said would come? Well, this is it. Everyone and everything is about to be destroyed. You, me, everyone. Only Noah and his family will survive. Take what little time is left and ask G-d's help to die quickly. I'm sorry I can't help you."

Turning, the trio raced toward the eastern gate, not seeing Kira'im and Ka'atibel face each other, grasp hands, and smile broadly as an enveloping shaft of light spiraled out of the clouds to take them home.

Chapter 19

Those people in the houses overlooking the market area heard the deep rumbling growl emitted from the earth. Staring out their second story windows or from rooftops, they watched as the two men seemed unaffected as the giant idols swayed wildly before toppling into heaps of dust, decimating the temple guard. A few watched as paralyzed witnesses as the two men attacked their temple, unleashing carnage upon the defending priests, and then to their horror, the sight of the high priest murdered, and his body thrown to tumble down the steps. When the two desecraters returned to the market place, those who had not fled the city, cheered as their rich patron enjoined

Noah's soldiers in battle. They even shouted with joy when it appeared the unwanted and frightening one in white was about to be vanquished, but what must have gone through their minds when Noah's angel suddenly rose up, and their champion ran away? Looking to the north and west, they retreated inside, slamming shutters, and cowering, remembering the words of the prophet Noah—too late.

As the black, boiling clouds swallowed the sun, day turned into the blackest night illuminated only by the eerie, blue light of now continuous sheet lightning punctuated by blinding hot-white bolts striking the earth vicious blows, causing the ground to spasm. With Amalekiel beaten, Manny had no idea what to do or where to go until Sher'i screamed over the deafening roar of thunder as if a hundred 747s were taking off at once.

"Let us go to the Ark. Uncle Noah will take us in."

"But it is only for the animals and his family," Manny tried to explain.

"But you are his family, remember? By G-d's command he adopted you."

Nothing in the scriptures of his day indicated anyone but Noah's family, his sons and their wives, went aboard the Ark. Nothing about children, let alone adopted children, but Sher'i remained insistent.

An uncertainty entered his mind. In the time of his birth, there was speculation and some proof of translation errors in the scripture texts. Of course, that was possible, what with going from one language to another several times by men with imperfect command of languages, and by design. He relented when she began pulling him along. Besides, where else could they go in the face of certain death? Then another dream flashed in his mind, the one of the mountain above the Ark where Noah prayed! Where he and Sher'i were sitting in the rain. Quite unexpectedly, Sher'i found herself pulled along by Manny, Ru'el following at their heels.

Now realizing Noah's warning was coming true, people choked the eastern gate in panicked flight, seeking higher ground. Some voiced the plan to board the Ark. Fighting to remain standing and not be trampled as some already had been—a woman, what appeared to be a child, a man in a garish, red and green robe with a silver and gold tasseled rope belt—the three were swept out of the city by the stampeding throng. Once clear of the city, a wind rose its terrifying howl, lifting the ground, and driving it in a blinding, stinging horizontal cloud.

Using what clothing they had, each covered their faces with eyes barely exposed. Those they attempted to shield with hands. Breathing became laborious. Walking upright was nearly impossible. Seeing the road was worse. Manny stumbled when his foot struck something. A person. Whether dead or not, there was no way to check in the blinding storm, nor time. Vision was reduced to mere feet. Manny had in fact passed the intersecting trail when Ru'el screamed above the howling wind.

"Manny! Here! I think this is it!"

Doubling back, he struggled to see, as the blinding cloud of dirt stung his eyes. He could barely see his feet. Dropping to his knees, he felt the single rock about the size of a large beach ball, recognizing the mark placed upon it.

"Yes. This is it," he said.

Manny stepped off the main road and looked down at his feet to find the trail. He honestly didn't hold out much hope seeing let alone follow it. The wall of dirt seemed to part. Yes. He could just barely make out the trail's outline. No one else would.

Despite the wind at their backs so the particles of dirt didn't sandblast their eyes, progress still seemed painfully slow, until splashing into the stream. Without a second thought, he made for the waterfall, climbed up the side, and began wading upstream. With only ankle deep water over a smooth bottom to contend with, they used the ever-deepening ravine as shelter from the raging wind as particles of dirt and small rocks hurled overhead. This was the stream passing the Ark. When it made a sharp, left bend, they scrambled up a long incline of melon-sized boulders forming another small waterfall to enter the dense forest.

The shrieking wind caused the trees to groan, but they held firm to buffer the onslaught.

Visibility improved some until reaching the clearing where Noah's camp was located. Without the windbreak, visibility again vanished. Manny tripped and fell face first into a tent ripped from where it had been anchored, and thrown into their path.

Up until now, he had only the vaguest idea where they were in relation to the Ark. Now he took hope. The raging wind made speech impossible, but turning around he conveyed through signs that this was the place. That's when he realized Ru'el was not with them. The last time Manny had seen his friend was when they began following the stream. A bolt of lightning had struck very close. Manny glanced back and thought to see Ru'el before resuming their flight, but they had somehow become separated. His heart yearned to go back, but there was no time as a large raindrop splattered on his shoulder.

With the burden of loss weighing upon his heart, Manny turned, faced the mountain, and started over the rise that would take them to the Ark. It was easier to see now as the wind slackened and a light rain scrubbed away the air-borne dirt. Quickly making the other side of the saddle, they found Noah standing at the base of the wide gangplank encouraging the remaining animals to enter. There seemed to be no problems as the creatures approached the ramp and entered with surprising order. Shem and Japheth stood at the top directing each pair to their designated place like stewards on a cruise ship. Calēb barked and loped out to meet them.

"Uncle Noah?" Sher'i said as they approached, trying to pacify the excited dog.

Turning toward them, his weathered face broke into a wide smile letting his arms envelop them both in a hug.

"I'm so glad you are safe."

"Uncle Noah," Sher'i began to cry, "Aran, and Abigail, and the baby," her voice cracked, refusing to form the words.

"I know," he said tenderly. "The L-rd told me. They are safe in his house. We must rejoice for they are far better off than any of us." Suddenly he backed away, his face taking on a solemn look.

Sher'i knew.

"We can't go with you, can we?"

"No," Manny interjected before the prophet could answer. "It is not written," privately grumbling that the translators had to get that right.

"I'm sorry," Noah replied, bowing his head. "When He had you sealed to me as a son . . . I thought that would be your escape, but the L-rd has another direction for each of you to take. Go to the mountain and seek Him out."

Turning, he scanned the valley one last time as if searching for stragglers. Shaking his shaggy head, he looked at his niece and adopted son again. Kissing Sher'i on the forehead and Manny on each cheek, he turned away to prod the last two animals, ponderous hippos, up the ramp. To Manny's shock, Calēb didn't follow, remaining seated, leaning against Manny's leg, whimpering softly.

"Father Noah," Manny called out. "What about Caléb?"

Noah didn't respond as he stood in the opening, looking for something.

"Father Noah," he called out again, trying to be heard over the approaching roar of wind and rain.

Noah waived one final time, nodded for his sons to pull the great ropes lifting the ramp up, and disappeared from view as the great gangplank sealed the opening.

"Come on," Manny said, giving the girl a gentle tug.

"Where?"

"The mountain. Where Father Noah always spoke with G-d."

The rain was now coming harder creating rivulets of water to cascade down the mountain with such force to carrying small rocks. It seemed as if every foot forward slid back, their sandals acting as surfboards on the sludge. Reaching back to the handle on his sword, he popped the short blade free, slipped it along his legs, and cut the bindings. Barefoot, he could dig toes into the oozing mass. He did the same for Sher'i. Caléb stayed close to Sher'i, allowing her to grip his neck as his great claws dug into the slippery earth and carry both upward.

Finally gaining the saddle overlooking the

Ark, they collapsed in exhaustion, sitting side by side, the Mastiff lying next to Manny, any whimper drown by heavy panting. Staring at the Ark, Manny had never felt such emptiness. That's when they felt it, a low, continuous rumble growing steadily louder. Looking over his shoulder, he spotted the grayish-white line moving toward them, becoming increasingly larger. Sher'i wrapped her arms about his chest, pulling as close as possible, shivering uncontrollably. The waters from the deep were coming.

The massive wall moved steadily toward them until enveloping the remains of camp. Striking the mountain, the wave split, wrapping around until meeting and surrounding the Ark. The great boat rocked, lift from the braces, and began to move upon the frothing waves.

"We need to go higher," Manny said, pulling the girl along as they struggled for the summit. Part way up he thought to glimpse two white deer, each with a golden horn. Were these the stragglers Noah had searched for? Whatever they had been doing, they had missed the boat, suffering their kind to extinction as would all humankind save for those on the Ark now disappearing into the darkness and into history.

Calēb, who was leading the way up faltered. There was no way for him to climb the near vertical trail. Manny searched for another route. There was none and the water was rising rapidly. Suddenly the great dog barked as if to say farewell and loped off in the direction of the abandoned deer.

After a short but slippery, hand-over-hand assent, the two sat on the uppermost peak, huddling close, both shivering from cold and fear, the water licking at their feet. Pulling Sher'i closer he looked into her huge, brown eyes and said, "I love you. I will love you forever," and they kissed. Moments later a wave ripped them from the mountain.

"Sher'i! Sher'i!" Manny cried out, but the powerful wave had torn them apart. Spinning around, he continued searching for her, crying out her name, choking on water. She was gone.

Suddenly he was gripped by the feeling of being totally alone; a terrible feeling, like the time he lay beneath the debris in the old hotel until remembering Noah's words, "You have the power to save yourself and Sher'i." Reaching over his shoulder, he pulled the sword from its sheath, reassured by the crack of thunder from a sky blackened as if burnt by the fiery bolts of lightning now reduced to sporadic, reddish glows. Then at that moment something touched his ankle, not hard like wood or rock, but pliable and soft. Fingers had locked onto his ankle.

"Sher'i?"

The fingers jerked him beneath the roiling water. He jerked the foot free. It couldn't be Sher'i. The grip was too strong. The fingers reached around his ankle and pulled him down again. He kicked free. "Amalekiel!" he choked, popping back to the surface.

Two hands gripped his leg. Taking a deep breath just before being pulled down again, Manny determined to die on his own without any help of his enemy. Drawing the free leg up, he shot it down striking something solid. Manny envisioned it to be Amalekiel's face. Freed, he popped to the surface, gasping to refill his lungs with air, but the rain was coming so hard now he inhaled too much water and began choking. He felt the hand grasp his ankle. Once more he pulled his knee up. Shooting the foot down he made contact again—solid contact. He pulled up and struck again. The third time there was nothing. He was free for the moment, but only a moment, knowing what must be done before his nemesis returned.

Raising the sword with both hands overhead, he pointed it toward heaven and smiled. It was coming, the twisting shaft with its fiery maw

For All Time and Eternity:
waters from the deep

Chapter 20

Manny closed his eyes, bracing against the searing sensation to seize his chest and radiate throughout his body, to be sucked into the twisting, gut-wrenching, weightless torment. Nothing happened. Eyes shut, he continued to be tossed about upon the waves. What had happened? Slowly, reluctantly he opened his eyes, afraid to discover that somehow he had missed the only ticket to survival, but it wasn't water that tossed him about, but the fog—thick, gray, entwining. He breathed a sigh of relief, nauseous, but relief.

He moved his legs to step forward, but as before, there was nothing to take hold of and propel him in any direction. Completely exhausted, he really had no desire to move, wondering where it would take him, and then if Sher'i was in here as well? He twisted to look around. It was all the same in every direction.

Something flashed. There was no light, yet for an instant, he had seen something. Sweat began beading on his forehead. A fuzzy, indistinct image materialized, shimmered, and faded. Frustration peaked, but by drawing in a long breathe Manny fought the feeling down and relaxed. After a time the images began to focus better and remain long enough to be recognizable. Faces—Sher'i, Noah, Aran, Ru'el, Shem, a laughing Japheth—passing in slow motion, each of their smiling faces filling his heart with warmth.

Then a nightmare! A little boy playing in an abandoned building slips. A wall panel topples onto him. He can't move. The heavy weight pins him tight to the floor. He kicks. There's no one to see him. He screams. There's no one to hear him. "Don't play in that place," a woman's voice admonishes. No one knows he is in the building.

"Mommy, I can't move," the little boy screams. "Mommy, help. I can't breathe!"

The child is buried alive! He fights to move, It is impossible. The great weight suddenly lifts. A grateful child stares at Benny who tenderly brushes dirt from the child's hair and face, and comforts him.

The fog returned spilling over the tiny boy held in Benny's arms and like the wave that tore he and Sher'i from the mountain, it poured over Manny as well, lifting him upward in its oppressive tangles, lifting him upward to float and twist, forcing him into a spin. His stomach sickened.

"Please, G-d, not again! Help me!"

A light. A bright pinpoint far off in the nebulous distance. His mind grabbed for it as he choked down the urge to vomit. Concentrating on that growing spot helped suppress the sickness. Drawing nearer, the fog began dissolving and the light became a brilliant, blinding white.

And then a voice called out, "Manny."

It was so far away. He tried to open his eyes. He couldn't. He tried to move his arms. Neither would budge. He couldn't feel anything. He couldn't move.

"Manny."

He focused on the voice. It was familiar. Yes! That voice! Praise be to His Holy name.

TO BE CONTINUED

Sean Patrick

O'Mordha

Sean moved to the Sparks/Reno, Nevada area after compiling an annotation of the first five Books of Moses of the Old Testament also known as the Torah, an eleven-year project. Drawing from material in that project, he began writing the series **For All Time and Eternity**. He brings to this first installment, **Waters of the Deep**, a unique combination of skills including those of historian, theologian, and researcher. Those who have enjoyed his series, **A Pirate's Legacy**, will make a startling discovery about the protagonist, Manny Guzman.

Sean has written a number of novels which can be found on his website.

http://oldguey.webs.com